3-20

D0455265

SAVING CICADAS

**Center Point
Large Print**

Also by Nicole Seitz
and available from Center Point Large Print:

A Hundred Years of Happiness

**This Large Print Book carries the
Seal of Approval of N.A.V.H.**

Saving Cicadas

Nicole Seitz

CENTER POINT PUBLISHING
THORNDIKE, MAINE

This Center Point Large Print edition
is published in the year 2010 by arrangement with
Thomas Nelson Publishers.

The text of this Large Print edition is unabridged.
In other aspects, this book may vary
from the original edition.
Printed in the United States of America
on permanent paper.
Set in 16-point Times New Roman type.

ISBN: 978-1-60285-678-3

Library of Congress Cataloging-in-Publication Data

Seitz, Nicole A.
  Saving cicadas / Nicole Seitz.
     p. cm.
  ISBN 978-1-60285-678-3 (library binding : alk. paper)
  1. Single mothers--Fiction. 2. Mothers and daughters--Fiction. 3. Domestic fiction.
  4. Large type books. I. Title.
  PS3619.E426S38 2010
  813'.6--dc22
2009038300

For Janie

'Listen!' said the White Spirit. 'Once you were a child. Once you knew what inquiry was for. There was a time when you asked questions because you wanted answers, and were glad when you had found them. Become that child again; even now.'

—THE GREAT DIVORCE BY C.S. LEWIS

Prologue
THE WINDOW

"Do you believe in . . . past lives?"

She's waited a week to get the gumption to ask him, but now she's second-guessing. Priscilla keeps her knees together and smoothes the flowers in her skirt. She pulls her hair to the right side of her head and stares at the big black book on his desk. "I mean, I know you don't, but—"

"Why?" he says. "Do you believe?" A flash of sunlight fills the room—a temporary break in the clouded sky. And then it's gone, and all is gray again.

"I'm not sure. I'm starting to wonder."

He swivels his chair and leans back, cracking his knuckles, one after the other after the other. "I can tell you, you're not the first to ask. We've got some Cherokees here, and the traditional belief of rebirth comes up every now and again. Usually when somebody loses a loved one."

Priscilla stares down at her knees.

"I certainly don't claim to know all the mysteries of God," says Fritz, "but I do know we all have former selves, pasts we've got to deal with and learn from. Otherwise we carry these former lives on our shoulders, unable to let go." Priscilla glances up at him finally, searching his face. "Some people remain stuck living *past lives*. But you can exchange that burden for something wonderful—"

"No. That's not really what I'm talking about, Fritz. I do understand what you're saying, it's just . . ."

"What is it, Priscilla?"

She tucks a strand of long blonde hair behind her ear and shakes her head, studying the lines of his simple pine desk. "She's . . . she remembers things. Things she can't possibly remember. She talks about family members, ones who've been gone for years now. I don't know, maybe it's the photographs, or maybe I've talked about them to her or around her. Maybe she's just extra sensitive, attentive. I can usually explain it away, except . . ."

"Except what?"

She looks him in the eye and says, "The window."

Fritz pauses and glances at the window behind Priscilla's shoulder. It's simple and unadorned, unlike the ones in the other room with their magnificent colors and stories. On the other side of the clear-paned glass, a mockingbird swoops to the ground and calls out *warning* beneath a blanketed sky. "Tell me about this window," Fritz says.

"She can describe it to me in detail . . . but I don't know how. I've never talked about it. To anyone."

"I see."

"It comes to me in my dreams. The window."

"You're thinking she can read your mind now?"

"I don't know, I—"

"Maybe you talk in your sleep."

"No. It's not like that," Priscilla says. "She's special. You know her. There's something . . . different about her. There always has been."

"If you ask me, I'd say she's a bright, loving child. Tell me: does she seem troubled by these memories?"

"No. She acts as if nothing is strange at all, as if it was just the other day or something. She goes on and on about that summer too . . . when we left Cypresswood. It just unnerves me." Priscilla uses her left hand to pull her right arm close to her side.

"If you'd like me to talk with her, you know I will. But maybe not just yet." Fritz leans forward and places his elbows on his knees. He clasps his hands together and looks just over her shoulder, then finally meets her eyes. "We each have something, Priscilla, some memory that haunts us, that shows up in our dreams. In your case, it's a window. Maybe what bothers you is not that your daughter remembers this window she can't possibly know, but that she reminds you of the thing it represents—something you thought you'd let go of long ago."

She looks up at him, and her lip trembles as if she may cry or speak. She does neither.

"She's a good girl, Priscilla. A blessing in your life. Sometimes God has a way of using children to speak to us. To lead us closer to him. If you want my advice, let her lead you. She may say something truly worth hearing one of these days."

Fritz takes Priscilla's free hand and squeezes it, and the two sit engulfed in the moment, oblivious to the fact that they're not alone. Hidden in the shadowy corner of the preacher's office, a lone head bows and whispers, "Amen."

Part One

THE MACYS
HIT THE ROAD

Chapter One
FLYING DREAMS

{Janie}

Come over here by the light and let me see what pretty pictures you drew. Oh, this one here is my favorite, Janie. Is this a car?

Yes, ma'am.

Can you tell me about it?

I trace my finger along the red and blue lines on construction paper, the green blurred trees, the yellow circles for faces—then I close my eyes. It's how I remember best.

It was about four years ago, the last trip we ever took together—my mother, sister, grandparents, and me. 'Course, we didn't know it at the time. You never know something like that, like it's the last one you'll ever get, till it's just a memory, hanging like mist. This is what happened that summer, true as I can tell it. Not a one of us was ever the same.

I sat in the front seat, all eight-and-a-half years of me, twirling my hair and trying to hum a happy tune. I did this, knowing Mama was nothing at all close to being happy after just finding out she was having another child. In fact, sitting so close to her, I thought my mama's fear and anger smelled a lot like dill pickle relish and red onions. Or

13

maybe it was just Grandma Mona, old and mean and full of egg salad, breathing down our necks from behind the seat.

Some things, like the smell of fear and anger—and guilt—are enough to drive anybody out on the road, even when gas prices are about to kill you.

A gallon of gas had soared to over four dollars that summer, and Mama said that alone might do her in. Not like she had a money tree or anything in the backyard. Hers was hollow, dead, and bearing no fruit—certainly no dollar bills. No, Priscilla Lynn Macy was a working woman, said she gave her life and youth to the pancake house. So you might think it strange we would set out on the highway. I did, anyway. But I would soon find out this was no regular summer vacation. We were destined to go.

Mama had stuck her long blonde hair in a ponytail, packed the whole caboodle into the car—the past, the present, the future—and we were barreling down I-26 at seventy-five miles an hour, and she had absolutely no idea where she was going, or maybe she did. Maybe she knew deep down she wasn't running away from her problems but hauling them right along with her.

Rainey Dae Macy, my seventeen-year-old sister, hugged a plastic baby doll in the backseat and watched the trees blur into a long green line. She didn't like change or surprise vacations, but she kept her mouth shut anyway. She was used to doing whatever pleased Mama, fearing her special needs made Mama's life just a little bit harder than most.

I was more or less a normal kid. Like most, I dreamed of saving the world someday. Not like Superwoman, but I don't know—making sure kids had clothes and enough to eat, making sure people like Mama had good jobs that made money and made them feel good when they went home each day, like they did something with their brains—like they did something to help the world in some small way. Not like they were wasting every second of every day of every year of their lives—like Mama had said, oh, more than a time or two.

Two nights before we left Cypresswood, Mama was tucking Rainey into her princess sheets on the top bunk when she asked her how many days there were until Christmas.

"About six months," Mama said.

"How many days?" Rainey insisted. She liked to count things. She was good at it. And she counted days like seconds, like sand.

"Let's see . . . a hundred and ninety, I think."

Rainey started to whine, "That long? I want it now."

My mother was sensitive to any talk about Christmas presents. She'd hear one and add it to her master list. That way, come holiday time, she wasn't scrambling to save money and frantic to buy. So she asked, full of hope, "Why, is there something you want for Christmas, honey?"

"Yeah, but . . . I cain't tell you," said Rainey.

"Why not?"

"I made a wish. On a dandelion. Won't come true if I say it."

"If you tell me, honey, I can help you write a letter and make sure Santa knows about it."

"Huh-uh," said Rainey. "God knows. He tell Santa."

I was lying in the bottom bunk, listening to the whole thing. I was wise for my age. Not meaning any harm, Mama often said things in my presence that aged me, partly because she was a single mother doing the job of two, and partly because she had a special-needs child and a crappy job and she was going gray early. Sometimes, she'd just about talk to the wind in order to get it all out.

So I, Janie Doe Macy, listening to the wish conversation and knowing my mother the way I did—how hard she worked, how hard she tried—felt sorry for her.

"Don't worry, Mama," I said. "I'll get her to tell me. I can help you make sure Santa gets the message."

Mama kissed Rainey on the cheek and on her flattened nose and on her upturned eyes. "Good night, sweetheart."

" 'Night, Mama. Don't forget Janie light."
Rainey knew I was deathly afraid of the dark.

"Good night, sweet Janie. Don't let the bedbugs bite."

" 'Night," I said.

Mama reached down and turned on the night-light, then she stood there at the door, not leaving, and smiled at us in a strange sort of way. She started counting on her fingers. Then she spouted out, "Oh good gosh, I'm late. I'm never late." She reminded me of the rabbit in *Alice in Wonderland*, and I wondered what she could be late for at this hour. The light from the window was turning sapphire blue.

When the door closed, I looked up to the top bunk and whispered, "Rainey, you can tell me your wish. Sisters don't count."

"Huh-uh. I wished on the dandelion. It won't be true."

"Rainey, just tell me. Please?"

It was quiet from the top. Then Rainey leaned over the edge and looked at me. Concern spread like butter across her face. "Oh, I prob-ly won't get it. I wish . . . I wish I had wings and flied around."

"Oh. Really? Like an airplane? Like a bird?" I bit my lip and turned my head to the wall, heart-sick, knowing the wings she wanted couldn't possibly come true. Not even Santa could pull that one off.

"Like a angel." I heard Rainey lay back on her pillow.

"Gee, Rain. I don't know if that one can happen. I used to wish the same thing when I was little. But I've had dreams where I've been flying. Have you ever had one of those? You're high up over the trees and the buildings and it feels like you can do anything at all, like nothing is impossible?"

"No." Rainey sniffled. The room was growing darker.

"You should tell Mama about the wings," I said. "You know if she can help it come true, she will. Remember how she put you in the Olympics and you won that pretty medal for running? 'Member that?"

"Yeah, I 'member."

My sister and I stopped talking after that and settled in for sleep. Knowing Rainey, she was praying even harder for her wings, never minding she couldn't get them.

In the bottom bunk, I lay there trying to remember that feeling, what it felt like to fly. And I fell asleep hoping, just maybe, I'd have one of those carefree, light-as-air flying dreams again, like I used to when I was much younger than the wise old age of eight-and-a-half. For some reason, I suspected my wings were too short to ever catch air and lift me off the ground—that some children, no matter how hard they try, will never fly.

Chapter Two
THE SMARTEST MACY

"It'll be all right, Mama. Promise it will."

Grandma Mona and me were watching Mama's face twist and curl in our tiny bathroom. It had a daisy shower curtain and matching soap dish, making it strangely cheery for such a dark day. We were sort of like good cop, bad cop, Grandma Mona and me. I was the good one. Hard to be bad when you're only eight. I would say something nice and Grandma Mona would say something nasty. Mama could form no real words at all, but for sure, she wasn't happy. There was a blue vein bulging in her left temple, and she was frozen, holding that little white stick. Like a wand. Like a little magic wand that would change everybody's world with just one *swoosh* of the wrist.

Normally, my mama was the prettiest lady I'd ever seen, blue eyes, creamy white skin. Other folks thought it, too, giving her looks in the restaurant, in the grocery store. In the small town of Cypresswood, South Carolina, most everybody was invisible, melting in with everybody else. Except for Mama. Nobody was prettier than her. Some ladies didn't like her so much because of it. Maybe they worried their men might take a liking to Mama more and want to trade them in for her. But Mama wasn't like that. She wasn't after anybody's man. 'Fact, she hadn't loved anybody except me and Rainey since the day my daddy left four years ago.

Mama might have been pretty, but it never went to her head. She thought her hair was too flat and wished it had some wave. Every now and again she got pink lipstick stuck on her front tooth or had it all cockeyed off one lip or the other. And she thought the ladies who drove those pink Cadillacs in Fervor, the ones who knew how to put on makeup right and such, were the ones to envy, not her. But those Fervor ladies never saw my mama sitting up late at night, rocking a scared Rainey who'd had a bad dream. They never saw her early in the mornings making smiley face pancakes and trying to cheer up her sad daughters and take our minds off Daddy, right after he left. No, no one ever saw that side of Mama. But I did. And sometimes when she was wearing a nice dress and had her face put on just right, I looked at Mama and got this feeling down deep in my chest—a feeling like I wished somebody would just walk on by and I could say, "That's my mama, and someday I'm gonna be just like her."

Right now Mama didn't look anything like that. Her blonde hair framed a tired face that was growing longer by the second. Her skin was all stretched back like it was tied behind her ears, and she was screaming. Not for joy neither. Scared me half to death. I wished I could save her, but it's not like there was blood or anything, something I could stick a Band-Aid on. I plugged my ears with my fingers and leaned my head against the cold hard wall. Hoping it would pass. "There, there, Mama." She rarely hollered, if ever.

"Well, isn't this just fitting," said Grandma Mona when the screaming died down. "This calls for a celebration, dear. Why don't I go pour you a nice gin and tonic?"

"Let *me* see," I said, shooting Grandma Mona one of her own nasty looks. She got the hint and left us alone. Mama set the stick on the counter and I leaned over, studying it. I stared at the picture on the box. A minus sign meant *not pregnant.* A plus sign, *pregnant.* My mother was definitely pregnant. I covered my mouth. It couldn't be. Daddy'd been gone for four years now. I figured maybe there was a mistake. Then I thought about it some more and thought maybe Mama *had* taken one of those ladies' men, just like they'd worried about. Maybe she'd done it down at the pancake house or somewhere when Rainey and I weren't looking. I was shocked my own mama could be so naughty. But then I thought on it some more and knew my mama wasn't naughty, maybe just forgetful on how babies were made. So then I was just shocked thinking about a new baby being in our house.

My legs went jelly, so I sat down on the cold

edge of the tub. I felt like I was floating, like my spirit might fly right off. Mama dropped the stick in the trash can and it made a *clunk* noise like a jail cell door. "How could this happen?" she said, trancelike.

"It happens." Grandma Mona popped her head back around the door. "How do you think it happens? Good gracious, child, you ought to know how it happens by now."

At eight-and-a-half-years-old, I didn't know everything, but being the smartest girl in the Macy family, I knew a few things, like, *never climb onto a strange, mangy dog, even if he* does *look like he's smiling*. My sister, Rainey, learned that the hard way, and she lost the tip of her right pinkie finger too. Had to get the shots and everything. I say I was the smartest Macy girl because my sister, she was older than me and she *was* smart, but she was special, you know, and sometimes could only grasp so much. Well then there was Mama. I guessed I was smarter than her now, too, because another thing I knew was, *you can have babies just by kissing a boy.* Why, every time on TV somebody was kissing, there wound up being a baby. Mama should have kept her lips to herself because she had two children already, but maybe she forgot how you make babies. She must have because she'd gone and done it again. Didn't look too happy about it, neither.

"That's good," I said, patting Mama on the

back. She was straddling the commode and quiet now. "Just take a deep breath. I'm sure it's not so bad."

My mother stared at floating dust. Her shoulders dropped low as if a heavy little devil and angel were sitting on either side. Then the devil and angel began to jump, and Mama's shoulders bounced up and down with them, keeping rhythm.

"How did this happen?" She wailed again and put her head on the counter beside the sink. She banged it a couple times, then rolled it from side to side, her arms falling limp past the toilet paper roll down to the floor. "How could I let this happen again? What kind of mother *aaaam IIII*?"

I didn't want this.

"Mama, it's not *your* fault you're pregnant." Hearing that word *pregnant* come out of my mouth made me want to crawl in a hole. And then hearing how dumb I sounded, I added, "Well, you didn't do it by yourself, anyway. Somebody musta kissed you back. Or maybe they kissed you when you weren't expecting it—surprised you or some such. Could have been like Sleeping Beauty and the prince, you know. She had no warning from him whatsoever. Just snuck up on her and *boom!*"

"Oh, thank you," said Grandma Mona. "That's just what I wanted, Janie. A nice little picture in my mind of your mother *being* with a man.

Lovely. And for an eight-year-old girl to know all this. I swanny. Just a disgrace." She walked away, sputtering and leaving a trail of venom behind her like snail slime.

"I'm eight-and-a-half!" I hollered.

"What's wrong, Mama?" My sister, Rainey, heard the commotion and filled the doorway, her hair still mussed up from sleeping. She had her hands covering her ears for the noise. She was eight years older than me but seemed more like my age, except for her body was a grown-up's. Go figure. I wasn't sure why they called it Down syndrome. They should have called it "Up" or something. Rainey was the most loving, positive, excited person I knew. She was like our Labrador puppy Bitsy was, always wagging her tail, just happy to be alive. Until she got run over, that is.

Anyway, Rainey saw joy in everything . . . unless she was scared or bothered or mad. "What's wrong?" she asked again.

"Oh, nothing, honey—"

"She's pregnant," said Grandma Mona.

"What's pregnant?" Rainey asked. Strangers had a hard time making out her words sometimes, but I'd been with her for so long, I had no trouble at all. Sounded more like "whad-ped-nat?"

Mama looked shocked at hearing the word. "It means having a baby," said Mama, holding her middle and looking like somebody kicked her in the stomach.

"A baby?" Rainey's face lit up like sunshine. "Oooh, we get the baby! Goodie!"

"No, Rainey, it's not a good thing," Mama said, straightening up. "It is not a good thing for an unmarried woman with no money and a crappy job to get pregnant."

"Oh." Rainey's eyes flitted from Mama to me. Understanding crossed her flattened face, and she looked at her shoes. "Mama bad. You the bad girl."

"No, no. I'm not a bad girl, Rainey. I just . . . I don't know how this happened . . ." Tears began streaming down Mama's face, and she excused herself to the kitchen for some water.

"Sit down," I told Rainey. I was more like the big sister in our relationship, and it was time to do big-sister things. I patted the toilet seat and Rainey sat down. I put my head in my hands and rested my elbows on my knees so my brown hair covered my face. "See, it's like this. Somebody kissed Mama and it might not have been her fault. Just because a lady gets pregnant . . . is going to have a baby . . . it doesn't mean she's a bad girl."

"No?"

"No."

"Like Mary!" Rainey squealed. I peeked at her between my fingers. "Mary had the baby," she said. "From the Bible."

"Yes! Yes, that's right. Mary had a baby, and that didn't make her a bad girl, did it?"

25

"Jesus was in her tummy," said Rainey, looking out the door to her book bin. She got up and hurried to it, lifting the lid and digging until she found the one she wanted. I followed her and plopped down on the couch, feeling like I'd gained five thousand pounds. I curled my feet up under me and Rainey brought me her book, flipping through its pages with thick fingers. "See? Here the baby Jesus. He come again someday. Mama having the baby?"

"Uugh." I put my head down and closed my eyes. I knew Mama wasn't happy about being pregnant, and I also knew the Jamisons at the Y had adopted a baby from Russia, so I knew Mama could give hers away if she wanted. If I thought on it, I felt sick inside. "I guess Mama's having the baby," I said. "But we don't really know yet, Rainey. It's up to her."

She was quiet for a second, so I turned to look at her. Rainey's eager look had turned to frustration. "Why?" she whined. "I thought Jesus coming to our house. I want the baby Jesus."

"Oh, Rain." Tears sprang to my eyes. They dripped down slowly, lingering on my cheeks. Rainey moved in and clumsily swiped at my face, trying to dry my tears. She thought of crying along with me, then smiled instead. "Don't be sad. I help. Baby Jesus stay in our room. I feed him and change the diaper." Then she pounced off the couch and ran away, hunched over with purpose, clutching her book of Bible stories. I could only imagine she'd gone to prepare a place for Jesus. Probably my bunk on the bottom.

And then it occurred to me. Mary was called a *virgin*, and God gave her a baby. If Mama truly didn't know how all this had happened, then it could very well be that she was a virgin, too, and God had given *her* a baby. I imagined Mary was just as upset as Mama was when she found out. Then I got excited and nervous and serious all at the same time. My mother was having a child of God like Mary did, so I hunkered down in the couch cushions, waiting for angels to come tell us the news. I knew it was something that might happen only once in a lifetime. Most folks, I knew, weren't this lucky, and I certainly was nobody special to deserve something as such.

Chapter Three
BIRDS AND BEES

I sat still and felt the lumps of the sofa. I closed my eyes and listened to the grandfather clock ticking. *Tick, tick.* Time was rushing by, Mama more pregnant with every second. I waited and waited, but no angels came.

I touched my own stomach, and my blood swelled. No matter how Mama got pregnant, a baby was coming to our house. Into our lives. And what would it mean for Rainey and me? No more late movies on Fridays nights with popcorn and Co-colas. No more roller-skating at the Y or half-price bowling every other Tuesday. Mama would be too tired for me and Rainey. Life, as we knew it, was completely over.

I could hear Grandma Mona letting Mama have it in the other room. "Why do you always go for men who use you, Priscilla? Who's the Prince Charming this time? I tell you, one of these days . . ." Mama stayed silent, taking all the abuse. Then she came white-faced from the kitchen carrying a glass of water, and she set it down with shaky hands on a coaster and sniffled. Pulling a balled-up tissue out of her pocket, she wiped her nose before sitting next to me. Mama and I didn't look at each other but stared straight ahead at the glass half-empty with a faded print of Donald Duck on it.

"I guess," she told me, "I really did it this time."

I kept my mouth shut, but Grandma Mona, of course, could not.

"Yes, you did, Priscilla," she said. She was hovering over Mama's shoulders like a gnat.

"Cain't you just leave her alone?" I said. "I really don't think she needs this right now. It might not even be her fault."

"But we talked about this years ago. Didn't we?" Grandma Mona ignored me. Her rouged cheeks were getting redder; her skinny hands perched on pointy hips. "I thought I was very open and honest with you, Priscilla Lynn. It made me quite uncomfortable, but I told you all about the birds and the bees. What about contraception? Don't you know about it? My goodness, Priscilla. There are so many kinds these days. There must be a hundred ways *not* to get pregnant!"

"Grandma Mona!"

Mama stayed silent. Beaten down. She swiped at her nose again. Then she said, "What am I going to do?"

"What do you mean?" I asked her. "You're gonna have a baby. It'll be okay, Mama. I know it will. We'll all help."

"I am single. I live in a tiny, nothing town with a terrible job slopping pancakes and sausages on a buffet for senior citizens. And then there's Rainey . . . she needs so much more than what I can give her. She doesn't get enough from me as it is . . ."

I turned and looked at my mother. Her eyes were closed and she was gnawing on a spot inside her cheek. Slowly, I melted into her side. I lay down on her lap, and her hand rested on the top of my head, unmoving. I wondered if she even knew I was there.

"Well? What are you going to do, Priscilla?"

"Grandma Mona, could you just leave us alone for a while?" I said from the tops of Mama's knees. "Cain't you see this is hard on her?"

"Back in my day, having a baby meant *having a baby*. I suppose in today's world it could mean a multitude of things. What in the world is the world coming to anyway?"

"Please, Mona."

"That's *Grandma* Mona to you, young lady. Don't sass me." She sped away to the kitchen where she liked to spend most of her time. I imagine the heat of the stove must have made her feel right at home.

Mama stirred, so I sat up. "I have no idea what I'm going to do," she said. "Or maybe I do. Maybe I know exactly what I have to do. I think I'm going to be sick." She put her face in her hands and pressed her eyes. "God, how could you let this happen?"

"Oh Mama, I'm sure there's a reason for all this. Right? God has his reasons."

I was finding it hard to keep my optimism. Apparently, being pregnant was akin to the end of the world for her. Were we really that bad? I tell you what, I knew I was never kissing a boy until I got married. That was the truth. Time seemed to have stopped for my mother. I wished so hard I could rewind it for her and undo all this. I took a deep breath and let it out slowly. My mother did the same. Then we heard Rainey singing "Rock-a-bye Baby" from the bedroom, and that just sent Mama over the edge. Her tears plopped down hard, making wet spots on her blue jean shorts.

Mama had a choice to make. Simple as that. This was America, right? She could just make a list of her options and choose the best one. She could do pros and cons for each option. She liked lists. I did too. I could help her.

Mama's eyes were closed. She had tears streaming down her cheeks. I hated what all this was doing to her. It should have been a happy occasion. It should have been.

"Oh Mama, I'm sorry," I said. I lifted myself off the couch and went to the bathroom to look at the stick again. Maybe this was all a big mistake and we read it wrong. Now that would be funny. That would be really, really funny.

I leaned facedown into the metal wastebasket. Keeping my eyes closed, I said a little prayer and smiled, imagining Mama's face when she found out how silly we were, reading it wrong. Oh, how silly.

Then I opened my eyes and stared at the stick. A pink plus sign was staring right back at me, like a cross or a boni-fied sign from above. Or like angels coming and bearing the news.

Chapter Four
THE KEEPER OF SECRETS

{Mona}

I was standing there in the kitchen with my back pressed against the door. I bit my lip and closed my ever-living eyes. I could hear Priscilla sobbing in the next room. I could picture her face, distorted and red, her faint stork's foot now splotchy across her forehead. I had to fight back the tears myself. It's a thing no mother can bear, the sight of her child in pain. And although I fussed at Priscilla as always, I had grown especially hard on her now . . . for her sake and for everyone else's. She had once again put herself and her family in a terrible predicament.

I wanted to throttle her. I wanted to tell her that this was not how she was raised! That she was once a proud young girl who knew how to say no and wouldn't take no for an answer! She worked hard at her studies. She was going to make something of herself. She kept her frilly room clean, took care to wash her hands and face. She brushed her long, beautiful hair a hundred strokes a day, just because I told her it would make it stronger.

That was back when she listened to me.

And then . . . well, sometimes people make choices that change their lives forever. Priscilla gave up everything and everyone to bear her burdens all on her own, thank you very much. In many ways she was still so proud now that she was all grown up. Too proud to ever ask anyone for help. That's why I knew it was time to take matters into my own hands.

When the lights were all out and the world was quiet, I slipped into Priscilla's bedroom while she was sleeping, knelt to the floor, and buried my head in her mattress. Silently I prayed that she'd make the right decisions regarding the child she was carrying—and that I might could help in some fashion. And an amazing thing happened right there in the quiet of her room. Alongside the sound of Priscilla's breathing, I heard something. A word from above? Perhaps. All I know is that I felt it down thick and wide and true in my soul: *She must go home.*

I opened my eyes and watched Priscilla's covers moving slowly up and down. I touched my fingers to her forehead and gently rolled them over her hair like I used to when she was younger. She'd left home so long ago. Seemed like another lifetime. She'd sufficiently cut the thought of home right out of her mind and clean off her family tree. What or who could ever make Priscilla go home now?

The one thing I knew about Priscilla was that

she was stubborn. Just like her mama. I knew anything I said to her would be the very *opposite* of what she did. It's just how our relationship had become. It didn't please me, no. It's just how it had to be.

And my granddaughters. I had to play it up for them. I needed them, Janie especially, to believe I was the detriment to the family. Why? Well, that would be revealed in due time. Let's just say it was one of the many sacrifices a loving matriarch must make.

She was tossing and turning now, so I straightened her covers. Before I tiptoed out of Priscilla's room and left her to her restless dreaming, I kissed my daughter softly on the cheek and whispered into her ear, "Go home, sweet child. It's time for you to go *home.*"

Chapter Five
GREAT MOTHER OF GOD

{Janie}

The light was coming in through the window, frosting Rainey's wild hair. I was mesmerized by the sound of her *tap, tap, clacking* on the keyboard. Our computer was one they were going to pitch from the Y, seeing as the screen went dark whenever it pleased as if a ghost were in charge of the on-off button. That, and the keyboard was missing the letter *Q*, but Mama figured we could get along just fine without our *Q*s, and occasional black screens wouldn't hurt anybody.

If it were up to me though, there would have been a law against letting people with Down syndrome Google themselves. There was too much stuff on the Internet to misunderstand. One time Rainey Googled her own name and cried when she read she'd died in a car accident. Today she'd made the honor roll at some Presbyterian college in West Virginia, so she was happy. Now, she'd found every single online baby store for Mama and was making a list of things we were going to need for the baby: a blue crib, blue blankets, blue baby clothes. She was very good with her letters and lists. And her reading. But I really didn't think this was helping much.

"Rainey," I said, annoyed, "why is everything blue? Not that we're getting any of it, because we don't know yet if we're even going to need any of it. Right? But why in the world do you think everything should be blue?"

"He the boy, silly," she said, matter-of-fact.

"Oh. A boy. How do you know?"

"Duh. Everybody know it."

Rainey was still adding things to her list, so I turned away from her and the computer screen showing blue baby stuff flashing, flashing. I thought I might scream. I wished the screen would go black. I was still clutching *my own* list. Mama needed something that could actually help her make a decision.

The one thing Mama did for us, good or bad, was to teach us how to make lists. They helped keep us organized. Rainey fought the whole list thing for the longest time, but Mama practically forced them down her throat. Me, I took to them naturally, and they really seemed to work. I loved to check things off my lists. It made me feel as if I'd accomplished something. Mama had them taped inside every cabinet in the house, listing all the contents—*medicines, batteries, misc. knickknacks.* She worked hard, trying to keep our lives in order. I wished it would work right now. Two days ago, I'd woken up knowing who I was, what my place was in this family, basically not having a care in the world. Today, it was as if we were on that teacup ride at Disney where you're spinning, spinning, and your stomach twists all up. It had been five years since we'd been to Disney, but I still remembered that twisty feeling.

I sat on the couch and stared at the TV. It being summer, I really had nothing to do. I sort of wished I did so the day would go by quicker. By ten thirty, it'd been a million years.

I pulled my crumpled list to within inches of my face and thought on it. Hard.

Choices for Mama
#1: Keep the baby.

Cons:
1. *Mama's too busy for a new baby.*
2. *And she's too tired.*
3. *Her life will totally change. All of ours will.*
4. *She won't be able to have any more fun or friends. Not that she has any now, except for me, and Alisha, who really isn't that much fun or that great of a friend.*
5. *She doesn't have money for babysitters or day care.*
6. *We only have a two-bedroom house.*
7. *I'm not sure who the father is, but he might want to marry Mama. Mama might not want to marry him. I might not want him to be my new daddy. He might not be good for Rainey.*
8. *The father might not want to marry Mama. This might hurt her feelings because maybe she loves him. Maybe he won't want anything to do with the baby at all. Mama will wind up raising the baby all alone. She'll have to take a second job working the night shift at McDonald's just to take care of us all. Such a hard, sad life.*

Pros:
1. *Babies love you no matter what, even if you happen to work at McDonald's the rest of your hard, sad life.*

2. *Mama won't really be raising the baby alone. She'll have Rainey and me to help. And Poppy and Grandma Mona too.*
3. *God must think Mama needs another baby, or he wouldn't have given her one, especially being a virgin and all.*
4. *Babies are cute.*
5. *And small. They don't take up that much room.*
6. *I might like to have one around. I'd like to be a real big sister.*

"Mama?"

I found her on the sunporch. It was really just a big closet with windows, but the sun came in this time of day, and if the windows were open, a real nice breeze blew through. It was Mama's favorite wind-down place. She was always here after getting off work.

Mama was wearing her black polyester pants and white short-sleeve blouse. There was a red stain on the sleeve where somebody must have rubbed up against her with strawberry sauce. She lifted her head from her romance novel and stared right past me, sleepy eyed. Her eyes were still puffy from crying, her hair dropping out of a ponytail. She looked old at this moment, much older than thirty-two. She might as well have been fifty.

"Hey," I said.

I sat down next to her, and she kept her bare feet

propped up on the glass coffee table. The plants behind her needed watering bad. "Mama, can I ask you something?"

She raised her eyebrows in a weak sort of way and plopped her head on the back of the sofa.

"Well, after Daddy left, you still had us two kids." I stared at the plant slowly dying behind her. "I mean, I know it's hard, being a single mama, but is it . . . awful?"

Mama teared up and lifted her hands to her face. She rubbed her eyes so hard I thought she might go blind. Then she stopped and let her hands fall slowly to her lap.

"I'm . . . I'm sorta glad you're having a baby, Mama. Rainey and me, we'll be good big sisters. I promise."

She looked toward me and tried to muster a sad smile.

"I'm just so tired," she said. "How can I possibly have another child? Oh, goodness. My life might have been completely different. I could have gone to college. I wouldn't be waiting tables for old folks who lick maple syrup off their fingers. I might have met a guy, a nice guy, and gotten married. Oh, who am I kidding? But being a mom . . . it's the only thing I'm proud of. Being a mother is the only thing that makes any sense to me at all. It's who I am."

"So you're saying you're gonna keep the baby?" My heart raced, and I looked out the open window at a green lizard scurrying up the gutter. Mama stayed silent, rubbing her temples.

"I just need to take some time to figure this out."

"Oh. Okay. But Mama, I've been thinking. I'm kind of excited about being a real big sister. I mean, I know it won't be easy and all, but, well, I can get a job bagging at the grocery store. I can help out. I can. It'll be good. You're a really great mama."

She interrupted me, screaming, "Uuugh! I am just so *angry!*"

I looked over at her in horror.

"Ha! You're angry? You ought to be angry. At yourself. Imagine, a single woman your age, expecting. It's indecent."

"Grandma Mona, please. I didn't even hear you come in."

"Well, I'm here now. And is that any way to welcome me to your home, Janie? I'm her mother; I'm needed at a time like this."

There was really nothing more I could say. My grandmother was a force to be reckoned with. And not in a good way. More like an iceberg. Since I'd turned about four or five, I could only remember a handful of times she'd left me feeling the teensiest bit warm and fuzzy. She wasn't always this way though. I could remember her kisses and hugs when I was little, her telling me she loved me. But not anymore. The older she

40

got, the meaner she got. And I had to protect Mama from her.

Rainey came at us waving a piece of paper. She had this strange look on her face. "Mama?" She showed it to her. "The world gonna end. When Jesus comes."

"Rainey, what?" Mama asked, confused and trying to reach for the paper.

"We got to get ready," said Rainey. "It says right here."

Mama studied the paper called "Jesus Is Coming," and shook her head. But I thought I understood it, and it just made me sad.

"She's talking about you being pregnant," I mumbled. "She keeps printing out baby things and won't stop. Would you please tell her to stop it?"

"Rainey? What's going on, honey?"

Rainey smiled as if she was fully in tune with what was going on for once and could contribute to our conversation. She often felt left out.

"You got the baby Jesus in the tummy," said Rainey, poking the paper. "Jesus is coming. And the world gonna end. He not the reg'lar person, Mama."

"Oh, this is rich," said Grandma Mona, folding her arms and leaning against the wall.

"The world is not going to end, honey," Mama said. "And would you please stop printing things? This paper costs money."

"Janie," said Grandma Mona. "You told that poor child your mother is having the baby Jesus?" Her voice was flat and critical.

I stood up, unable to take any more and screamed, "No I did not, Grandma Mona! She figured that out all on her own. And I tell you what, I've been waiting for angels to come and tell us about this baby, but I haven't seen any! Not a one! So I don't know. Is Mama carrying the Son of God, or not?!" I waved my finger in the air. "She could be, for all you know! Mama's a good girl. You might be carrying the Savior, Mama! You're gonna save the whole world as we know it!"

"That is quite enough!" said Grandma Mona.

I closed my fists and burst out of the room. I didn't even look back. I wasn't sure what'd come over me, but I was crying and scratching at the door to the bedroom. The knob always stuck. When I finally got it open, I shoved all Rainey's clothes off my bottom bunk and flopped down on it. Then I remembered I'd left my list of pros and cons—and my poor pregnant mother—in the other room with the meanest, most unhelpful woman on the face of the earth. Some daughter I was. No wonder Mama was so upset about having another baby. Who wouldn't, with a child like me?

Chapter Six
THE WIND AND THE HOLLOW

By the time I woke up, it was lunchtime. I stood in front of the dresser mirror and stared at the red hand mark pressed in the side of my face from lying on it. I tucked my hair behind my ears and stumbled to the kitchen where I found my mother mashing hard-boiled eggs like a maniac. There were three cartons on the counter, all open.

My grandmother was leaning on her elbows, smiling, but not in a nice way. "There's a sandwich in the fridge for you," she said. "Or two. Or three."

My mother was mashing, mashing away, and I couldn't imagine eating all these eggs, but I didn't ask. She stopped long enough to open the refrigerator door and pull out a gallon of milk and an egg salad sandwich on wheat bread, cut into halves lengthwise. She set it in front of me. *The Young and the Restless* was on in the other room, and I watched a little through the doorway while I nibbled. This one man was crying on his knees while this lady stood over him, seeming happy about it.

Mama went back to egg mashing.

"That's a lot of eggs," I said.

Grandma Mona piped up. "Apparently they were on special. Can't you see?"

43

Mama picked up the jar of mayonnaise and scooped a spoonful, plopping it in. Then she squeezed the mustard, which made farting noises, spitting a glob out now and again. "Dang, dang, dangit," she said. Her face scrunched up like she might cry. She bit her lip and turned away from me, resting her chin on her shoulder.

"You okay?" I asked.

Still looking away, she said, "I'm out of mustard. I can't do this." Her shoulders started to shake. She grabbed the big bowl, wrapped some cellophane on top with a fury and said, "Well, I'll just go to the store and get some. You have a problem, Priscilla, you just go take care of it. No big deal." She was talking to herself the whole time cleaning up.

"I can walk to the store if you want, Mama."

She looked at me as if she'd forgotten I was here.

"No, no," Grandma Mona shooed at me. "Obviously she needs to get out of the house. I'll go with her."

"You really shouldn't do that. I mean, really. You shouldn't do that."

"I'm her mother."

"Rainey?" Mama called. "Rainey, going to the store. Back in a few minutes!"

"When you're done, Janie, why don't you go check on your sister?" said Grandma Mona. "She's in the backyard. Been out there for a while."

44

"Okay," I grumbled. Mama slung her huge brown leather purse over her shoulder and grabbed her keys from the hook next to the door. I heard her sigh. Then they were gone.

The bread was a little soggy, so I scraped out the egg salad with a fork. Eggs. Chicken eggs. Little baby chickens.

I pushed the plate away and looked at all the egg cartons staring at me with their empty cradles.

Pregnant.

I just couldn't believe there was something growing inside my mother. The back of my neck grew hot, so I picked up a glass of milk. Milk. Kids need milk. Babies *need* milk.

I had to get out of there. I wasn't even hungry.

Our backyard was a small patch of yellow grass, scorched from Mama's overfertilizing and lack of sprinklers, and then there was a great big oak tree surrounded by a chain-link fence. The tree was completely hollow. The only reason we kept it was because it would cost too much money to take it down, *and* it was leaning *away* from the house. Mama being so pretty, Mr. Rufus down at the hardware store offered to take it down for next to nothing, but Mama said it was no real risk to us if it did happen to fall. Plus, it gave us shade and Rainey liked it. That was the end of that.

I saw Rainey's bare foot sticking out of the hollowed-out part. For some reason, she was blessed with the most flexible joints ever. It came with having an extra chromosome, I guess. She liked to sit cross-legged with one foot over her shoulder, leaning facedown. Maybe it made her feel like she was in Mama's belly again. That's what it looked like anyway.

Mama's belly. Ugh.

I approached the tree carefully. Rainey retreated here when something was bothering her. One time it was because this silly lady wouldn't let her take her groceries to her car. That was her *job*. The lady obviously wasn't a regular shopper at Jerry's Supermarket or she would have known that you *always* let Rainey Dae Macy walk your cart to your car. She took her work in this world very seriously. Rainey ended up squabbling over the cart with the lady, screaming, "I can do it! I can do it myself!" You never told Rainey she couldn't do something. She'd always prove you wrong.

"Rainey?" I said, announcing myself. Her foot stirred. "You in there?"

She sighed real loud.

I scooted to sitting on the dirt and on the buckling roots in front of the hole. Rainey's head was down, foot over her shoulder.

"Is something wrong?" I asked.

She lifted her head and sat up, pressing her foot down into the ground. She looked like she'd been sleeping. The cavern around her was dark, and I knew for a fact that bats lived in the upper part of the hole. I'd seen them. And one time we saw a real live skink in the bottom part. How she could love being in here, I just didn't know. It creeped me out.

There was a baby doll lying naked in Rainey's lap, its tiny dress lying in the yellow grass behind me. The sight of it hurt me.

"Is that your baby?" I said.

"Uh-huh. It like the baby Jesus. He like God. I listen for God in here."

"You're listening for God in a hollowed-out tree?"

"Yeah. 'Cept for the bats squeak sometimes. God don't squeak."

"Well, what *does* he say? What does he sound like?"

The wide space between her almond-shaped eyes grew narrower, and she squinted up into the void at the hiding bats.

"He sound like the wind."

"Huh," I said. I did not know that.

"You feel like coming out now? Mama made a truckload of egg salad."

"No thanks. I had cheese toast."

"Okay." I thought of going back inside, but I didn't really want to be alone. "Mind if I sit here with you? I promise I'll be quiet." I leaned up against the bark and closed my eyes with the sun on my face. It felt so warm, and the backs of my eyelids turned orange and glowy. "Let me know if you hear from God again," I added. "Tell him I have a few questions for him."

"Okay," she said. From the rustling in the tree I could hear her moving back into position. After a minute or so she sat back up again. I startled when something cold pressed into my arm.

"God said you want the baby, so here." The bald-headed doll's little eyes stared up at me from my forearm.

"No, Rain. You keep it." I pushed the doll away, leaned back and closed my eyes again. "Let me know if he says anything I don't already know."

"Oh. Okay," she said. And we sat in silence for an hour or so—until Mama came to check on us. She left the door open and let the screen swing shut. I got up to talk to her, to put my arms around her or something, but I could hear she was on the phone.

"Oh, hey, Alisha," she said. Mama worked with Alisha. She wasn't my favorite person. She drank too much and smoked, and sometimes when Mama'd been hanging around with her, going out on her nights off and all, Mama turned . . . different. Like somebody else. "No, took a test already," she said. "Yep. Ohhhh, yeah. I don't . . . I just . . . I can't believe it. I don't know yet. Please don't say a word. I don't know what I'm going to do."

To be honest, I still didn't know who the father was. It's not like Mama ever brought anyone to the house. Not in a very long time anyway. She tried to keep men away from us, I think, so we didn't get attached to one and have him leave and break our hearts. It had happened with Daddy. Mama was tapping her foot and pulling her hair on the side of her head while she talked. It was a bad habit. One of these days, I figured it would fall right out.

"No, he doesn't know," she told Alisha. My stomach churned, thinking of her secret. I wondered when Mama was going to tell the father. She had to. Or did she? It was strange, knowing women had so much power over men.

Mama sighed and said, "I just don't think I can do this again. I will. Listen, we're, um, we're going to take off for a while. No. I don't know. I have to go. I've got to think about all this."

"Mama?" I whispered, seeing how upset this was making her. Rainey was next to me now, watching Mama and looking confused.

"Five weeks or so," she said, turning away from us and trying to talk softer. "I've got— what?—a month, two tops, to figure this out. I just can't believe it. Not again. Listen, I need to go. I'll call you when I get back, all right? I really . . . have a good . . . Bye."

Mama strangled the phone and made sure it was

49

dead before she pressed it to her forehead and turned away from me. She took two slow steps into the house, then said, quiet but firm, "Go pack your bags."

"Why?" Rainey said, alarmed.

"Yeah, why?" I asked.

"We're leaving."

"Where we goin'?"

Mama sighed again. "Rainey, I don't know. Just do what I said, all right? Pack some bags. We leave first thing in the morning."

"We go on ba-cation, Mama?" asked Rainey.

My mother faced me, and her pretty blue eyes were extra-double-bagged and droopy. "Yeah, something like that. I don't know. We're just . . . going anywhere. Far away. Just . . . not here."

Rainey, not one to spring things on, looked panicked. She put her hands over her ears like she always did when she was really upset. So Mama took her hands and brought them to her lips. She smiled and kissed them. "It's summertime, baby. Let's go see the world, okay? Life is out there, waiting. We just have to find it."

Rainey lit up. An adventure didn't sound so scary.

"Like Dora! We get the treasure. We go over the bridge, cross the forest . . ."

And just like that, our world changed. Mama was the heart of our family, the center of our world. Rainey and me, we loved Mama, and we'd follow her anywhere—to heaven and back or further if needed. As long as it made her happy. It was all Rainey and I ever wanted—for Mama to be happy. Right now, she was anything but.

Chapter Seven
TRAVELING IN STYLE

There was something special about our transportation. After my daddy left, my mother visited this used-car salesman named Carl down at the car place. Carl was about as exciting as a rock, but the pickins were slim in Cypresswood. Mama might have seen him only once or twice, but before she broke it off with him, Carl sold her a white 1996 Crown Victoria Police Interceptor. She said it was a steal but paid real money for it, so it wasn't really stealing. Police cars have to have all the police stuff stripped off of them before being sold. Carl made sure the car was stripped, and then he added a few things back in for my mother after the sale, hoping to get on her good side again.

Mama got rid of Carl right quick, but our car turned out to be a keeper. It had a siren and front lights that flashed and everything, stuff that came in handy every now and again.

Rainey was sitting in the middle of the wide backseat, her feet bouncing up and down on the rubber floor.

"Put your seat belt back on, honey." Mama was looking in the rearview mirror.

Rainey moved to the seat directly behind Mama and worked on stretching the belt around her puffy hips. She'd always been a little on the heavy side, never giving second helpings a second thought.

"Do you need help?" I asked her. But I knew what she'd say.

"I can do it myself." So I watched as she stretched and fumbled. Finally, I heard a click and relaxed.

"Nice day for car ride," I heard her say.

"Sure is."

"I'm having fun." I turned and watched her pull her feet up cross-legged, cradling her left foot. The look in her eyes showed she was worried, so I smiled at her to let her know everything was going to be okay. Then I heard the distinct sounds of my grandparents shuffling over.

". . . from a perfectly good nap, Grayson. Why do I have to go anyway? This is about her. It's her life." It was Grandma Mona and my grandfather, Poppy. Poppy was the only man in my world. Usually, he was the voice of reason and the total opposite of Grandma Mona. I wasn't sure how he put up with her to begin with, but they'd been apart for a good long while. I wasn't clear on the particulars, but they'd only gotten back together a year or so ago.

"Because we're a family, Mona. And families stick together."

"Coming from somebody else, I might believe that," she said.

"Just get in the car."

"Mama," I whispered, "you really want them to come? *Grandma Mona*, I mean?"

"I heard that," said Grandma Mona. "Don't think I didn't hear it."

My grandmother slipped in to the middle seat beside Rainey, and Poppy sat behind me, next to her. He was a little man, shorter than Grandma Mona, but he had a big heart. And he loved me, this I knew. He still had dark hair, not so much on the top but more on the sides. His hands were small and aged. I reached back over the seat and patted the headrest. Poppy touched my hand and squeezed it, letting me know he was right there behind me. Always there for me. I felt the warmth of his hand, and it calmed me.

"Okay then," said Mama, buckling herself in and turning around one last time to smile at Rainey. "All aboard. Who's ready for a little adventure?"

"Me!" said Rainey, grinning full throttle.

The rest of us—me, Grandma Mona, and Poppy—sat quietly, eyes closed or staring out the window. God only knew what we were really in for.

• • •

The sky was bright blue-jay blue with clouds dotting around here and there. The sun was shining on the back of us, so no need yet for sunglasses. I was quiet, studying my mother, who was concentrating on her driving so intently that at times her eyebrows touched. She looked tired as usual, but had attempted to put some makeup on—mascara, pink lipstick. I wasn't sure why.

"We know where we're going yet?" asked Poppy.

"Who goes on vacation with no destination?" said Grandma Mona. "And with gas prices so high . . ."

I turned around and glared at them both to be quiet and not to push. Mama sat back and positioned her hands on the wheel. I was afraid she'd cry again, and I didn't think I could stand that.

"What did you tell Bob?" asked Poppy. Then, turning to Grandma Mona, he whispered, "What'd she tell Bob? Did he let her off work?"

"She told him where he could shove his little two-bit job."

"No she didn't. Really?"

"I don't know, Grayson," she said. "Priscilla doesn't confide in me with these sorts of things. Knowing her, he's holding the job for her until she gets back."

"That's good," he said. "Girl's got to have a job. Having another baby and all."

I squeezed my eyes closed. I was praying my mother didn't lose it, listening to those two. They could go at it for hours, talking about you behind your back like you weren't even there. It was maddening.

We pulled into the parking lot of Hardee's and waited in the drive-thru behind about seven cars. The line moved slower than a funeral procession. I never did understand why fast-food lines seemed to move so slowly. When we got up to the window, I imagined myself on the other side, scooping up hash browns, dishing out change. I'd probably be slow at it, too, someday. A bagful of sausage-and-egg biscuits later, we were back on the road.

"Who's hungry?" Mama sang.

"Me!" said Rainey.

"Not me," I said. I was too jittery to eat. Mama reached a biscuit over her head to Rainey, while Grandma Mona and Poppy stayed quiet. Eating wasn't on their minds either.

Traffic was picking up, and my mother turned on the radio. A country music crying song was on.

"I can't stand this music," said Poppy. "Don't you have anything with a horn in it? How 'bout some jazz. Dizzie or Chet."

"Sorry, Poppy," I said. "Nothing like that in this town. We do have a couple cassettes though. How about John Mayer?"

"Never heard of him."

"Mama, play John Mayer," said Rainey.

"Okay, honey. Just a minute."

Mama ripped open a packet of mustard with her teeth and squeezed it on her sausage biscuit while driving. She took a mouthful, and I smelled her coffee, breathing it in. The smell had wafted to the backseat too.

"You really shouldn't drink that coffee, Priscilla."

Mama's cheeks looked like a chipmunk's.

"But she has to have her coffee, Grandma Mona," I said, sticking up for her. "One cup of coffee won't matter much."

"What do you mean it won't matter? Are you pregnant or not, Priscilla?"

Poppy said, "Leave her alone, Mona. You know she is."

"Then it matters," said Grandma Mona. "I'll have you know I didn't drink alcohol or smoke when I had Priscilla. I did, however, drink a pot of coffee a day. Draw your own conclusions."

Mama picked up the coffee and inhaled. She wrinkled her nose. Thinking, thinking . . . We were all watching to see if she'd drink it when she rolled down the window and poured it out. Just like that. Brown spray flew up against Rainey's window.

"Oh, that's nice. Look at that," said Grandma Mona.

"A perfectly good cup. Gone," said Poppy. "She acts like money grows on trees."

"I hope you're happy," Grandma Mona said to my mother.

"I hope you're all happy," I said. "You're upsetting Mama. Why don't we just play the quiet game? Whoever's quietest wins."

"I gonna win," said Rainey. "I always win, right, Mama?"

"Yes, honey. You are a winner."

This was going to be a very long trip. It'd been years since we went anywhere with Grandma Mona. The last time was Disney. Mama and Daddy saved up for two years to take us there. This time, well, I had no idea how much she'd saved up. 'Course, how much money did we really need, going on a trip to nowhere?

We eased out onto Northview, which led to the interstate. I knew how stressed my mother was, so I was trying to leave her alone about the whole where-are-we-going thing. I waited to see if she was heading east toward the ocean or west toward the mountains.

"Mama?" said Rainey. "Roll up the window."

What she meant was "down," and this being a former cop car, the doors and the windows wouldn't work from the backseat. Better to keep the prisoners in, I guessed. Mama flicked the switch and Rainey's window went down with a slow *whoosh*. She stuck her head out as far as she could with the seat belt holding her back. I craned my neck, watching her face light up in the wind, her shoulder-length hair blowing furiously around her. Rainey's eyes were tightly closed as if she was thinking hard, as if she was listening to God out there in the wind. I watched her and wondered, *what in the world is he saying to her now?*

"Close your lips, Rain. You're gonna get bugs in your teeth."

She closed her mouth and slipped back inside, her hair crazed. Her eyes were smiling, and she moved her tongue around, checking for bugs, just in case.

Mama was still nibbling on her biscuit, and Grandma Mona said, "Let me know if you start feeling sick or anything, Priscilla. We'll have to put you in the backseat with the rubber floor." I looked at my mother and suddenly wished I was in the backseat and out of her range.

She signaled right, and we pulled onto the ramp for I-26 West. We were going to the mountains. The last time we went to the mountains, it was right after my daddy left. Mama said he was headed for the hills, so off we went, chasing after him. Never did find him. I wondered what we're doing now, how long we were going to stay up in the mountains. Were we going to find Daddy? No. I pushed the thought out of my head. Maybe Mama'd get tired and miss our house. Maybe we'd run out of money and she'd head back to the egg salad nesting in the freezer. We'd probably be home in our own beds tonight.

"I know you're not going where I think you're going," said Grandma Mona.

I heard the wheels humming below us and watched the trees getting taller.

"We don't have to go anywhere, you know," I told Mama.

"Yes we do," said Grandma Mona. "Priscilla does. Don't you, Priscilla? Like when she was pregnant with Rainey, she just took off. Isn't that what you do, Priscilla? Tell your daughters. They're old enough to know."

Mama hadn't mentioned this before. She'd never really talked about her giving birth to Rainey. But something about the movement of the car allowed her to start talking. Maybe it was that she didn't have to look us in the eye.

"I was almost your age when I found out I was having you, Rainey. My mother was not nearly as understanding as yours. She told me what she expected me to do. She would have forced me if I'd stayed."

"To do what?" asked Rainey.

"Yeah, what did she want you to do?" I asked.

"That is quite enough, Priscilla," said Grandma Mona. "Why don't you tell her the truth? How you wouldn't stop running around with that Johnson boy. Now there's a good story."

"We were living in Yuma, Arizona, at the time,"

59

Mama said, ignoring my question and Grandma Mona's meanness. "Daddy's job had moved us there. 'We've only been here a year, Priscilla! Now what will everybody think?!'" Mama did an impression of Grandma Mona that I thought sounded a lot like her. Grandma Mona didn't think it was so funny though.

"Well truly. Everybody did think it. They did. You know I was right, Priscilla. We were living in different times."

Mama sniffed and wiped her face with the back of her right hand, and I wished I could open the door, jump, and roll right out of this pressure cooker. But I couldn't. Mama needed me.

"So you left home," I said. "You drove to Cypresswood, South Carolina, by yourself?"

"I hitched a ride to California, thinking I'd like it out there. But it was too close to home. So I waited tables for a week and took a bus all the way across country. I'd get off at each stop and look around, but I never felt like staying anywhere. The ground was too dry and dusty—hard like my home had been."

"It wasn't so hard," said Grandma Mona. "Your mother's exaggerating, girls. Isn't she, Grayson?"

"I was sixteen and pregnant and not an ounce of sense in me. I decided to stay wherever it was raining, and three days later, I'm in Cypresswood in a big thunder-boomer. I was a little disappointed I didn't make it all the way to the ocean."

"If you want the ocean, why you got off the bus?" asked Rainey. It was a very smart question.

"I told you. I loved the rain. I'd made a deal with myself."

"The clouds should have held out at least till Forest Pines," said Grandma Mona. "If it hadn't rained in Cypresswood, you might never have had Harlan in your lives."

Hmm. Well, that shut Mama up. Harlan was my daddy. He rode a Harley-Davidson named Marilyn after Marilyn Monroe, a dead movie star. I hardly remembered Daddy, seeing as he left when I was four. I did remember his brown hair was long in the back. And it was going gray down the sides too, so when the wind had caught it just right, it looked like he had two white wings coming out the back of him. I also had this memory of him and me riding to the Dairy Queen in Fervor, me holding on for dear life. Sometime after he left, my memory of my father started to fade. It's a terrible thing to forget your father's face, but it happens. At times, all I remembered of my father was an angel on a motorcycle.

Mama really loved him, and she cried a whole long while when he left. Some for her, but mostly for Rainey and me. We cried too. Rainey practically lived in the hollow tree for a month. I remember she'd even take her meals out there.

Driving down the road, every time a motorcycle would zoom past us, I'd check to see if it was him. Just an old habit. Mama said my daddy had a wild hair up his rear, and he finally ran off with Marilyn. I hoped they were happy, wherever they were.

Mama looked up at the clouds and said, "I loved the rain so much, I named you Rainey, honey."

"I like my name."

"Yeah, me too," said Mama. "Fits you better than Thunder or Boomer, don't you think?"

Mama smiled for the first time in days and set her head back on the rest, and Rainey pressed hers on the window. Poppy was already snoring in the backseat, and Grandma Mona had pickled herself quiet.

For the rest of the morning, we drove in near silence through the state of South Carolina, Rainey having finally fallen asleep, and none of us wanting to disturb her. I felt like a little window had opened between my mother and the rest of us, and I didn't want to close it. I looked up at the clear blue sky when we crossed the state line into North Carolina. Secretly, I was praying for rain and that Mama could finally stop running.

Chapter Eight
THANK GOD FOR
GROCERY STORES

Mama had this thing about not wanting to press her opinions on Rainey and me. She wanted us to express our "own self." I guess it all went back to her mother, Grandma Mona. Mama was just the opposite of her. I wondered what kind of mother I'd be when I grew up, the overbearing kind or the have-it-your-own-way kind? If we always do the opposite of how we were raised, I feared I might be cruel. I guessed it all depended on what you believed in. I wondered what Mama believed when it came to her having this new baby. All I really knew about Mama's beliefs were, you always tip a waitress no matter what, and you always pack an umbrella. Just in case. I patted my list of options folded in my pocket, to make sure it was still there. I'd work on it some more when nobody was watching.

Rainey and Poppy were awake now, but Grandma Mona was still unconscious. It was how I liked her the most. "Let me know when you're hungry," my mother said. "I'll find an Arby's or something."

"I could eat," I said, sitting up straighter in my seat and blinking to adjust to the noonday light.

"After lunch, I go work," said Rainey. "I need put my apron on."

"Oh. Right," said Mama. "Well, guess what? You're not going in to work today, honey."

I bit my lip, hoping Rainey would handle this well.

"But I got work," said Rainey. "Got take groceries to the car. Pack 'em up real good."

Mama squeezed the wheel and flipped her face all the way around to look at Rainey. We were speeding seventy miles an hour down I-26.

"Mama!" I screamed. "Look out!"

"Oh, sweet Mary, hold on!" Poppy was hollering, and Rainey was frozen up.

I mean it, we almost ran a guy off the road! He was honking and we were swerving. I grabbed the wheel while Mama was screaming, and finally we got it straightened out. I nearly had a heart attack. I was grabbing at my chest, and my mother looked discombobulated like she'd just woken up and happened to be driving a car.

Mama eased onto an off-ramp and then into the dirt on the side of the road.

"What in tarnation are you doing?" Grandma Mona shrieked.

"It's all right, she got it," said Poppy in his soothing kind of way. "Everybody just calm it down, now. Nice and calm."

We came to a stop, the hazards blinking, and Mama leaned her head on the steering wheel and banged it a couple times. Then she said calmly, "Rainey, I told Mr. Mooneyham we were going on a little trip, honey. He said it's perfectly fine and to have fun. Fun, he said. Isn't this fun? You can go back to work when we get home, all right?"

This change in routine was not sitting well with Rainey. She was trying to process it all and deal with it. I could tell by how she kept tilting her head to the side and mumbling to herself. She was holding her baby doll and fiddling with its fingertips, counting each finger, trying to stay calm. Trying. She couldn't hold it in any longer and threw her hands up to her ears, letting the doll roll to the floor. "I want go work! I want help people with the grocery. Let's go home, Mama. Time go home."

I watched as my mother's pretty face stretched back into a painful grimace and she started crying. And not just a little cry, but a deep, rip-your-heart-out kind. For a woman who was mostly quiet except for occasional bouts of self-talking, these outbursts were becoming right regular.

"Goodness, it's okay," said Poppy. "Oh, now. She'll be fine. Won't you, Rainey? You'll be fine, right? We're going to have fun! The Macy family on the open road!"

"I got go work." Rainey pleaded. She was really beginning to fret, with the bottom lip shaking and all.

Mama cried harder. The sound completely filled the car and bounced off my eardrums, pinging from window to window. We weren't even in our own state anymore. We were hours away from Rainey's happy place in the hollow of the backyard tree. I looked up at a flashing sign for cigarettes at a Zippy Mart, and that's when I had one of my smartest ideas ever. "Mama, go find a grocery store," I told her. "They're bound to be in every town, right?"

Mama must have thought it was a good idea, too, because we drove around, and when we found one, Mama went in and explained our situation. She asked if my sister could bag a few groceries. Maybe take them out to a few cars. There just happened to be another developmentally challenged person who worked at this particular store, but he was sick today. Bad for him. Good for us.

Chapter Nine
MOUNTAINS TO MOVE

{Mona}

The grocery store manager was more than happy to have some free help. My granddaughter Rainey was smiling and just bagging away. She was doing a very nice job putting the frozen foods together and the produce together. Very smart girl. Better than I could do. But the plastic bags were causing her fits. She was used to paper, so she mumbled about how hard and slippery these "bad bags" were. "Need the paper bags," she said. "Not these bad bags." Adorable child.

Grayson and Janie roamed the grocery aisles, hand in hand, marveling at how much things cost these days. Every now and again, they'd come back to tell us that a gallon of milk was over four dollars. "Might as well put that in the gas tank!" said Grayson. "Can you believe it? Four-dollar milk and four-dollar gas. What's the world coming to?"

"I know it, honey, I know it," I said.

"Come on, Poppy," said Janie, grabbing his arm. "Let's go see how much cakes and cookies cost!" And off they'd go.

Priscilla and I sat in the little café, sipping water, watching Rainey, waiting. I counted five sips of water before I held my breath and then let it out. "I know what you're doing, Priscilla," I told her. She froze up and grabbed her glass with two hands. "I understand you miss the man. I do. But honey, this is no way to act. You can't just come traipsing through the mountainside looking for a ghost." A man walked by Priscilla and tipped his cap to her. Priscilla halfway smiled, then crossed her legs and turned her head toward me. "He's gone, Priscilla," I whispered. "I know you don't want to believe it, but honey, it's true. He's gone and he's not coming back. The sooner you can accept this, the better it'll be for everyone. I just don't want to see you hurt—"

Just then, Janie bounded up and eyed me hard. She had fire in her eyes and hands on hips, ready to strike. So I played it up. "And when we get back on the road, please, for heaven's sake, use some sense around those tractor trailers! You're gonna get us all killed, and I'll tell you 'I told you so' soon as our feet hit the other side."

"Grandma Mona . . ." Janie scolded me with her tone. My goodness, she was so much like her mama when she was a girl. I wanted to grab her up and pinch her cheeks. I wanted to pull her into my arms and hug her tight like I used to. But I didn't. I couldn't. Not yet anyway. I wasn't actually bitter toward Priscilla anymore, just the contrary. But I played the charade just the same in front of Janie. It killed me, but as keeper of the family secrets, I had to be cruel—tough love, rather. I had to maintain my distance from her and everyone else just a little while longer. Just a little while . . .

Janie sat down in front of me, next to her mama. She looked over at her, and they both watched Rainey. "She's doing a good job, isn't she, Mama?" Janie was so tickled her plan for Rainey had worked. It did my heart good to see. "Thank you, God, for putting grocery stores in every single town," she said on folded hands.

"Amen," said Priscilla. Her eyes were closed as if she was praying too. She didn't seem to do that much anymore. I was praying she *was* praying. She needed all the help she could get. Then she opened her eyes and chewed on her bottom lip.

"What? What is it?" Janie asked.

"Oh, what I wouldn't do to just go back in time," said Priscilla.

Amen, I thought. But this time I stayed quiet.

Priscilla took a deep breath and watched Rainey hard at work. Janie studied her mother's face, like she always did. It was her gauge for how things were going. Janie only saw the best in her mama, as many children do. Not mine, anyway, but many. In between sips of water, Janie caught her mother smiling now and again, and the little girl's face lit up, grinning from ear to ear. She shuffled in her seat and sat back like she was at a picture show.

As long as Priscilla was smiling, my sweet little Janie was happy. Watching Janie's lips curled up, I was tempted to smile too—except that I had a vague feeling for what might be coming next. Yes, it would be a long hard road, but I knew if and when Priscilla finally found what she was after, Janie's world, as she knew it, would end completely. In many ways, it already had.

• • •

"How much longer are we going to stay here?" I piped up. "It's cold in this grocery store. Cold, I tell you. I'm freezing."

"You can wait outside, then," said Poppy, rounding the corner from produce. "Can't you see how happy our granddaughter is?" I gave him a raised eyebrow that told him all he needed to know.

We couldn't get Rainey to stop bagging groceries. It made her feel important. "What time is it?" she asked when we said it was time to go.

"It's already three thirty, Rainey. We need to get on the road, okay? Come on. You've done a terrific job. I'm proud of you." Priscilla took hold of her arm.

"Not time yet." Rainey grabbed a package of toilet paper and stuck her tongue out, trying to fit it into a small plastic bag. Amazingly, she got it in. Priscilla looked at her with tired eyes. Anyone could see she didn't have the energy for an argument.

"Do we have to go, Mama? Cain't we just stay?" asked Janie.

Priscilla made fists by her sides and took a deep breath. When the color rushed back to her face she said sweetly, " 'Scuse me, miss, what town are we in?"

The cashier assessed my daughter and assumed she'd inhaled drugs. She said, "Swannanoa."

"Swannanoa. Swannanoa . . . is Black Mountain near here?"

"Sure is. Next town over."

"Okay, honey. Would you like to spend the night here? Tell me . . . Arlene—" Priscilla read off her name tag—"what's there to do around here?"

"Flea market's up the road 'bout a mile and a half," said Arlene. " 'Course there's the mountains for hiking. Couple lakes if you like water and stuff. There's the airport in Asheville, if you're flying somewhere."

And just like that, Rainey got to work a full shift, and Priscilla bought a map, staking out a Sleep Tight Inn right next to a lake. I figured a dumpy motel room might be just what she needed to zap back to her senses and make her way home. Either that or she'd run out of money or gas, one. I was just betting Priscilla would run out of steam first. If it was possible for a person to age ten years in a day, my daughter had done it. I truly hoped she didn't find what she came up here to the mountains to find. Why, unearthing Harlan might delay her prodigal homecoming indefinitely. And I knew I could speak to her till I was blue in the face about the girls' father, but she'd never listen. What was a mother to do?

Chapter Ten
CLOSE QUARTERS

{Janie}

Sleeping in the same room with two old people who snored was about as fun as a rainstorm on the Fourth of July. The only good thing was, I had my own little sofa, and Rainey crawled into Mama's bed. Poppy and Grandma Mona took the other one.

I'd never liked waking up in the middle of the night. Everything looked scary in darkness, the what-ifs and what-if-nevers. Most of the night I worried about my mother. Worried about the new baby. Worried I might not be as good a big sister as I thought I'd be. Wondered how Mama would be able to survive another baby and a second job. Worried she might wake up any minute and start puking like they did on the TV when a baby was on the way. Wondered what an eight-and-a-half-year-old girl could possibly do to help her.

Mama never woke up puking, thank goodness, but it was like listening to a chorus of jigsaws all night. I lay there with a pillow covering my ears and another dangling off the sofa, and when Poppy would start snoring, I'd bop him on the head with it. Then Grandma Mona would go. *Bop, bop, bop.* All night long.

I was so tired, I thought I might cry.

"Poppy, y'all snore worse than anybody. Ever."

"That is not true," he said, pulling his trousers up over his briefs and working on the belt buckle.

"Oh, yes it is! Do you know how much I slept? Zero. Ze-ro, Poppy. You too, Grandma Mona." I held my finger up in an *O* and looked at her through it to press my point.

"Well, I didn't hear anything," she said, gazing over at Rainey, who was still lying in place trying to touch her tongue to her nose. She couldn't quite get it, but she tried over and over. Finally, Rainey grinned and said, "What we do today, Mama?"

"Well, I don't know, I . . . we can do anything we want, I guess. We're free as the wind." Mama leaned over and kissed Rainey on the forehead.

"I want read the book," said Rainey. Mama made her way to her hard white suitcase and pulled out a *Corduroy the Bear* book. She plopped down next to Rainey again, who grabbed her baby doll and kissed it. "This what I gonna do baby Jesus, Mama. I kiss him all the time."

"That's just lovely," said Grandma Mona. "I'm going to take a shower. A hot one. When I get out, can we *please* talk about going home, Priscilla? This doesn't quite feel like a vacation. No one's relaxing. And shouldn't you be going to the doctor soon?"

"Nobody asked you to come along," I said

under my breath, knowing it was extra fresh, but I was so tired.

"I'm going to pretend I didn't hear that," said Grandma Mona. "Why don't you lie back down and take a nap."

My mother squeezed her head between her hands and leaned into Rainey's pillow, saying, "Oh, Rainey, make it stop. Can't I just close my eyes and go to sleep for a long time? Couldn't we just take a whole day off and sleep?"

"That no fun. You sleep at night," Rainey said.

"I mean it, Priscilla," said Grandma Mona. "Seriously consider going home to your own bed today. I don't think this trip is any good for you . . . in your condition. I'll be out in a few minutes."

Mama picked up the book and started reading about a little bear that gets lost in a department store. I'd heard the story ten thousand million times.

After Grandma Mona was through with the bathroom, Poppy slipped in there. A second later, it was my turn. I hated motel bathrooms. Not that I'd been in too many of them. There was the summer Mama took us to Disney. I guess that was really the only place I'd been. That motel had roaches. Then another time, our air-conditioner broke at home in hundred-degree weather and we had to go stay in a hotel just to survive. Anyway, there I was in the bathroom. I wondered what other person's rear end had been sitting on the commode. Then I saw a hair that didn't belong to me. I was hoping it was Poppy's. *Please be Poppy's.*

I looked over at the puffy little skid-stickers and nasty cracks in the tub, and I didn't really want to bathe. I freshened up with a washrag and toothbrush instead. When I came out of the bathroom a few minutes later, I smelled something familiar. "Coffee?"

"Yes, she's drinking coffee. I suppose she does not care at all about the baby in her womb," said Grandma Mona, smoothing her white hair back.

"What a thing to say, Mona. That's enough." Poppy grinned at me and said, "There's my sunshine girl." The lines in his face were round and happy like somebody had drawn him.

"Nice and hot," Mama said, ignoring me and everybody and smelling the Styrofoam cup in her hands.

"I thought caffeine was bad for—" I cut myself off when I looked into the trash can and saw the green wrapper. "Lookit, it's decaf," I said, like, *duh, Mama knows what she's doing.*

"Just drink and be happy," Poppy said. "That's my motto. Drink and be happy."

"Lovely, that's what we'll stick on your tombstone, Grayson." Grandma Mona stared out a slit in the curtains. It was a wonder to me how those two were ever married.

Rainey was sitting on the edge of the bed, and

she wrapped her arms around my mother. I'm guessing she'd read *Corduroy* at least ten more times now. "I love you, Mama."

"I love you, too, honey. Why don't you go use the potty, okay?"

Rainey stretched her arms straight up and out and made grunting noises, then she stepped out of bed and shuffled to the bathroom. I heard her singing, but couldn't quite place the tune. It was more of a medley of cartoon theme songs, lullabies, and the ABCs all together.

I put on fresh clothes and observed my mother sipping her cup of decaf Folgers, feet curled under her, watching the Weather Channel. A guy with stiff hair was saying how a band of showers would be sweeping through the East Coast by lunchtime.

"Soooo . . ." she said.

"So what?" asked Grandma Mona. "Can we drive back home today?"

"Another town, another grocery store." Mama stared blankly at a commercial for new cars.

"That's what I mean," said Grandma Mona. "You really want to spend your whole vacation sitting in Piggly Wigglys and Bi-Los?"

"For goodness' sake, Mona. She might be okay."

"Oh, come on, Grayson, you know she won't. And then what about tonight? Janie won't be able to sleep again!"

"Can't you see she's not ready yet, Mona? We'll get Janie some earplugs. Or I'll wear some of those nose-strip thingies. We'll make it work."

"Or you can sleep out in the hall," Grandma Mona huffed, folding her arms across her chest. "I'm going to wait outside. It's cold in here."

I sat on the edge of my sofa, watching Mama drink her coffee. I couldn't help but think she looked mad at the world. I couldn't really blame her. I bet she was wondering why she ever allowed my grandparents to come along. She should have listened to me. "This coffee sucks," she said.

"So don't drink it," I said. She didn't answer me, and I felt I'd pushed my limits with my sassy mouth, so I opened the door to go hide away and was *overcome* with the most horrible smell.

"Oh, good gosh! Rainey!"

"Hi, Janie," she said from her porcelain perch, smiling. "See what I do?"

She was trying to balance the roll of toilet paper on her top lip. Super. I leaned out the bathroom door for clean, fresh air and took a deep breath, filling my lungs and cheeks. Then I rushed back in and grabbed a comb before nearly gagging and running to the dresser.

"Mama, you do *not* want to go in there. I promise you."

So to spite me, or to prove me wrong, or maybe just to tell me she was not going to do *anything* I told her to, my mother walked directly into the bathroom to take a shower. It was like watching a woman go to the firing squad.

"Mama, this is fun," said Rainey. I could hear her loud voice even over the water running. Then I heard the toilet flush. My mother, no doubt, had flushed it because for some reason, even though she was seventeen years old, my sister could not bring herself to flush the commode. Do not ask me why. It was just one of those frustrating things I didn't question anymore. Let's just say, sharing a bathroom with her had always been interesting.

When my mother emerged, freshly showered, I did not say a word. I was all packed and had a smile on my face. Poppy was rubbing his whiskers, pondering whether to shave or not.

"Well, you sure look better, sweetie," he said to her. "I think I'll go wait outside with your mother. Come on out when y'all are ready."

Mama stared at herself in the mirror over the dresser and towel-dried the hair hanging over her left shoulder. She let her other towel fall, and I caught a glimpse of her skinny body. She was too skinny now, causing a couple dimples to run down the back of her legs, and her chest was beginning to droop. It was like seeing a scary image of my future. I pinched my eyes shut and turned toward the window, curtains still drawn.

Rainey was engulfed in a Tom and Jerry cartoon. Tom was chasing Jerry down a dock. When they jumped off into the water, she turned away and said, "Mama, we go home now?"

Mama struggled with her bra, back toward me, and then turned to face me, holding her shirt up to her chest. Wearing a strange, I-mean-business look—very unusual for her—she said, "Not another word about going home. It's time we stopped whining and started acting like grown-ups."

I raised my eyebrows. Rainey looked shocked. I hadn't thought she was whining at all, but maybe being pregnant, Mama was hearing things differently. Then Mama realized what she said and who she'd said it to and crumbled. She got on her knees next to Rainey and hugged her. "I'm so sorry. I'm just . . . I'm just confused. I really need to stay away right now. I know you don't understand—"

"I 'stand. Okay, Mama? Love you."

"Thank you, baby. I love you too."

Mama put her shirt on and fluffed her hair, then moved to the mirror again, stretching her skin back at the temples so she looked younger. Changing her tone, she said, "I think I need a face-lift. What do you think?"

I thought of saying something back, but it wasn't very nice so I decided to keep my mouth shut. Rainey just watched her cartoon again.

Mama looked at me in the reflection and nodded, determined. Then she moved to the little table between the beds and turned on the light. She opened the drawer, pulled out a Black Mountain phone book, and flipped through the pages till she found what she wanted. She stared for a minute, set the book back in the drawer, and closed it tight.

"Everything okay, Mama?" I asked.

She rubbed the back of her neck and said as she was getting up, "Yes, I guess that's how it's got to be." Mama moved to the mirror again and sighed, looking at her reflection. She smooshed her hair up into a do and let it fall. She puckered her lips and smacked them a couple times. "Just give me just a few minutes, troops, and we'll get out of here."

"Where we goin'?" asked Rainey, peeling herself away from the television. Tom just got bopped on the head with an anvil.

"Put on your walking shoes, honey. We're going to a lake." Then turning away from Rainey so she couldn't hear but I could, Mama mumbled, "Maybe drown my sorrows and just get it all over with . . ."

My throat tied up in a little ball, and I pictured myself having to dive in and save my mama neck deep in water. I knew it was just something grown-ups said, *drowning their sorrows*, but still . . . I hoped and prayed I'd be strong enough if and when it ever looked like Mama might go under.

Chapter Eleven
LAKE TOMAHAWK

The water in Lake Tomahawk was real peaceful, no waves like the ocean, but ducks trailed and swam all here and there—brown ones, white ones, and a little ugly duck with a poofy hairdo, looked like Grandma Mona. Oh, and there were these little round ripples blossoming all over the place.

"What that, Mama?" Rainey asked, pointing to something lying on the surface. There were hundreds of those somethings everywhere. "Oh, Mama, help!" Rainey walked over some boulders and into the water with her shoes on, scrambling and picking up bugs. She splashed and cradled them in her shirt.

"Rainey!" Mama hollered. "Don't go in there. Come on out this minute!"

"She's a real good swimmer, Mama," I said.

"I can swim, Mama."

"I know it, but you don't know what all's in there. There could be snakes! I don't like snakes. Now your shoes are all wet, I declare!" Mama moved next to Rainey and leaned head and arms out over the lake, careful not to get her feet wet. I guessed I wouldn't worry anymore about Mama drowning in that lake if she didn't want to get her feet wet even. "Would you look at that?" she said. "My goodness. Cicadas."

"They sure are, Priscilla," said Poppy, coming to us from over a little footbridge. His face was glowing in the reflection of the sun off the water. Behind him, the peaks of the Seven Sisters fanned out like a peacock, blue and grand.

"Look at 'em all!" I said. "Hundreds!" At my feet I saw cicadas lying on their backs or right-side up, walking slow. A couple flew by me all in a tither, trying to land on anything solid. "But don't they usually make noise? They're so quiet. I've never seen this many before."

"Poor thing," said Rainey, still working on pulling out the drowning bugs. The ducks looked at her like she'd lost her mind.

"These are special cicadas, girls," said Poppy. "They're magicicadas."

"Magic cicadas?" I said.

"Something like that. They come out by the hundreds, the thousands even, all over the place. But they only do it once every seventeen years."

"I seventeen," said Rainey with pride.

"That's right honey," said Mama. "Did you know these bugs were out like this the very year you were born? I'll never forget it. I thought it was a sign from God. Or a plague . . . like the locusts."

"They're not locusts and they're not a plague," said Poppy.

"So what are they doing?" I asked.

"They're dying," he said. "They mate and they

lay their eggs in the shoots of new green trees. Then they live for about a month or so. And then they die."

"But that's so sad," I said.

"Maybe," said Poppy. "But it's nature. It's how God designed them."

"But they only live a month. Can you imagine if you only had a month to live?"

"Actually, honey, at my age, I can imagine it. But cicadas live longer than most other insects. See, when the eggs hatch, they drop off the trees as larvae—sort of like caterpillars if you want to think of it that way. Then the larvae burrow down deep into the ground. They live that way, eating the roots of the trees like the big old maple over there. Then, after seventeen years, they all rise up at the same time, turning into adults with wings and big red eyes and such—like they are now."

"How do you know so much about them?" I asked.

"Back in the day it was my job to know about bugs like these. All kinds of bugs and plants and animals. It was my job to help the crops grow. Farmers would hire me to help them get over droughts and infestations and such."

"Poppy?"

"Hmm?"

"How do they all know when to rise up at the same time?"

"The magicicadas? I don't know, sweetie. It's a mystery. Something only God knows."

I thought on this some and watched the hundreds of millions of bugs all over the lake, the ground, and I thought, *my goodness, y'all were under our feet all along and nobody even knew it.*

"Poppy!" I said, excited I'd figured something out. "These magic cicadas are just like the baby in Mama's tummy! 'Cause we cain't even see it yet, don't even hardly know it's there. But it is there, right?"

"It sure is," said Poppy.

"It the pretty one, see?" said Rainey, holding a cicada up to Mama's eyes.

"Yes, it sure is," said Mama. She watched Rainey snuggle the bug on her finger and pet its back. Mama sighed. "That is a pretty one."

There was a gravel walkway all around the lake and a nice gazebo. In the middle of the lake was an island where the ducks liked to go. A white man and woman and a little black boy walked right past us and headed around the trail. I could hear them crunching by on the ground. The grown-ups were holding the boy's hand and swinging him in the air. He giggled and begged for more. I saw Mama watching that family, and I wondered what she was thinking. Was she thinking, *must be nice to have a man help with your child*, or was she thinking, *that little boy must not really be theirs, must be adopted*, like I was thinking?

Then I looked around at all the bugs and at Rainey and at Mama with the baby in her tummy, and all of a sudden, I started crying. It's not something I normally did. I plopped down on the ground and cried for all those bugs just a-dying. I cried for how we never knew till this very minute they were even alive. And I cried for the baby growing in Mama who didn't have a say-so in the matter of whether or not to rise up. I cried and I cried and I waded down in the water to help Rainey scoop out as many of the buggers as we possibly could. Somebody had to save them. Somebody just had to. Might as well be Rainey and me.

Mama saw us crying and told us to follow her. It was time to go.

"We gonna take the bugs?" Rainey asked.

"Oh, honey, we can't."

"Please! Mama, please!"

"Oh . . . okay, but just one."

"Not enough!" Rainey hollered.

"That's all we can do." Mama was real stern, and we saw it in her eyes. Rainey and I each held a bug in our palms and followed Mama's footsteps, trying hard not to step on any magic cicadas.

"I'd like to take one last look in the gazebo, Grayson," said Grandma Mona.

"You all go on," said Poppy. "We'll catch up."

"Where we goin' now?" Rainey whined, not so happy anymore, sloshing in her wet shoes. Mama was holding her free hand.

"Listen. I need you on your best behavior. Can you do that, please?"

"Yeah," said Rainey, looking at her bug.

"Yeah, I guess," I said, sniffling.

"Good. Thank you." I watched as my mother left us sitting on a park bench. She looked back once, then straightened her shoulders and headed for a white house. There were houses all around this lake, some directly looking over it, some farther up the hill. At this particular house, two chickens and a duck were waddling around the yard. Wild blue flowers reached up and brushed Mama's shins as she walked up to the back door. She was still within listening distance if we acted up, I reckon.

"I the ugly buggy, can you help me swim," Rainey sang, kicking her feet and bopping her head from side to side. "Can you help me drive the car? Can you help me—"

"Hush, Rainey, not now." Rainey loved to make up songs about silly stuff. Sometimes we did it in the car together. Drove Mama batty. Right now, I couldn't sing. I was focused on Mama and what she was doing up at that house.

Mama held her hand a couple inches away from the door. She knocked and looked behind at us.

"What's she doing?" I asked Rainey.

"Don't know. Look the buggy." Rainey was cooing at her cicada and rubbing its back. Mine didn't look too long for this world because it hardly moved at all. Or maybe it was already gone, I couldn't tell.

The door opened up some, and Mama talked with an old woman in curlers. She had a plastic bag on her head and a purple dress. The woman scratched her bag and cackled, "Harlan Bradfield? Don't care if I never see him again. But you find him, tell him he owes me a new washing machine. Commode don't work, neither."

My daddy? Harlan Bradfield was my daddy's name! I couldn't believe it! Mama'd known where he was all along? And he was here? He'd been in that very house? My heart skipped and ached a little. I'd tried long and hard not to care about my daddy, but hearing his name set me back.

"Oh," said Mama. "I see. Sorry to bother you."

The door closed and Mama put her hands over her face. She stood there frozen for maybe twenty, thirty seconds. Her shoulders bounced up and down again like they always did when she cried. The sight of her hurting hurt me. Somehow it was worse than missing my own daddy. Mama stood up straight again, smoothed her hair across her head and came toward us, smiling all fake-like.

"Why didn't you just say you were coming to find Daddy, Mama?" I said quietly, carefully. "Why didn't you tell me? Where did he go?"

Chapter Twelve
WAR OR PEACE

"All for nothing," Mama said, her words like dripping ice. "All this way for nothing."

"Nothin' for nothin'," said Rainey, grinning to beat the band. She was holding her cicada out like a consolation prize.

"Oh, goodness, you're just what the doctor ordered," Mama said. She looked at me and gave a sad little smile like she was sorry it didn't work out the way she planned, coming up to the mountains to find my father. She was not one for long explanations, but I knew at some point she'd tell me what she knew about Daddy. She would.

"It's okay, Mama," I said. "I'm sorry you didn't find him."

"Come on, now. It's time to go." Her eyes went wide. "We're off to find an airport!"

Just like that Mama sprung *airport* on us. First the trip, then my father, now this. Mama was completely out of control and we were just flailing right after her. Grandma Mona had wanted to go home this morning. For the first time in my life I was thinking she might be the voice of reason. That alone made my stomach twist all up.

We followed the signs to the Asheville Regional Airport, and I could only imagine my father

worked there. Or maybe he was flying somewhere and we were off to catch him at the last
minute before he got on the plane like they did in
the movies. Maybe we'd won a trip or something.
Mama bought lotto tickets sometimes and stashed
them in her sock drawer. Maybe she'd won and
been trying to keep it a surprise. Lately, that's all
she was, surprises. I was too afraid to ask her
what this was all about. Rainey was still holding
her cicada, but turned out, mine was already dead
before we got in the car, so I was just sitting there
empty-handed, grieving my bug.

"Look at that," said Poppy to Rainey. "Look
right there on its wing. What do you see?"

Rainey pulled the cicada so close to her eyes,
they crossed.

"Do you see a letter of the alphabet? Right
there?"

"A dub-ya," said Rainey.

"That's right. Every time the magicicadas come
up from the ground, they grow wings with either
a *W* or a *P* on them."

"Really, Poppy?" I said.

"Really. And you know what those letters are
said to stand for?"

"Huh-uh."

"War or Peace." We all stared at the critter, everybody except Mama, who was driving. "Now that
might be an old wives' tale, but you know there's
always a war or peace somewhere in the world,

so in a way, the cicadas are right—every time."

"Wow. Every time," I whispered. Rainey was truly marveling now.

"Well, this is interesting. We're flying somewhere, Priscilla? With what money? And I thought you hated flying." Grandma Mona was in the front seat because she'd been complaining about being carsick in the back. Poppy was right next to me in the middle of the backseat. He was holding both mine and Rainey's hands, the one without the bug in it.

"Mama, I see airplane!" Rainey's eyes were peering up, her smile wide.

"Yes, honey, see that? There's lots of airplanes over there."

"We're really flying somewhere?" I'd never been on an airplane. The thought of being so high in the air, so small, just a speck in the sky, both excited and scared me.

"I gonna fly!" Rainey squealed.

"Better than that," she said. We pulled into a big grassy area, at least two football fields away from a fleet of planes lined up like soldiers. Mama stopped the car in the shade of big tree, took a deep breath, and said, "When I was a little girl, Daddy used to bring me to the airport whenever it was just the two of us. Maybe just a handful of times, but I remember them."

"I do, too, sweetie," said Poppy. "Oh, what a treat. What a great idea."

"We'd do this," said Mama. She turned off the car and got out, then opened Rainey's door and unbuckled her. "Come on out, Rain."

Poppy followed, then me, and we four stood in front of the old Crown Vic, watching as an airplane took to the air. *Whooooooosh* . . . Our heads tilted to follow it as it flew right over.

"What in the world are we doing?" said Grandma Mona, refusing to get out of the car. She sat there, eyes sharp, cheeks shriveled up like an apple doll.

Climbing on top of the hood of the car like four big kids, my mother, my sister, my grandfather, and I lay flat and watched the clouds move through the big blue sky. I could feel the hardness of the car in my back and sense my mother's presence beside me. I pictured Poppy lying on the other side of her, the way they used to when she was little, and it made me so happy. Knowing Mama had left home when she was younger than Rainey and how she didn't see her parents for a very long time—having everybody all together again, in a way, made this trip all worth it. No matter what happened. Even if we never found my daddy again.

"Look, the angel," said Rainey, arm outstretched and pointing to a cloud with two wings flowing out the sides.

"Sure is," said Mama.

"And that's a flower," I said. "See the petals? Right there. To the left of the angel."

"Oh, yeah. I see," said Rainey.

For the first time since we left our house yesterday, I was feeling like I could finally take a breath.

"I gonna pick flowers," said Rainey. "Get some for buggy." She sat up and slipped off the hood.

"I'll go with her," Poppy said. Mama and I propped ourselves on our elbows, watching Rainey hunched over in a field of dandelions. Poppy handed one to her, she made a wish, then blew it and stared at the puffy parts floating away on the wind. Then again and again. Poppy handed her a flower, and Rainey wished on it. It was Rainey's faith in action. So simple. Just taking things as they come. Then, believe it or not, she set her beloved cicada free. She watched it fly about three feet, then it disappeared into the grass. Poppy was patting her on the back, assuring her it was the best thing for it to be earthbound again, but Rainey decided to search and save it again.

Suddenly, I felt the weight of all this, remembering the baby growing as we lay here, slowly but surely. A baby. Mama was having a baby.

"Mama?"

"Mmmmm . . . this feels good," she said, letting a band of sunshine cross her eyes.

I remembered that boy and his parents at Lake Tomahawk, and all a sudden, there was something I really had to talk about. "Did you . . . did you ever think about adoption . . . a long time ago?" The words sounded foreign to me, talking so frank. "I mean, you were only sixteen. It must have been hard to be a mama so young."

A plane sped by in the distance, faster and faster until its nose tipped off the ground and it escaped the pull of earth.

"Oh, yes."

"Well, what did you think? I mean, you didn't give away Rainey. Or me."

"Oh, God, what am I going to do?" Mama sat up suddenly and wrapped her arms around her belly. She looked down at it. "I just couldn't give this baby away, could I?"

"I don't know, could you?"

Mama and I grew silent and watched the clouds. I realized I needed to add "adoption" to my list of options and pros and cons so I could help Mama out. Let her study on it in print. Rainey was still blowing dandelion puffs in front of us, the air swirling white.

After a minute or so, I asked again, "Are you thinking 'bout giving the baby away?" I couldn't see her face, so I couldn't tell how she felt about this.

"What if I put the baby up for adoption and nobody adopts it? That could happen. It *could* happen. Then it would grow up in an orphanage or go from foster home to foster home. Oh, I couldn't live, knowing I had a child out there, somewhere . . . I just couldn't live . . ."

"I . . . I don't know, Mama. I guess it could happen. But there are hundreds of people waiting for babies, right?"

Grandma Mona piped up from within the car. "Good heavens, if that's true, why do so many people go off to China and Russia and Timbuktu to adopt children?" The roar of an airplane shook our car and rattled the inside of my chest. "These days, seems it's easier to do it out of the country," Grandma Mona kept on. "Less red tape or something."

"But that's not right, is it?" I said. "This is America. It doesn't make sense."

"No. It doesn't."

"Look, Mama." Rainey carried a bouquet of flowers as if walking in a wedding. "These are for you."

"My angel." Mama reached over to caress her cheek before taking them. "Can I make a wish?"

Rainey nodded, eyes wide, as if this is exactly the moment she'd been waiting for, living for. I watched my mother close her eyes. She took a while to think on it. When she finally blew her dandelions clean, I wished, I *wished*, I knew what she was wishing for. I knew what I was wishing for, that Mama didn't give our baby away.

"All righty, this has been nice, but it's time to hit the road," Mama called from the hood of the car.

I'd slid off long ago and joined Rainey and

Poppy hunting flowers. "Where are we going this time?" he asked.

"Yeah, where we goin'?" asked Rainey.

Mama said, "Um, Forest Pines."

"Is that far?"

"No. Well, sort of," said Poppy. "It's in South Carolina."

"South Carolina?" I said. "But we're in *North* Carolina, Mama. We drove *up* to North Carolina." Part of me was wondering why we were giving up on finding Daddy so quick. Seems like if she wanted to, we could keep on looking. Mama opened the door and got Rainey situated with her baby doll, her *Corduroy* book, her cicada, and a pillow across her lap, then she climbed in and started the car. Grandma Mona was still huffing in the front seat.

"You excited about going, Mona?" asked Poppy. He slipped into the middle backseat again. I could feel his heat pressing into my side.

"Why? What's in Forest Pines?" I asked. I was completely, totally, not in control, a consequence of being a child. Mama reached into her huge brown purse and pulled out the map.

"Gosh, Mama, it's all the way back down there, close to Cypresswood," I said. "You mean we came up all this way just for nothing?"

"Not for nothin'," Rainey said. "I made wishes."

"Mama, you came to Black Mountain on purpose, didn't you? Just to find Daddy?" I already knew the answer.

"Your father went to the North Carolina mountains four years ago," said Grandma Mona. "Yes, your mother knows that."

Mama looked in the rearview mirror at me, both of us knowing it. What, was she going to take me to see him? Was he down in Forest Pines? In the back of my head, if I was honest, I was thinking it. Hoping it? No, maybe that was saying too much. I had to change the subject.

"All right, so when did you decide to go to Forest Pines?"

"Just now, when Rainey made her wish," said Poppy. "Right, honey? Well that, and I sort of suggested it back at the motel."

I looked at Mama, my eyes wide. "*Who* is in Forest Pines, Mama? Did Daddy go there?"

"It's not *who's* there, honey, it's *what's* there." Grandma Mona crossed her arms and looked all satisfied with herself. Mama paid her no mind and pulled out her lipstick, sliding it around her puckered mouth and checking it in the mirror. Then she looked behind her and began to back out.

When the car hit pavement she said slowly, "I spent a lot of time in Forest Pines, honey. I loved it there. Was happy there. Would have gone back some, too, but I was dead to everybody who knew me there."

"You dead, Mama?" asked Rainey, concerned. She'd learned what dead meant after Bitsy our dog went to heaven.

"No, not really, honey. Nothing to worry about." Her voice went softer, almost talking under her breath. "I left home when I was almost your age, and my parents made it very clear that *I* was dead to *them*. They wanted nothing more to do with me."

"That is not true! I am not going to sit here and take this kind of talk, young lady." Grandma Mona turned her head to the window.

"Hush now, Mona," said Poppy. "Just listen."

"Your grandparents lived in Forest Pines for a very long time," Mama said, spiting Grandma Mona by going on. "It was your great-grandparents' house, and when my folks were young and married they lived there with them. I did too. I'd like to go back, I think. For old times' sake. Anyway, at this point we have nothing left to lose, right? It's not like you can get even deader to somebody."

"Grayson Macy, I want you to stop this right now. Make her stop this car this instant and let me out. You hear how she's poisoning these girls against me? Against us?"

"Nobody's doing that, Grandma Mona," I said. "What's past is done and gone. That's what you always say, isn't it? I'd like to go see Forest Pines, Mama. But maybe you should be getting to a doctor now. For the baby? And we're almost out of gas. Why don't we just go home, Mama? It sounds so much easier. Let's just get back to life as normal." I knew it as soon as I said it—we were anything but normal, what with the pregnancy and all. Even without that.

"Let's go home, Mama," said Rainey. It broke my heart to hear how honest she was. All the time.

"Honey, even if we did go home, I . . . I got nothing to go home to. I don't have a job anymore." Mama broke the news like it was no big deal, like we were out of eggs or milk or something. But I knew better. I knew this changed everything. Again.

Chapter Thirteen
HEADING SOUTH

I shook my head to clear my ears. Mama had said she had no job, but that was impossible. She'd always had her job at the pancake house. "What, Mama? I thought they were holding your job for you." A station wagon full of teenagers slowed beside us with feet and hands dangling out the windows.

"I threw my apron down yesterday and told Bob to go blank himself. Or maybe in different words." Oh. Wow. Mama was serious. The job she'd had for the last ten years, before I was born.

Gone. "So, we might as well keep on driving, right?" she said.

"Mr. Mooneyham gonna let you do grocery. He real nice. You work with me."

"That's sweet, honey. Thank you. Maybe I'll look into that." Rainey couldn't see the worry on Mama's face, but I could hear it in her voice.

"And we got good bags, paper. And you walk the grocery to the car. Put 'em in the back. It real nice, Mama. You like it."

"You really mean to tell me you quit your job, Priscilla?" Poppy was beside himself but seemed to be working as hard as he could to keep his cool. He wrung his wrinkled hands. "You think that was the wisest thing to do, what with your condition and all?"

"Now, Grayson. If Priscilla was aiming to do the smartest things in life, do you really think she'd be pregnant right now and driving halfway 'cross the south just to go back to a haunted old house? And with gas prices being so high? I mean, truly."

Well, I guess that about summed it up. I was pretty much speechless, so I just settled in for a long day of driving. I pulled my feet up Indian-style and leaned my head on Poppy's shoulder and let myself wonder if we'd see us some real-live ghosts in that haunted house in Forest Pines. And I wondered what the ghosts would look like, if anything, or if they'd have names like Rainey Dae or Janie Doe or Casper the Friendly Ghost.

• • •

It was a long, dark trip back to South Carolina. The sky looked like gray blankets of wool covering the sun and all heavenly things. Only a couple times did the clouds pour on us, and when they did it was hard and fast. Then it was over. Mama didn't stop, just kept on going. The sun hadn't shone since Asheville, and I was beginning to wonder if it ever would again.

We were driving in the passing lane because Mama liked to drive faster than most folks. Not too much faster, but just enough to make her feel like she was getting somewhere first. I told her we'd all get there sometime, no need to hurry, but she did what she wanted. With us being in an old police car, people would look in their rearview mirrors and think we were the police. Maybe undercover. Mama had fun with that some. She'd pull up on somebody real close, and as soon as they saw it was a Crown Victoria, they scooted over real fast into the other lane and then slowed down to a crawl, worried we'd give them a ticket.

On Highway 26 we came up on a line of tractor trailers carrying military vehicles on the backs. Slowly, we passed them, one by one. I could see the letters and numbers on the tanks. I could see the big nuts and bolts holding the giant tires on.

"Wow, would you look at that," said Poppy.

"Look what they are now. In every war, Janie, these tanks have been painted a different color. Back in World War II they were olive drab. Same as in my father's day."

"What war was that?" I asked.

"Korea. Your great-grandfather, my daddy Adolph Macy, was a hero. Saved a whole platoon when he jumped on a land mine."

"Goodness," I said, imagining it must have hurt pretty bad.

"We gonna see your daddy?" asked Rainey.

"Well, he's in heaven, sugar. The land mine killed him."

"That sad!"

"I know it, but that's just the way it is. He sacrificed his life so the others could live. That's a true hero, honey." Looking back at the tanks he said, "No, not until after Vietnam were these tanks painted in camouflage so they could mix in with the jungle and not be seen. Look at 'em all now. See the color? What does it look like?"

"Sand," I said.

"You're right. So where do you think these are going?"

"The beach!" Rainey squealed, so pleased with her smart answer. Everybody knows there's sand at the beach.

"Almost," said Poppy. "How about the desert? These new tanks, all painted fresh and such, they're going either to Afghanistan or Iraq, my guess."

"Why?" asked Rainey.

"'Cause it's where the wars are being fought," said Grandma Mona, turning her neck to look at Rainey. I was beginning to think Poppy was the smartest man in the world, what with the magic cicadas and the tanks, so I was surprised when it seemed Grandma Mona knew something too. I couldn't see her face since I was directly behind her, and the headrest was covering her up. I could see her thin white hair on the back of her head, though, and I thought on what she said a minute, about the wars and how the tanks were leaving this country to go fight them.

"So there aren't any wars here in America?" I asked.

Grandma Mona turned her head around the other way and peeked at me with one gray eye in the sliver of light between the seat and the window. "Oh, there are wars here, honey, just not any you can see."

"But I don't like war. It scares me."

"Me too," said Rainey.

"Nobody likes war," said Poppy. "But just the fact you don't like something, doesn't make it any less so, I'm afraid."

"Amen," Mama said.

We passed the seventh and final tank, and I secretly prayed for the people who'd be driving them soon—to be safe and for nobody to get killed. And for none of us at home to ever run into those invisible wars.

Mama'd been really quiet. Maybe it's because Grandma Mona was next to her. I sat there in the backseat, trying to put myself in Mama's shoes. What would it be like to be traveling back to the place you used to love, the place where you knew love and were loved and everything was good and happy and simple?

I wished my mama's life was easier.

I wondered how close we were to finding my daddy in the mountains.

Did Mama have that same empty feeling eating at her like I did sometimes? That what-if feeling? That poor-me-I-don't-have-a-daddy feeling? Sure, Poppy was with us now, but he'd been gone for most of Rainey's life. He'd just popped back into Mama's life and Grandma Mona's—and mine, for that matter—after all the hard needing part was over. I had to get away from him for just a second. To breathe. I leaned up on my elbows and studied the slight lines showing in my mother's face. I loved my mother. Loved every single one of those lines. Her hands looked fixed like wax forever on that wheel.

I wondered if I'd ever be able to forgive Poppy and Grandma Mona for what they did, letting Mama go off all alone like that when she was a girl. With a baby in her tummy to boot. I was fuming now, thinking of how Rainey might have been better off with more people who loved her, with better schooling . . . *if.*

Well, what's done was done. There was only the future now to tend to.

Chapter Fourteen
WELCOME TO FOREST PINES

When we passed the sign that said WELCOME TO FOREST PINES, Mama must have had the stomach jitters because lo and behold, we had to pull over so she could get sick in the grass.

"Mama? Mama sick!" Rainey was troubled and pressing her face up against the glass. With the windows and doors not opening from the back, she couldn't get out of the car to help her. It was all she could handle, hands over ears.

"She'll be okay," said Grandma Mona. "You all right, Priscilla? Let me know when it passes. Oh, gracious, I hope your pregnancy isn't as bad as mine was."

Mama reached into the glove box over Grandma Mona's lap and grabbed some napkins, wiped her mouth, got ahold of herself, then slid back in, leaving the door open. "It's okay, Rain. Mama feels better. Don't worry about me."

"Wanna hold the baby?" Rainey tipped the doll's hard bare feet over the seat and touched Mama's ear.

"No, no. That'll just . . . no thank you, sugar. That's awfully sweet of you though."

"Let's just wait a minute," Poppy said. "Maybe you should get in the backseat, Priscilla, with the rubber floor and all."

"No, she's fine," said Grandma Mona. "When it's done, it's done. At least, that's how it was with me."

"Are you sure?"

"I'm sure. Sit tight." And off we went.

Driving through the town of Forest Pines, I took note of every grocery store we passed, marking them for later . . . Piggly Wiggly, Food Lion, Bi-Lo. The act of list making in my head soothed me, enough to say what I'd wanted to for a hundred miles or more.

"Why haven't you ever brought us back here, Mama?"

Mama was quiet, thinking. We were stopped at a light in front of a big white Baptist church. There were tons of Baptist churches in this town. I figured everybody must be Baptist here. Maybe it was a law.

"Strangest thing," said Mama. "I ran into an old high school friend, Marsha, about six, seven years ago. She told me Daddy'd moved back here."

"You mean you knew where he was? Poppy, you were here in Forest Pines all that time?" I just didn't understand. He was such a sweet man. I didn't want to be disrespectful of him, but it didn't make sense how he could be so close but neglect his family for so long.

"Oh, honey. There are some things you don't understand yet. But you will someday, I promise."

"Tell me now, Poppy! Tell me, please. I'm not a little kid. Honest!"

"Oh, sweetie," said Poppy, grabbing my arm and holding it tight. I let it lay limp in his hands. "You're my girl. Just hold tight, all right?"

We started rolling again and turned left down a tree-lined street. "This is where your roots are, Rainey." Mama looked in the rearview mirror and smiled. Rainey was barefooted and cross-legged. She pressed her hand in the window as if there was something special she could see outside.

"There it is. There's the old house. Wow, that was a long time ago. I was just a child."

"Mama and Daddy's house, God rest 'em," said Poppy, putting his hand over his heart.

Before I knew what was happening, the car had slowed to a stop and we were parked out in front of a blue Victorian house that looked just like a great big dollhouse. It had white twisty spindles for the porch railing, and all these little details and doodads along the pointed roofline. There was a round gazebo on the right side of the porch like that one we'd seen at Lake Tomahawk, and with everything in me I wanted to go sit there under the shade of it, looking over the lawn. I was drawn to it as if the house and its lawn were not Mama's memory, but mine. But I knew I'd never been there before. Then it dawned on me. I did know this house.

The Christmas after my daddy left, we woke up to find Santa Claus had all but forgotten us. Rainey and I only got one toy, a plastic doll. The *same* doll. It had a green dress with yellow yarn hair. I didn't even like dolls much. Santa had to know that. And I'd been really good that year. Extra good, I thought.

My mother on the other hand, looked like a queen next to Santa. I'd watched her working for days and days, baking, pressing, squeezing, sticking, until she had made the most amazing gingerbread house I had ever seen. Rainey and I were afraid to touch it. We didn't dare try to break off a piece of candy or a corner of the rooftop for fear it would be gone once we ate it. And if it was gone, we wouldn't be able to lie there anymore, elbows on the countertop, watching the house, the little door, the little windows, imagining we could be *in* that house, living there, a full family, with a father, even.

I had no idea a gingerbread house could grow up out of the ground and come to life, right in front of your very eyes. But *this,* the house now tall and grand in front of me, was our gingerbread house.

I looked through the black wrought iron fence built up on brick and stucco peeling away. The gate was closed, and beside it, I saw faded brass numbers, 628.

"You mean you never saw your grandparents again?" I asked my mother. "When you ran away from Yuma? You never came back to Forest Pines?"

Mama licked her top lip slowly and shook her head.

Watching her eyes water, I understood something for the first time. My mother had a whole different life before Rainey and me. She wasn't a pancake-slopping waitress with bags under her eyes, trying to make ends meet. She wasn't tired all the time. She *became* that way because she had us. She gave up this blue Victorian house and everything that came along with it. For us.

And with no help from the old folks in this car.

I thought I might be the one getting sick now, but thank goodness, I held it together. Mama didn't need any more messes to deal with. Her past had gone and grown up out of the ground.

Chapter Fifteen
A Step Back in Time

{Mona}

Glory hallelujah! At last. I could not believe what I was seeing. Could not believe that the moon and stars had aligned just right so that my daughter would come within a hundred feet from where we once lived. But she had. She was here, in the flesh. I wanted to reach over and hug her, but I didn't. I sat there, arms crossed, tense, and wondering if we could ever get her inside. *Hold your horses, old woman*, I told myself. *She's here, isn't she?*

Next, a sense of dread filled my bones like an arthritic ache, pulsing, pounding. Heavens, I did not know what to expect. All I'd known was that we needed to get her here. Well, she was here! I simply didn't know what else was in store for Priscilla. I looked back at Rainey and then Janie. Their eyes were filled with wonder and awe at being in such a strange place, familiar to everyone but them. I wanted so badly to reach my hand back behind the seat to squeeze my little Janie and tell her . . . well, just tell her how much I loved her. That's all. But I didn't. Grayson, thank goodness, was doing the honors in my place.

"Are we going in?" Janie asked. We'd been sitting there, car idling, for about five minutes. Priscilla was still clenching the steering wheel. Every now and again I saw her mouth some words, talking herself into doing it, I suppose. "Let's just go up to the door and knock," Janie said. "Maybe somebody'll open the door."

"You know idling makes you use up lots of gas, honey." Grayson tried to let her be, but he just couldn't stand it. A man is a man is a man. The lawn outside the window was dark green and overgrown with weeds in places. The rail on the front porch, once white, was now streaked with gray and mildew. I would have hoped it had been kept up a little bit nicer, but oh, to see the old place. It did me good.

Priscilla hesitated, inhaled, and held her hands to her chest. Then she grabbed the wheel again and put the car back in drive.

"I can't do it," she said. "I can't."

"Are you kidding me?" I snapped. "We came all this way, wasted all that gas, just to see the house from the street? That's it?"

"Oh goodness," said Grayson, putting his hand on Priscilla's shoulder. "I can't blame you, sweetheart." Sitting back, he said, "Mona, think about the last time she was here. Don't you remember? We were happy then. It was before we moved to Yuma. Oh, why did I ever move us to Yuma? Drought or no drought. Priscilla was just a young girl, just a few years older than Janie the last time she saw this house. Give her some space. Priscilla honey, take all the time you need. I'm right here for you. We all are."

Of course, I knew all these things, and tears burned my eyes at the thought. I knew how happy my child was here. How content all of us were. The car was quiet except for the hum of the engine burning the gas Priscilla couldn't afford. I turned around and watched Janie assessing the house. Her eyes traveled up and rested at the windows up top, dark and shrouded with curtains.

"Didn't you say the house was haunted?" she said. "Why's it haunted, Poppy?"

"Oh, honey, that's just . . . when your Grandma Mona and I lived here, she used to swear she could hear footsteps, voices, and such. My mother heard it too, though I never heard a thing. So if you ask me . . ."

"It was the ghost of your Aunt Gertrude, Grayson," I said. "She would move things. And throw spools of thread. I saw it with my own eyes."

"Oh now, that's enough. Don't scare the poor girls before they even go in."

"Gracious, let's just—"

"Let's go find a motel room," said Priscilla, changing the subject. "Maybe have us a nice supper. I bet tomorrow I'll have the nerve to go in. I bet I will. What do you say?"

"Time go work," Rainey said. "Need get my apron on."

"Oh, I know, baby. I know." Priscilla sighed long and controlled.

"You've got to be kidding," I said. "Again?"

"You know your granddaughter, Mona. Don't act like you're so surprised. I expect every day of this trip will be more of the same. Not to mention, you should be proud she's got such good work ethic."

"I'm not complaining," I told Grayson. "I know who my granddaughter is, thank you very much. And I'm very proud of her, but . . . listen, how about just open the door and let me out here."

"Don't pout, Mona."

"I'm not pouting; I'm just tired of being in this car, is all. Let me out, Priscilla. I'd like to walk around and get a feel for the old place. See if there's anybody here I still remember."

"I'll go with you, then," said Grayson.

Rainey unbuckled herself and pushed on the door. "Open, Mama."

"Honey, we're not staying—" she said, but I unlatched the door from the front and Rainey stepped on out. Grayson followed her. Rainey stretched her legs and her arms way up to the sky. Priscilla gave her a minute, then said, "Come on back in, Rainey. We're going to try and find you a grocery store. Would you like that?"

"Yeah, 'cause I scared-a ghost."

"There's nothing to be afraid of, honey," said Priscilla. "Come get up front with me."

I slipped out of the car when Rainey came in. I grabbed Grayson's hand and squeezed it tight.

"Y'all go do your fun and we'll be waiting here for you," he told them. "On the front porch, maybe. Suppertime."

"Don't be late," I added.

So Priscilla, Janie, and Rainey drove off, my girls, leaving Grayson and me in front of the old house. We needed to see who was still around, see what all had changed. And we needed to spend time alone, away from our loved ones, to pray and prepare and wait for what must come.

Chapter Sixteen
THE SECRETS OF MOCKINGBIRDS

{Janie}

The Snooze 'n Eat Inn in Forest Pines was just like Mama's pancake house back home, but with bedrooms sticking off behind it. She went ahead and paid for a room, slipping her change purse out and digging like there was gold in there and she didn't want anybody to see it. She set her money down, ran her hands through her hair, and turned back to look at us. She smiled on thin lips and said, "Let's get checked in. Let me make a phone call. Then maybe we can have a look around town and grab some supper."

"Gotta go work, Mama," Rainey said, like, *Duh. You ought to know that by now.* Mama was trying to slip one past her.

"Oh, shucks, 'bout forgot, sweetie. Okay. Just give me a few minutes and we'll get going, all right?"

Room 103 was dark and smelled funny. There was a big brown stain on the carpet beneath the air conditioner. It *drip, drip, drip*ped a little tune.

Mama was quiet and set our white suitcase by the closet. She looked at a bed and sat down on the edge like she was trying hard not to let her skin touch the bedspread. She picked up the phone and pressed buttons. Rainey and I were on the other bed, flipping through TV channels.

"Alisha? Hey. Forest Pines." I heard Mama talking real low. To my favorite person. Not that she was so awful, but she didn't bring Mama up any. I thought she was jealous of how pretty Mama was. Alisha looked like a mixed breed to me, wiener dog and Chihuahua. "No. Huh-uh. Has he said anything?" She twirled the white cord around her fingers. "Well that figures. No. Tell him you don't know where I am. Let him wonder . . . So how've you been?"

Mama turned to look over at us, and I faced the TV real quick so she didn't think I was eavesdropping. Which I was.

"That bad? Gee, I'm sorry, but you're getting twice the tips, right? Me? Oh, I don't know. Probably a cashier job at the supermarket. I'll find something. Yes, she's fine. Better than I expected. We're getting ready to find her a grocery store. She's got to bag every single day no matter where we are. No, I'm not kidding. Don't laugh. It's important to her, so it's important to me. All right, then. No. Still don't know what I'm going to do." Mama grabbed her belly and said, "Three choices and not a one looks good. How about you choose the least worst for me?"

I didn't hear much more after that because I was caught up on that last part she said. The part about having three choices. I could tell the conversation had switched to the baby. Mama had three choices about the baby? I dug in my pocket and pulled out my list. I ran into the bathroom and flipped the light switch. There it was. Option one and option two. Keep the baby or give it away. But she'd said three options. What more could there possibly be?

After spending a fair amount of time in the Piggly Wiggly, we drove by the old blue house again. Mama came to a stop right in front of the walkway and stared as if she was imagining walking it. Grandma Mona and Poppy were waiting for us, just like they said they'd be, so they hopped in and off we went to find the motel.

"Y'all have a nice time?" asked Poppy, holding his knees and chipper as usual. His bow tie was a little crooked. He was the only man I'd ever known who wore one every day, red with tiny black dots like a ladybug. "We had a nice walk, didn't we, Mona?"

"Yes. Except for seeing Clarabelle Shoemaker. I didn't care if I ever saw her again."

"Hard to miss her, though, when she's right there across the street."

"Well, I know but—"

"Rainey did such a good job, they gave us some leftover sandwiches from the deli," I blurted out.

"That so? That's wonderful, Rainey." Poppy leaned over and gave her a kiss on the cheek.

"We got tuna fish and egg salad. Ham and cheese, but I don't like ham. I took it off."

"That's right, honey," said Mama. "You did a fine job. You're a real hard worker. I'm proud of you."

Rainey's face beamed in the blue light of dusk. For her, there was nothing more important than making Mama proud of her. I guess that went for me too. There was nothing better than putting a smile on Mama's face.

Rainey and I sat in the backseat nibbling two halves of a cheese sandwich. Mama grabbed egg salad, but Poppy and Grandma Mona said they'd have their tuna fish back at the motel. There was nibbling, teeth chomping, and paper crinkling until we rounded the bend and were almost there.

"Great, I'm almost out of gas," Mama said. "Tomorrow I'll ask Mr. Stevens if he'll pay you in actual money. These sandwiches are good, but they can't fill up the tank."

"Okay, Mama."

"You mean you're actually planning on staying in the same town for more than one night?" said Grandma Mona. "I'll believe it when I see it."

"Come on, let's go in," said Mama. "Get some sleep. I have a feeling tomorrow's gonna be a big day."

We finished up our food and stuffed the wrappers in a plastic grocery bag, then everybody slid out and headed for the building. I took Poppy's hand and pulled him back at the last second, letting the others go on ahead into room 103. "I need to talk to you," I told him.

He turned to me, eyes dark brown and crinkly. "What is it, sugar? Something wrong?"

"I just need to talk."

"Okay." He leaned in the door and whispered, "Mona. Janie and I are going out for a few minutes."

"I wanna come," said Rainey, cradling her baby doll in her arms. Her cicada was lying in a plastic sandwich box on the dresser, not much interested anymore in flying. Mama was fussing over the suitcase, emptying the clothes into the drawers. Don't know why she did it when she'd just pack them up again tomorrow or whenever we'd head to wherever we were going next.

"I got to talk to Poppy, Rainey. Just give us a minute."

"Poppy?" Rainey was all fretful, so Poppy said, "Oh honey, it won't harm for her to hear. She doesn't care. Right, Rainey?"

Rainey grinned. There was a glob of sandwich bread stuck in her teeth. "Goodie," she said, so the three of us paced back down the concrete sidewalk and out to a little fountain in the parking lot. It was an odd place for a fountain, and it gave the impression it'd been here long before the lot was paved, maybe back when the place was grander than it was now.

Rainey took her shoes off and dangled her feet in the black water. She leaned down and collected coins lying in the bottom, left over from desperate people's wishes. I was nervous about what I was going to say, so I was happy to have distractions. They came in all forms. An old yellow car about the size of a boat cruised in and around the parking lot, then bumped back onto the street. I heard a bird singing. Then another and another. When the songs were over, a single mockingbird flew out of a tree and dive-bombed us. Poppy saw me watching the bird and he said, "You know why they call them mockingbirds?"

"Huh-uh."

"Because they mock other birds. They can

listen to a birdsong, then copy it exactly. They sing over and over, then switch to another song. It can fool you sometimes."

"I thought that was three birds."

"That's what I mean," he said.

"Are they making fun of them . . . of the other birds?" I asked.

"Not sure about that. What I do know is it has something to do with staking their territory. Protecting their young."

"So . . . they pretend to be something they're not, so you can't see them coming when they dive-bomb you? Our next-door neighbor Miss Carson used to complain about mockingbirds attacking her cats."

Poppy looked at me and said, "That's how it appears, yes. God has a way of providing every creature a way of surviving. Some are just more creative than others. Remember the magicicada? It protects itself by coming up out of the ground in great numbers. The mockingbird does it by changing its voice."

I turned around and watched the trees for more mockingbirds.

"So what's all this about?" asked Poppy, his arms now crossed. His feet were shoulder width apart, hips tucked under like he was planting himself against a gale wind. "What did you need to talk to me about that was so important? I know it wasn't mockingbirds."

"Well . . . I know I'm not supposed to listen in on conversations, but I promise, Mama said everything right there in front of me and Rainey. She was talking to Alisha on the telephone."

"And what did she say?"

"She said she has three choices with this baby and none of 'em look good."

Poppy's chest fell flat and he raised an arm to rub the back of his neck. "I see," he said.

"But I don't see," I whined. "See this?" I reached into my pocket and pulled out my list of pros and cons. There were a lot more pros listed for adoption already, like *Mama won't have to make any more money than she already does* and *We won't have to find a bigger house to move in.* Poppy stared at the list, his eyes flicking from *Keep the Baby* to *Give the Baby Away.* "There's only two options I know of," I said.

Poppy scratched the top of his head. "That's a tough one, Janie. I'm not sure I'm . . . uh, Rainey, how 'bout you go on in and grab your grandmother for me. Tell her, her lovely presence is needed in the parking lot."

"No!" I said.

"Please, Janie. I'm not so good at this sort of thing. Your Grandma Mona can tell it better than I can, being a woman and all."

Woman things. I didn't think of that. I supposed Grandma Mona *was* a woman. "But she's so—"

"What?"

"Mean."

"Yeah . . . sometimes she is." Poppy touched my shoulder and turned me to him. He bent down on one knee, and I was thinking to myself, *My mama was the luckiest girl ever, having Poppy as her daddy.* In that second I wondered what in the world she could ever complain about. At least she had her daddy with her now. "See, some folks have a hard time telling you how they really feel," he said. "Sometimes they put up a firm face, a sharp tongue, even, when really, they don't mean it."

"So they're pretending . . . like the mocking-bird?"

"Sort of. It's just their way of coping with things that hurt them."

"So everything hurts Grandma Mona?"

Poppy laughed, not at me, but in a nice way, and said, "Just about. But really, she's had a world of hurt in her lifetime."

"Like what? Like you leaving for so long?" My face burned hot when I realized what'd come out of my mouth.

"Yes, like what?" said Grandma Mona, arms on hips, ears flaming and eyes angled crossways at Poppy. I'm betting he didn't know she was out here already. I sure as all get-out did not.

"Janie and I were just talking . . . about Priscilla."

"Mm-hmm. That so?" she said.

"And Janie had a question for you. It stumped me."

"This should be good." Grandma Mona stood there a minute, but I was too afraid to speak. It wasn't at all like talking with Poppy. Grandma Mona reminded me of a snake up in the air, ready to strike. "Well what is it, child? Spit it out."

"I don't know what the third choice is." I blurted.

"The what?"

"She means . . . Janie overheard Priscilla talking on the telephone about three choices having to do with the new baby. She already knows two choices—keep the baby or give it up for adoption—but she doesn't know what a third choice might be."

Grandma Mona's eyebrows rose like hot-air balloons, then they deflated and fell to her nose. "That so?" she said. "Well, I'm not sure this is appropriate talk for a young girl."

"She's asking a question, Mona."

"I know it, but she's an innocent child."

"Innocence never protected anyone." Poppy and Grandma Mona exchanged a look that spoke of things I knew nothing about.

"Oh, good heavens. I guess you'll learn this sooner or later." She shook her head as if the thought was unpleasant and she was trying to squeeze it out. "The third choice is not to have the baby."

"You mean give the baby away?"

"No, I mean *not* to have the baby."

"But I don't understand," I stammered. "The baby's in Mama's tummy. Right?"

"Technically, yes," said Grandma Mona, "but your mother can choose to *not* let it be born if she wants to."

I tried to let that sit a minute, but my mind was scrambling, imagining angels reaching into tummies and mamas making deals with God to take their babies back. "It doesn't make sense. Poppy?"

"Don't look at me honey, I don't make the rules."

"Who does?" I asked.

"Well, the Supreme Court," said Grandma Mona, "and everyday people like you and your sister, your mother, me. Just good people, trying to do what they think is right. Trying to survive."

"I thought God made the rules." I was so confused I could spit. I sat down next to Rainey and put my hand in the water, reaching for a coin. Then I remembered hearing something about God not liking lukewarm water. I didn't like it either, so I pulled it out and dried my hand off on my shirt.

"So how?" I asked. "How do you not be born?"

"There's a procedure," said Grandma Mona. "With a doctor and all. Sort of like . . . being born, but the opposite of that."

"What happens to the baby?" I asked.

"It just . . . doesn't exist, honey," said Poppy. "It just—"

"Tell her what the procedure is called," said Grandma Mona, grave, staring at the asphalt.

"I really don't want to," he said.

"Remember why we're here. Why we needed to come along."

"I can't," he said.

"Fine. Abortion." Grandma Mona's lips were shut tight and wrinkled like she ate a lemon, like the word tasted bitter on her tongue.

"Jesus the baby," said Rainey, piping up. "He in Mama tummy . . . with that 'bortion. How you spell it?" Her eyes were working hard to picture the letters. She loved learning new words.

"Oh honey, don't you mind. Now run along. We'll be there in a minute."

"A-b-o—"

"Mona! She might look it up!"

"I am aware of that. A-b-o-r—"

"Mona, please."

"Grayson Macy," said Grandma Mona, and I knew it wasn't good because she used his full name. "This is America. Rainey is a young woman in America. You are not. She may need to know this term someday, especially if her mother is considering it as an option."

Grandma Mona's eyes meant business, so Poppy said, "Oh gracious, I suppose there's no way around it." Then he spelled that word for us, the one that meant un-borning a baby, and we all headed inside to the damp, musty motel room, deadly quiet. No more words between us. I guess it was because that one new word we learned was quite enough to speak of for the night.

Chapter Seventeen
THE LITTLE THIEF

The next morning, I woke up in the motel room before anybody else did. I saw the darkness first, then a sliver of light coming in at the bottom of the curtains. I listened to the saws and snorts from Poppy and Grandma Mona, while Rainey kicked her feet.

I tried not to make a sound, but there was no way to go outdoors. Somebody would hear me. I was a captive of the room. I looked over at Mama sleeping. I couldn't see her face, just a long lump under the covers. Her hand was dangling off the bed onto the nightstand. It rested beside a digital clock.

I took a deep breath and closed my eyes again, pulling my knees up under my chin. I thought about Forest Pines and that pretty blue house. I thought about our house at home, and all I could remember was Mama wailing and making egg salad. I began to pray. *Lord, please give Mama some peace. Please help that baby in her tummy. Please help me know what to do to help.*

I opened my eyes and the first thing I saw was that big brown purse of Mama's. I got a naughty idea, and I knew it was naughty, but at the same time, I knew it was what I had to do.

After Mama woke up, Rainey got up, then Poppy and Grandma Mona. I let them all do their morning things, getting ready, taking showers, the whole bit. I stayed quiet, invisible on the couch. I was excited because I knew we were headed for the blue house that morning. I felt like my mother's life had become a big mystery, and the key to her had something to do with that house.

When it was time to go, Mama reached in her pocketbook to find her lipstick. She screamed when she couldn't find her change purse. She looked and hollered and poured her purse out on the bed. Poppy was trying to reason with her, saying practical things like "Just think about where you had it last," or "Try and retrace your steps."

Finally, Mama called the Piggly Wiggly and cried over the telephone. The manager said he'd keep an eye out for it. Mama said she didn't believe she'd ever see it again.

"I can't believe this," she said. "I cannot believe." She balled her fists and looked up at the cracked gray ceiling. "Why?" she said. "Truly. Why? We have nothing. Absolutely nothing."

But really, I knew where her money was; it was safe. And I knew I was making her unhappy for a while, but deep down I felt I was supposed to do it. I don't know why. It's the first time I'd ever felt that way. It was strong and forceful. A knowing beyond knowing. I always figured if God asked me to do something it wouldn't involve stealing. But I was only eight and a half years old. Who was I to question the maker of the universe?

We went back to the grocery store and Mama talked to everyone there, asking had they seen her change purse. She even said there was a reward if somebody did find it. Not sure what the reward was, but nobody claimed it. After Mama gave up looking and finally stopped crying, we found ourselves standing on the porch of the blue gingerbread house on Vinca Lane, where the Macy family went back a hundred and forty-three years. Poppy was running his fingers over the railing and woodwork, admiring it, remembering it. Grandma Mona stood taut, clutching her red purse in her skinny fingers and clearing her throat every second or two. Rainey was looking at me with nervous eyes, petting the wings of her dying bug for good luck, and Mama was standing limp shouldered, hand over doorbell, waiting—for nerve or for somebody else to relieve her from her task.

"Just open it, for heaven's sake," said Grandma Mona. "Ring it already. You're not getting any younger."

Mama took a deep breath and punched the white button surrounded by fancy etched flowers in brass, then she pulled away quick like she was embarrassed to have made a sound. An old lady across the street in a yellow Victorian not as nice as this one was watching us from her front porch. She was pushing a broom back and forth, sweeping slow like a person who wants to seem like she's cleaning but mostly's trying to hide the fact that she's nosing around in the neighbors' beeswax.

The door started to open, and Mama gasped. So I held my breath. I was nervous as all get-out and didn't rightly know why, like maybe a ghost would be standing there. But it was no ghost. There was a tall, skinny man, older than Mama but younger than Poppy, and he looked a whole heck of a lot like Grandma Mona. Except for not so mean.

"Fritz," Mama said.

"Oh my—Priscilla? Is it really you?"

Mister Fritz seemed to be taking us all in and could hardly believe we were standing there before his very eyes.

"Fritz," said Grandma Mona, "it's been a long time."

"Well, my goodness, come in," he said. "I'm . . . I was hoping I'd see you. After all these years." Mister Fritz spoke with faraway stars in his eyes.

"Yes," said Mama, still tight-lipped. "It's been a long time."

Mama looked at Fritz, and he looked back at her, and then all of us said our hellos and shuffled into the house like nothing at all was strange about us being here after all these years. Nothing at all was strange about meeting a man you didn't know existed, who just happened to look a lot like your Grandma Mona. Nothing at all was strange about stepping into your great-grandparents' house that was said to be haunted with ghosts and family secrets, with gladiola wallpaper going up the stairs to the rooms where your mama once played when she was young and happy and life was simple.

Before she left home, dead to the family, alone in the world. And now she was back, her fatherless children in tow.

No, nothing at all was strange about that.

Part Two

EATING THE
GINGERBREAD HOUSE

Chapter Eighteen
WHICHEVER WAY
THE POT FALLS

Mister Fritz looked like he was young and old at the same time—no wrinkles or anything—but there was gray around his face. He towered over Poppy, who, at this moment, seemed he'd died and gone to heaven, staring over all the faded brown portraits of people on the walls.

Grandma Mona was not much for saying howdy-do and got that out of the way real quick. Now she was in the sewing room that sat off to the right of the front door. She was pressed up to the little sewing table, turning spools of colored thread and thimbles in her fingers. I hadn't realized she liked to sew. Watching my grandparents here in this house was sort of like seeing them when they were younger. Like their heads had filled with olden days. I looked back at the front door and wondered if we'd walked through a time machine.

Mama and Rainey were sitting with Mister Fritz in the fancy living room on the other side of the hall. He'd gotten them cups of iced tea, but I declined. I was standing there in the middle of the hallway, torn between rooms, trying to take it all in.

I had never walked into a place and felt that I

had history, or roots, in my life. It was as if all my life I'd been just waiting to come to this very house. Everybody—Poppy, Grandma Mona, Mama—seemed to have found pieces of themselves here, like they weren't really themselves until they got here and the house popped in that last piece of the puzzle.

Rainey was strangely quiet and well behaved. I could tell she liked this Mister Fritz. She was usually a good judge of character, except for mangy dogs, so I supposed I'd like him too. Rainey was sipping her tea and had her knees pulled together on the sofa, like Mama did. Rainey was copying everything Mama was doing. Every time she took a sip, Rainey took a sip. If she turned her body or crossed her legs, Rainey did it too. It was how Rainey learned what to do in situations she wasn't used to. She was real smart that way.

"It's good to see you, Priscilla," I heard Fritz said, "and so wonderful to meet you, Rainey. I see you're every bit as beautiful as your mama."

Rainey grinned bigger than I'd ever seen. She forgot being graceful and pulled her shoulders up to her ears like a little girl. Don't you know, she spilled her tea on that pretty rug?

"Not to worry. I'll get that," said Fritz, standing up, sort of taking his time, and heading to the kitchen. I wondered if he was walking so slow because he couldn't move fast or because he didn't want Rainey to think it was a big deal, spilling tea on a rug that was probably a hundred or more years old. I was guessing it was a bigger deal than he was letting on, and it made me like him even more. Soon as he was out of the room, Mama said in a hush, "Rainey, can you please be more careful? My goodness, when I was little I wasn't even allowed to take a drink in here. My grandma would have had my hide!"

"Sorry, Mama." Rainey turned all galumph-y again. She'd quit trying to be Mama and was just Rainey now, her head sagging low. She eyed her calm cicada on the doily beneath the window.

"Why don't you go on and look around the place? But please, honey, don't touch anything, okay? Everything in here is a precious antique that used to belong to somebody important in the family." Then she said real low, more to herself, "I can't imagine what all this stuff is worth now."

"Let's go upstairs," I said. "Poppy's looking at pictures."

So Rainey and I started to climb the stairway. It was in the middle of the hall directly in front of the door, and rose-colored carpet rolled up the middle with dark wood sticking out the sides. The rail was fancy, with a curly-q and wood pickets carved with swoops and swirls. Must have taken somebody a long time to make those pickets.

"Look here, girls," said Poppy. "You see this? This is your great-grandfather, Adolph Macy. Remember I was telling you about him?"

"He dead," said Rainey.

I flitted down the steps for just a glimpse of my mama. I wanted to make sure she was all right now that she and Fritz were by themselves. He was sitting an arm's length away from her on the sofa, looking down at her feet. Mama had her elbows on her knees and her hands covering her face. It was perfectly quiet, but I could tell she was upset. About what, I didn't know. I knew they were waiting for me, so I climbed back up to join Rainey and Poppy.

"Everybody in these pictures is dead, Rainey," I said. "It's no big deal. This one died in the war. On a land mine. We were talking 'bout him in the car."

The picture of Adolph Macy was brown and faded all around the edges, so it made him look like he was just floating there with no body or anything. His eyes were colored in blacker than normal and real serious. Maybe somebody had come along with a marker. Made it look like he was staring right at you, or like you could see right into his head. He was real young to be Poppy's father. Didn't look much older than Rainey. She had his chin, though, square and fat, so I knew he was family.

"And this one right here? This is my mother, Madeline Macy. She had some Indian in her, though we never did figure out what. Wasn't really anything folks used to talk about. But see her cheekbones? Janie, you favor her a lot." That was the first time I'd heard a grown-up say I looked like anybody at all, and it made me feel like I belonged. Maybe I did have a place in this family.

"She was a good woman, my mother," said Poppy. "Hardworking. She took care of me and my brother all by herself after Daddy went off to Korea. And when he didn't come back, she just kept on as if nothing had ever happened. In my book, my mother was a hero, just like my father."

"You can be a hero just for acting like nothing ever happened?"

"Absolutely. My mother never let us see her cry, even though I knew it was hard on her. It had to be. Because of Mama being so strong, my brother Jimmy and I just went on like nothing had ever happened either. It made it easier that way."

"Who's this?" asked Rainey, putting her leg over the railing like she was going to slide down. She was pointing to the portrait to the left of Great-Grandma Madeline.

"Get off the rail, honey. That won't hold," Poppy said. Rainey minded him and sat on the stairs. She never liked to be scolded. It wounded her for a few minutes before she could go on. Always had been that way. She was pouting, but I showed Poppy I was all ears for him. He got real animated then and said in a spooky voice, "This . . . is your Great-Aunt Gertrude. Her ghost is said to still be in this very house."

The *s* in *house* lingered on his tongue like the hissing of a snake, and my mouth dropped open. Rainey got over her pouty self, and her bottom lip reared back like a smiling dog's. Her eyes went wide. "Where is she?"

"They say she's in the attic," said Poppy.

"She *is* in the attic," said Grandma Mona from the sewing room. She'd been listening in on us this whole time.

"Why?" I ask. "Why's she in the attic?"

" 'Cause that's where she died."

"Somebody died *here*?" I was thinking this wasn't such a great idea. I had known about ghosts, but I didn't like the idea of somebody having to die to become one. "Let's go," I said. "Can we go now? Go back to the motel?"

"Oh, honey, she's harmless," said Poppy, pulling me into his lap. He was resting on a step three up from Rainey.

"I thought people go to heaven when they die," I said.

"Yeah, hebben," Rainey echoed.

"Well, sometimes they do," said Poppy. "And sometimes, they don't. Like if they've been real bad or if they have business to tend to."

"Was Gertrude bad?" I asked.

"Well, it's not for me to judge, but the story is, she tried to kill her husband, your great-uncle Remorse. For some reason, Gertrude thought he

138

was two-timing her, and . . . well that's just not something we know for sure. But what we do know is one afternoon, she put a pot of boiling oil up on a rafter in the attic. Then she called him to come up there for something, luring him into a trap, you see. Next thing you know, Aunt Gertrude's the one lying on the floor, covered in grease, not Uncle Remorse. Burned three-quarters of her body, it did, and she died not long after that. Died a painful, terrible death from all those burns."

I covered my mouth and spoke through my fingers, horrified. "She was really trying to kill him?"

"Legend has it," said Poppy. "Funny how life works, isn't it? Had the pot fallen the other way, Uncle Remorse would've been killed instead of Gertrude. Word has it that Gertrude is still so mad about the whole thing, her ghost stays up in the attic, trying to figure out what went wrong."

"What do you think went wrong?"

"Truthfully? I think God works that way. All things work for good for those who love the Lord. I'm guessing Uncle Remorse loved the Lord a little more than Aunt Gertrude. Otherwise, she wouldn't have been working so hard to kill him, now would she?"

"You believe she's still up there?" I asked.

"I don't know, honey. Your Grandma Mona seems to think so. Some folks need a good reason to up and leave the earth, I guess. If she's not in heaven, I suspect that old attic looks better than the alternative . . . down there." He pointed to the ground and said, "And I'm not talking about the basement."

"I don't want to go in the attic or the basement," I said.

"Me too," said Rainey.

Poppy closed his eyes and laughed. "Now girls, this is all good and fun, all right? There's nothing scary about this house. There is nothing at all going to hurt you here. I can promise you that."

Rainey and I looked at each other and made a silent secret pact not to go anywhere near the attic or the basement.

"Come on down, honey," Mama called us from the back of the house. "Uncle Fritz is gonna show us the garden in the back. You won't believe it. It's all grown up and even prettier than I remember it."

Couple things I'd just noticed. One, Mama actually sounded happy for the first time in a week. I wondered what all had happened while Rainey and me had been sitting here having our wits scared out of us. Last time I saw Mama she was looking upset. Or was she? Second, Mama'd just called him *Uncle* Fritz which, in my book, if he looks like Grandma Mona, would make him Mama's *brother,* and I had no idea she even had one. I looked up at Poppy all alarmed with my suspicion, and he whispered to me, "We'll talk about this later, all right?"

"But she said—"

"I know it, honey. In a little while. We've got some things to explain to you, and we will."

And here I'd thought Mama was an only child. My whole life I was thinking this. She'd never once talked about an Uncle Fritz before—even in her childhood stories—and neither had my Grandma Mona. Neither had Poppy. It made me nervous and wondering, heaven knows, what else had they been keeping quiet?

Chapter Nineteen
UNCLE FRITZ

We were standing in the garden behind the house on Vinca Lane, all of us family, Fritz even. It seemed a lot less scary out there with the sunlight and nobody's dead eyes looking out at me from portraits on the wall. Blue gingerbread doodads covered the back of the house, and a blue trellis hung over the walkway, covered in jasmine. The smell was next to heaven. Uncle Fritz stooped down and showed Mama an herb garden with rosemary, chives, and basil. It was in little squares all nice and neat, a different herb in each square. Then the strawberries. They covered the ground, flopping all this way and that, and Rainey went to grab one and Uncle Fritz said, "Eat all

141

you like, they're perfect for pickin' right now. And look there. You see that tree? Know what it is?"

"Oranges?" I said.

"It's a peach tree," he said. "They're not quite ripe enough yet, but I tell you what. Soon as they are, I'll have you out here to help me pick 'em. Would you like that?"

"Yes," Rainey said, tickled to be included.

"Wonderful. I'm hoping your mama takes me up on my offer too. What do you say, Priscilla? This house is just sittin' here, empty. I'm only up the street a couple blocks. You should stay here while you're in town. Stay as long as you like. There's no reason to be in a motel. Truly."

Mama looked around at us all and then at the flowers, and her eyes softened, almost like Rainey's, sweet-like. Then, they firmed up again and she said, "No. Thank you. But no, we're fine where we are."

Fritz looked at Mama and put his hands up, "I won't press you, then. Just know you're welcome . . . and entitled to be here whenever you decide."

"I appreciate that," said Mama.

"Can I talk you into some tomato sandwiches though? They're all ripe, and I've been trying my best to can 'em and make sauce, but they're coming out my ears now. They're nothing fancy, but good."

"Thank you. That would be very nice. Rainey, what do you say, are you hungry?"

"I like-a eat," said Rainey. She was sitting on the walkway, running her fingers through the chives like hair. She smiled and Mama seemed to melt. She was so proud of Rainey, and rightly so. She loved Mama so much. Rainey was her heart. I was more of the one she dealt her troubles to. Her confidant. But lately, since she'd found out she was expecting a baby, she'd quit talking as much to me. If I was honest, I was starting to feel a little closed off. Maybe it was having Grandma Mona and Poppy around. I hoped that was it and I could get some time alone with Mama soon.

The kitchen had old appliances in it, but they'd been kept nice. It felt a little like walking back in time. Grandma Mona got so excited, oohing and aahing over every little thing, the toaster, the fridge, the stove, the linoleum on the floor. And she had a story for each one. She was almost like a child again.

"You see this mark on the wall, Janie? This is where a pot of lima beans started a kitchen fire. I kid you not. Your Poppy was frisky back in the day."

"Oh, come on, Mona."

"No, she'll like this. I bet it's hard for her to imagine us young . . . and in love."

I looked at Grandma Mona and tried to imagine her young. It was harder than picturing her in love because for a split second, I saw her eyes light up when she looked at Poppy. His cheeks flushed red, and Grandma Mona kept on. "I was fixing supper one evening. Your Poppy had just come back from a trip out west. He'd been gone for three or four days, and things had gotten quiet around here." She looked at Mama. "Priscilla was, oh, 'bout eight or nine years old at the time. She liked to spend time sitting up in the window seat in her bedroom upstairs. Didn't you, Priscilla? You'll see it in a little bit, girls. Anyway, so she was quiet. I think Grandma Macy was out taking a walk or something. Anyway, I'm standing here cooking and your Poppy walks in, grabs me around the hips, and kisses me on the neck. Liked to scare me to death."

"She jumped so high, she knocked the pot of beans over and grease spilled out. I spent the next few minutes fighting a blazing fire like you never seen. Liked to burn the whole place down."

"It wasn't quite that bad, Grayson."

"For sure it was." He reached his hands up high to show how big the flames had gotten, stood up on his tippy toes and everything.

"That's what your kisses used to do for me. Start fires."

"Oh Mona, stop it. There's children in here."

"You like the kiss," said Rainey, pointing to Poppy and giggling. I was thinking in my head I knew how they wound up having Mama, what

144

with all that kissing going on. I was sort of surprised they didn't have more children.

After lunch, Rainey and I explored the rest of the house. The downstairs had the living room, sewing room, kitchen and dining rooms, a little tiny bathroom, and that same gladiola wallpaper everywhere. It was faded in places close to the windows and dark in places where the sun didn't shine. We climbed the stairs slowly with fear and reverence, passing the portraits of Adolph Macy, Madeline Macy, and Gertrude the ghost, and hoped we wouldn't be seeing her anytime soon.

I was surprised to see how light and bright the upstairs was. It was even nicer than the downstairs, and I couldn't decide which room to stay in longest. There were four bedrooms, two on the front and two on the back of the house. There was one bathroom for every two rooms. The ones on the front overlooked the yard and Vinca Lane. I could see all the houses on the street from there, including the yellow one with the old lady who liked to sweep and snoop. These rooms had great big beds like Mama's at home except taller, and they were covered in patchwork quilts I imagined were sewn in that very room downstairs. I was right. Mama and Fritz followed us after a few minutes and walked in each and every one, explaining things as they went.

"Mama and Daddy's room," said Mama, standing with her hand on the doorframe.

"You can go on in," said Fritz, so we all did. Poppy and Grandma Mona were somewhere outside, probably settled into the rocking chairs on the back porch.

"Daddy used to keep his billfold right here," said Mama, running her fingers along a dark wood dresser beside the bed. "And every night, he'd put his change out like this, lined each piece up, one after the other. I'd count them for him, and he'd tell me what a rich man God had made him. You know, just this minute, I realize he wasn't talking about money."

She turned to look at Fritz and he smiled at her, a kind, knowing smile. Rainey was sitting on the bed. She flopped back onto the quilt. "Your Grandma Mona made that quilt, Rainey. She was always in that sewing room. I can't imagine how much it must have hurt her to leave it behind when we moved to Yuma. Far as I know she never did any more sewing."

I'd never heard Mama say anything in a kind way about Grandma Mona before, so I studied that quilt like it was treasure. It had squares of blue and lavender, and green diamonds. Embroidered on it in cream-colored thread was a great big sprawling tree.

"Come on, let's go look at the other rooms," said Fritz. Rainey got off the bed, and she and I led the way.

"Look in here!" I said. We'd come into a room

across the hall that looked out over the garden. Green light filled the air, putting a hue on every-thing, the walls, our faces, a trundle bed. It felt cool and calming to be in there.

"Oh, this was my room." Mama's eyes glowed green with the rest of her. Then they welled up with tears. "My goodness, I can't believe how hard this is. I can't believe how many years it's been."

"Sometimes when you come home like this after so many years, it makes you wonder why in the world it took you so long," said Fritz.

"You're right. You're exactly right," said Mama. " 'Course, you would know about that, wouldn't you? I can't imagine what it was like for you when—"

"It was hard," said Fritz. "I can't tell you how much." And my ears perked up because sitting on that window seat where my mother used to sit when she was my age, looking out over that garden, I could hear in Fritz's voice that some-thing had changed. And if I got real quiet and still like I did with Mama sometimes, they might even forget I was here and open up about the secrets they'd been keeping from me. About how Fritz was the uncle I never knew I had. And how Mama could go from being sad to happy in no time flat.

Chapter Twenty
THE INVITATION

Sitting there in the green room, trying to be invisible, didn't work. Mama and Fritz didn't spill any family secrets. Instead, we just joined Poppy and Grandma Mona again on the back porch. They were walking around the garden so Mama and Rainey took the rocking chairs. *Rock, rock, rock, rock...*

"You sure I can't change your mind about staying here?" said Fritz to Mama. A nice cool breeze blew through my hair. "I mean it, it's no trouble, and it'd do the house some good to have company. I'm not here as often as I'd like."

Mama rocked. I thought about how he'd put that ... about the house needing company. I pictured it blue and ornate and lonesome ... with a soul, even. Mama rocked some more. Then she looked over at Rainey and me standing beside her.

"I get Mama's room," I said.

"I get Mama room too," said Rainey. Poppy and Grandma Mona creaked up the steps to show us a ripe tomato.

"I ... I don't think so," my mother said.

"But Mama . . . please? We'll be good, I promise!"

"Priscilla, for heaven's sake, take him up on his

offer," said Poppy in her ear. "You've lost all your money, remember?"

"Please, Mama?" There must have been something about the way Rainey begged, because Mama changed her mind right then. I don't know if it was because she was born special or what, but Rainey seemed to pull more weight with Mama than I did.

She breathed out. "Well, all right. If you promise it's no trouble, Fritz, I guess it can't hurt. It can't be worse than sleeping in a tiny motel room. I haven't rested well since we left home. Even before then. Yes," she looked up in Poppy's warm eyes and said, "it would be nice to spend some time here again like old days. Maybe get my head on straight."

I was looking at Poppy and wondering if he was thinking the same thing, that this offer to stay was like a miracle, what with Mama losing all her money and such. It made me feel good about what I'd had to do, taking it and all. Made me feel like I'd played a real part in bringing us here.

"That's what I wanted to hear," said Fritz. "Your daddy's pleased, I'm sure."

"I just can't tell you how much, Priscilla. Thank you, Fritz," said Poppy. "Having us all here in the old house, well, it's more than I could have imagined."

"It's settled, then," said Fritz, pulling a red cap out of his back pocket and pulling it over his pepper hair. "I'll be stopping back with some groceries for supper in a little while."

"You don't have to do that," said Mama.

"Not at all. You just make yourselves at home."

And then, Fritz was gone, and Mama and I were standing there, looking at the jasmine, smelling it. Poppy and Grandma Mona had rediscovered the rocking chairs, and Rainey was chasing a happy yellow butterfly. If I didn't know better, we looked like some family out of a storybook.

I had never had an uncle before. Never had a blue gingerbread house before, neither, but even though Mama had brought us here in an ailing sort of way, I had the strong suspicion I was going to like it here. And I hoped for her sake we'd stay for a while.

The manager at the grocery store, knowing Mama had lost her change purse, offered to pay Rainey real money for bagging groceries and taking them to people's cars. That second night in Forest Pines, she came home with twenty dollars and a bagful of leftover deli meat, cheese, and two loaves of bread. Mama stuffed them in the fridge and declared we'd be eating sandwiches for a while.

"Are we staying, Mama?" I asked.

"Janie wanna stay," said Rainey. "We stay here?"

"Oh, goodness, I'm not sure. Maybe a short—"

But before she could finish her sentence, Rainey and I were jumping up and down, hollering. We were excited about something for the first time in a long time. We went running through the house, claiming the trundle bed in the upstairs green room. She got the top part, and we pulled out the undermattress for me, almost like our bunks at home. We played upstairs in all the bedrooms, lying in all the beds, trying on clothes left over in closets and chests, and pulling books off the shelf. A few were left over from Mama's child-hood: *Anne of Green Gables, Catch-22, Heidi.* We never showed our faces again until it was time to eat.

Uncle Fritz came over for supper that night. He brought a pork roast, butter noodles, and sliced tomatoes and onions. Mama had a pitcher of iced tea waiting, and we had a real nice time for a while, all of us in the dining room.

And then Rainey spoke up.

Sitting there at the old oak table with fancy plates hanging on the wall, Rainey looked over at Uncle Fritz in between mouthfuls of noodles and said, "You look like Grandma Mona."

I was shocked she'd said it so brazen and equally happy she'd brought it up. I watched his face to see what he'd say. I wasn't sure if he could understand her or not, so I repeated for him, "She says you look like Grandma Mona."

Fritz looked at Rainey, baffled or amazed, like

151

she was real smart and had figured out a puzzle. In his confusion, he looked even more like his mama, who was sitting beside him on the right.

"Oh gracious, here we go," said Grandma Mona. And she picked up her plate and carried it to the kitchen. "Call me when y'all are done. I'll be out back."

I looked at Poppy and Mama, then Fritz. He'd set his napkin in his lap and looked to be thinking about folding it up again. Mama cleared her throat and said, "You know, it's funny you brought that up, honey. There's a picture upstairs of my mother that looks the spitting image of Fritz right now." She looked at him for help maybe.

"Rainey," said Fritz. "I've got a secret to tell you. A really neat secret. Your mama and I . . . we share the same mother. That's why I look like her, your Grandma Mona. Your mama and I are brother and sister."

I'd been suspecting as much, what with Mama calling him Uncle Fritz and all, and I was eager to show my smarts with a question. "And Poppy?" I asked. "Poppy's your daddy too?"

"No sweetie, I'm not his father," said Poppy, and my noodles liked to slipped right out of my mouth.

Chapter Twenty-one
THE PAST LIFE OF
GRANDMA MONA

"Who your daddy?" asked Rainey, not real impressed with any of Fritz's announcements. She grabbed her glass of iced tea with both hands, concentrating on not letting it fall. The condensation dripped down to the table and left a big wet spot on the wood. Rainey slurped.

"Apparently, my mother," said Mama, "was married to another man before she met my father. It's not anything she ever talked about. I'm not even sure Daddy knew about it."

"Yes, I knew about it," Poppy said. "I just didn't like to talk about it much. Or think about it. It was your mother's private business."

"Grandma Mona was married?!" I found it strangely unsettling to think of my grandma having a life with another man before Poppy. It made me feel icky inside and unglued.

"I was born," said Fritz, putting his elbows on the table around his plate, "while my father was away, fighting a war. My mother, your Grandma Mona, got news he'd been killed in action, and well, rightly so, she fell apart. She didn't think she could care for a baby all by herself, so she put me up for adoption. I was adopted and raised by a very loving couple, Sue and

153

Christopher Rosier, whom I called Mom and Dad."

I couldn't take this in right. It wasn't quite jibing with me. Not only was Grandma Mona married before Poppy, but she had a little baby boy, Fritz, right there in front of me, all grown up. And she'd given him away? How could somebody do that?

"She gave you away?" I asked, flummoxed. "You were a little baby, and she just gave you away?"

All of a sudden, Rainey started crying. Her upslanted eyes got even slantier.

"Don't cry, honey," Mama said. "There's nothing to cry about. Your uncle Fritz here had a wonderful life. Right?"

"I did! I absolutely did. The best. Wonderful parents. I went to school, I even went to seminary. Why, do you know I have a church right here in town where I preach on Sundays? Would you like to come there with me sometime?"

Rainey sniffled and nodded a little, but I wasn't going to let this go just yet.

"How come I never knew about you?" I asked Fritz. "Mama never mentioned she had a brother."

"She didn't know," said Poppy. "I didn't either, for that matter. Not until Fritz here came to find his mother years later. He was twenty-three at the time, I believe. Priscilla was fifteen. We'd just moved out to Yuma."

"When I finished seminary, Rainey, I felt called to go and look for my birth parents. I found my mother after six months. She was remarried to your grandfather, Grayson Macy."

"That's right," said Poppy. "Now listen, there's something I want you to know about your Grandma Mona. Just because she had a family before doesn't mean she loved me or Priscilla any less. She's a good woman. She really is. And she did what she thought was best for her son at the time. She thought her husband had died in the war."

"But my father hadn't died in the war like they told my mother," said Fritz. "He'd been captured. And when he finally did come home, well, the marriage just fell apart after all that had passed, after I'd come and gone. I never did meet him. He died before I could track him down."

"It was terrible timing," said Mama, putting her hand lightly on Fritz's hand. "Sometimes God and babies have terrible timing, don't they?"

"I know what this is about!" I squealed. "You're gonna give our baby away, aren't you?" I put my head down and sulked, face in my plate.

"Don't give baby 'way, Mama!" Rainey wailed, hands over her ears. "I want the baby Jesus! I want the baby!"

"Oh—" Mama inhaled and covered her mouth, fretting. Then she excused herself real quick to go to the bathroom, her chair falling off the edge of the rug and scraping the floor.

"Maybe this was all too much too soon," said Fritz.

Poppy, Fritz, and I were left trying to console Rainey. I was finding it awful hard to do, seeing as I was the one who needed consoling. And then when she stopped crying and I looked at Fritz and Poppy, tears in their eyes and such, I felt sad for the whole wide world—that women lost husbands and had to give babies away. That babies grew up wondering who their parents were. That Grandma Mona, the meanest lady I ever met, was maybe not as mean as I might have been, had I suffered all that she had.

And I ran out on the porch to find her. I hugged her harder than ever before. I pressed, and I cried, and she hugged me back for the first time in years, and I prayed that just by touching her warm skin, I could somehow take her hurting away.

Chapter Twenty-two
THE LADIES OF FOREST PINES

The green room glowed with the blue of nightfall. Out of a little arched window above the curtains, I could see the stars out in full, but the moon had withered to near nothing. There was a faint smell of mothballs on my pillow. "Rainey?" I said, the sound of my voice settling on the air.

"What?"

"Are you scared . . . about being in this house?"

"No." She answered with no hesitation.

"Me neither," I said. "I thought I might be, with the ghost and all. But I think I like it here. I hope we stay a long, long time."

"Me too."

I turned over and closed my eyes. I reached my hand up on Rainey's mattress and touched her on the arm.

"Huh?" she breathed.

"What do you think of Fritz, I mean, being Mama's brother and all? Grandma Mona, Poppy, Mama . . . nobody ever said a thing about him. Do you think it's true?"

Rainey stayed quiet a minute, and I thought she might have gone to sleep until she said, "When baby comes, I gonna be the big sister."

"I'm gonna be a big sister, too, you know," I said.

"Nope," she said.

"Yes I am."

"Huh-uh."

"I am too!" Rainey usually never made me mad, but I was steamed. Here I was, trying to be all happy and hopeful in this house which had been in the Macy family for so long, and my sister chose this moment to make me feel small, hardly a part of the family at all. So I said, "When the baby comes, Mama's gonna let me hold it first."

I waited to hear how my words had stung her,

but all I heard was Rainey's breath. It grew heavier and slower as her mind drifted away.

I couldn't sleep. There were noises in the old house. Squirrels scurried on the rooftop, and the fan above me clicked every time it made it all the way around. But I wasn't scared. I reached under my pillow and set out to find my mother.

Her room was across the hall and to the left. The door was open a little, so I spied at first. A little light glowed from beneath the pink shade of a small lamp. The window looked out over the front lawn and a large bushy tree, I wasn't sure what kind. My mother had some reading glasses on, and she was propped up in bed reading a book with no picture on the cover. The glasses were dark brown, square, and fit her low on the nose. They gave her a wise look and reminded me of Poppy for some reason.

I squeezed in the door and she glanced up. "Hey, Mama," I said. "This is a really neat house. I'm glad we're here."

Mama took the glasses off and nodded. She studied them and put them on the nightstand. "Oh, goodness, what it means to be back. I always did love this house."

She set her book down too, and I saw the gold letters, *Of Mice and Men* by John Steinbeck. I'd never seen Mama reading a book like that with no man on the front. But seeing her here, and not at home, it looked right. Funny how it seemed a person could change into whatever surroundings she was in, like a chameleon.

"Time for bed, young lady," Mama said in a funny low voice. Almost like she was imitating Poppy.

"I know, I just . . . well, I wanted to give you this." I pulled out my list of options for her and set it on the nightstand right beside *Of Mice and Men*. I flattened it out real well, and Mama looked at it. Then at me. "It's not much," I apologized, "but it's got two options for you, pros and cons, just like you taught me. I know there's another one but I'm not clear on it yet, so when I am, I'll add it. Okay? Maybe this can help you for now . . . deciding about the baby and all."

Mama took a deep breath and closed her eyes tight. I wondered if I'd upset her, taking it upon myself to get in her business. She thought a minute, then said, "Thanks, I needed this."

"You're welcome, Mama. Oh, and . . . if you keep the baby, maybe you should let Rainey hold it first. I think she'd like that."

Mama held her tummy and turned out the light.

"Good night." I warmed all over from head to foot and went out feeling that even though Mama's load was heavy, I'd done my part in helping her carry it, if only a little.

Next morning, I had barely opened my eyes when I saw Poppy standing above me, chipper and

159

dressed in his usual ensemble, brown slacks and shoes, white short-sleeve button-up shirt, and red bow tie. There was always a gleam in his eye, too, but this morning it was as if the sunlight was coming from him and not the window.

"Girls? What do you say we go for a little walk?"

I smelled sausage and coffee, and everything looked different, the light fixture, the wallpaper. It took me a minute to realize where I was, this being the third different bed in as many nights. When I realized I was in this pretty place with so much to explore, a feeling welled up in me like I might burst. "I'll go!" I hollered.

"Me too," said Rainey, trying to wake up.

"Good. Get dressed and come on down to the kitchen. We'll have a bite and then set off on an adventure."

"Where are we going?"

"Well, I can't exactly say . . ." he said, "but I have it on good authority there's a library within walking distance."

"The library!" I jumped up on the bed and hooted. The library was my most favorite place, so quiet, so many books, a different life in every one. You could stay there for hours and never look at the same thing twice. And, the library was free. In Mama's book, that made for a real good time. At home we went about every month to the library so Mama could stock up on romances. She traded them back and forth with Alisha.

We did as Poppy asked, and by nine o'clock we were off and exploring, Poppy, Rainey, and me. Every house on Vinca Lane had crape myrtles, tall and reaching up, white and pink heavy blossoms dipping down like fruit and tickling us as we walked. Pink petals littered the street curb. Every house had color, every yard, flowers. There were no wire fences, no barking dogs tied to stakes, no dried mud rivers waiting to melt with the next rain. Vinca Lane was nothing like our street in Cypresswood, and seeing this place made me see our house for what it really was.

Funny, I'd always thought we lived real nice.

We passed the yellow house where we'd first seen that old woman sweeping the porch. Today she was sitting in a fancy hammock made for one, hanging from the porch ceiling. More like she was wrestling with it, hands and bony arms poking out every which way.

"Mrs. Shoemaker, that you?" asked Poppy, being real polite.

"Yeah, it's me," she growled. "Who'd you think it was?"

"I just . . . it looks like you might need a hand."

"Naw, no, I got it. I . . . Oh, come on, then, and hurry it up. Help me outta this crazy co'traption. What was she thinkin', anyway? This ain't restful."

Poppy walked us across the street and up to Mrs. Shoemaker's porch. Somehow, she'd sunk a leg in crossways and looked like a crab stuck in a shrimp net. Rainey and I stood there on the sidewalk, a healthy distance away, trying not to laugh. For two folks who didn't seem to care much for one another, there sure was an awful lot of grunting and limbs and carrying on.

After Mrs. Shoemaker was free, she caught my eye and scrutinized me. Then Rainey. Poppy said, "These are my two granddaughters, Rainey and Janie."

"That rhymes," said Mrs. Shoemaker. Her white hair had pulled loose from bobby pins like strands of yarn across her brow. She wore an apron covering a brown housedress. "I don't like it when names rhyme."

Poppy looked at us and did one of those funny eye rolls, letting us know Mrs. Shoemaker wasn't all there and not to take her seriously. She must have seen him do it because she turned uglier all of a sudden.

"I see you got one reg'lar grandbaby and one . . . special one." She said *special* like it was something nasty.

"Don't say nothin' about my sister!" She really set me off.

"It's okay," Poppy said. "She didn't mean it."

"But it's not nice to make fun like that," I said.

Mrs. Shoemaker was pointing a shaky hand our

162

way, and I was itching to let her have it again. "That one's got her grandma's spunk, I see. All I meant was—"

"We'll just be going now," said Poppy. "We're on our way to the library."

"I gonna see books," said Rainey. "They got all kinds . . ." She put her hand up and counted fingers. "Picture books, word books, Bible books . . . I gonna get the book."

"That's real nice," said Mrs. Shoemaker, apparently trying to make up for her meanness.

We started to walk away when Poppy stopped and addressed her again. "I see you're back. It's been a while, hasn't it? You staying with your daughter?"

"Yep. Been a while. I reckon she needs some help 'round here. Not much an old lady can do, though. I see you're back too. Must be nice, having all the family together. Don't know how you can stand Miss Mona, though."

"Oh Clarabelle, you two are like oil and water. I'll be sure and give Mona your love and kisses."

"Tell her she can kiss my—"

"Bye now, Clarabelle."

I turned back around and watched the old lady watching us go. Then I stared down at my feet. I knew I'd been ill-mannered, mouthing off to a grown-up and all.

"She wasn't very nice," I said.

"You weren't very nice to her, either," said Poppy.

"But she said—"

"It doesn't matter, Janie. People say things all the time. What's important is to know *why* they say those things. You need to look at people the same way God does . . . look on the inside."

"She's probably got worms and stinky cheese on the inside."

"Janie Doe Macy." He said my name to shut me up, but I sort of liked the way he said it. 'Fact, I didn't mind him fussing at me neither. I was just glad somebody was paying attention to me in some fashion or another.

The sidewalk was old white concrete with cracks and crevices along it. Green grass and yellow daisies grew up from the cracks, and I remember thinking, *How amazing is it you can pour concrete on top, but that still don't stop the life from shooting up?* The flowers in the sidewalk spoke hope to me, and I took note of every single survivor.

Then I heard a yelp.

Running up behind us, Mama came fussing like a mockingbird. "I asked you to wait for me! I told you I was finishing the dishes."

"Sorry, Mama," I said. "But Poppy—"

"Sorry, Mama," said Rainey.

"It's all right. I like libraries too, you know. And this one, the one we're going to, is the very one I went to when I was little. Mama would let me go there by myself once I got older, and anytime I went missing, she could find me there. Sort of like your tree back home, Rainey."

Mama looked nice this morning. She had a pretty flowered skirt on and a pink short-sleeved sweater set. It fit her snug, but her tummy wasn't big yet. I wondered how long before it got that way. Her hair was curled a little and she had flat navy shoes on. She didn't look anything like the Mama I knew back home in Cypresswood. I liked it. I wondered if there were some clothes here that I could put on too. Maybe in the attic? But no, I couldn't go up there, what with the ghost and all.

"Well, my stars and garters, is that Miss Priscilla Macy?" A cream-colored car rolled up to us at a stop sign, and a window came down. At the wheel was a lady with a jeweled headband covering curly brown hair. She was fancy with gold bangles on her wrist and pretty pink fingernails. The bracelets clinked when she shook her hand. "I declare, it *is* you! Why, look at you!"

"All grown up," said Mama. "Kelsey Piper, how long has it been?" Mama's voice sounded different. There was a soft lilt I hadn't heard except when she'd talked with Mr. Carl a while back about buying our car. She smiled real nice and approached the window.

"It's been long enough for me to not be Kelsey Piper anymore. I'm married to a doctor now . . . Mrs. Kelsey Arielle." She dangled her fingers at Mama to show she did indeed have a shiny ring.

To my knowledge, Mama never had a pretty ring like that one.

"How wonderful," Mama said. "This here is Rainey." She showed her off like, *see what I've done with my last seventeen years?*

"Well, hello, Rainey. What a lovely name. Are you enjoying your time in Forest Pines?" Rainey nodded and looked at the sidewalk flowers. "I do hope you'll be staying here awhile."

"We goin' to library," said Rainey, not shy anymore. "They got books. I can read."

Mrs. Kelsey Arielle melted and grinned. Rainey had that effect on people sometimes. If they chose to look at her and address her at all, they often swooned and carried on. It embarrassed me for her. "Oh, how lovely," she said. "Of course you can read. And I adore the library. All those books!"

I looked over at Poppy waiting across the street for us. He grinned at me, and it gave me the gumption to speak. "I'm Janie," I said. "I'm eight and a half, almost nine. I can read too."

"So nice to meet yewww! And so nice to see you again, Priscilla. What a sweet family you have, and pretty as a picture. Listen, I know it's last-minute and all, but I'm having a little Bobby Sue get-together next Saturday. You think you girls could make it? The more the merrier."

"I'm afraid not," said Mama. "I don't—"

"Oh, come on, Mama, it'll be fun." I was

hoping this might be a nice friend for Mama to have. I liked her better than Alisha anyway. She smelled better. Drove a nicer car.

"Yeah, we gonna have fun," said Rainey, putting her arm in Mama's and hugging her side.

"Oh . . ." Mama looked at Rainey and said, "All right, then. But I'm in between jobs right now, so—"

"Not to worry, you don't have to buy a thing," said the lady. "I just want to catch up and spend some time. Oh, and there's door prizes."

"Next Saturday it is, then. Thank you."

Mrs. Arielle clapped her hands together. "Perfect! Well, I won't keep you now, but we're at 154 Mercy Street. You know where that is? Big white house, can't miss it."

"We'll see you there," said Mama.

The car started rolling slowly, but Mrs. Arielle was waving her arm. "Twelve thirty, now. I can't wait to tell the girls. Bye-bi-iiiie!"

And off she went in her nice clean car. Mama waved, then pressed her hair down and straightened her dress. I couldn't tell if her face was flushed because she was hot or happy or pregnant or scared.

"Let's just keep going," she said. "We're almost there."

Chapter Twenty-three
THE LONGEST WALK EVER

The library was nothing like the one we had in Cypresswood, where a little-bitty building held a few books and a grumpy old man who couldn't see very well. For some reason he was always at the card catalog, looking for something he must have lost. This library was grand to walk up to, with big white columns out front and big letters across the top saying FOREST PINES PUBLIC LIBRARY. The lawn was manicured, and a sidewalk down the middle to the front door made me feel like a princess approaching her castle. Reading books was a big deal here in Forest Pines, I could see.

Inside, there was a whole separate children's section with pictures of Dr. Seuss on the walls and colorful banners—stuffed animals, even. I headed straight for it. Rainey's eyes lit up, too, the second we walked in, but she headed for a place in the middle just past the checkout counter with long tables and computers lined up. "Mama, Google!"

"Oh, super! All right, honey. You go ahead. I'm gonna be right over there. See those bookshelves? You need me, I'm right there."

Rainey nodded and rushed to an empty chair. I decided to follow her. The picture books could wait. There was a young black man sitting across from Rainey, and a white-haired lady two seats down. I sat beside her and Poppy stood behind, hand on Rainey's shoulder. "Amazing what you can do with these computers today, isn't it?" he said.

"Uh-huh," said Rainey, tongue sticking out. Somebody from before had left Internet Explorer up, and Rainey was already typing with her right index finger, *w . . . w . . . w . . .*

"What are you going to look up?" he asked her. She paused as the page for Google came up. She liked this page more than Yahoo because it had less going on. Simpler was better for her. She could focus on the search box. "Um, I dunno."

I looked over and saw Mama running her fingers along the edges of books in the fiction aisle. A nice-looking man with blond hair walked past her, but she was staring so hard at the books, she didn't even notice. He certainly noticed her, though, and turned around for a second glance, books in hand. Finally he walked to the check-out desk.

I thought about Mama. I thought about that man looking at her like she was so pretty, but I bet he had no idea about the secret inside her. I remembered that word Poppy had told us. "I know, type in *'bortion*. That's Mama's third choice!" I was thrilled to be able to help her even more. I wondered if her list was still on the nightstand, and was excited to figure this out so I could add it to it. "How do you spell it again?" I asked Poppy.

He sat down in a seat on the other side of Rainey, slow as if his joints ached. He took a deep breath. Then he said, "A-b-o-r . . ."

Rainey plunked her fat finger on every single letter, just as he said it. She was really good with the keyboard. But she must have hit "search images" because instead of a list of Web sites coming up, a gallery of pictures popped up, row after row after row.

I swallowed. Hard. This wasn't right. I was supposed to be seeing cute babies in fat tummies with beautiful angels taking them away. Instead I saw bloody, dead things.

Some ripped to pieces.

Tiny body parts lying over fingers.

Mangled baby faces.

Black and blue.

Red and white.

Fingers and legs with no bodies at all.

I thought I might throw up. Rainey started screaming at the top of her lungs, hands over her ears. She couldn't pull her eyes away from the computer screen.

All of a sudden people rushed over, the old lady with white hair, the black man sitting across the way, the people behind the check-out counter, the man with books who thought Mama was pretty, all of them trying to help Rainey out of her chair, and she was kicking and screaming, and Mama ran over and kneeled down. That's when she saw what we'd been looking at. They all did. Mama's face turned green, and she said, "It's all right. It's all right, honey, shhhhh." She hugged Rainey tight and screamed, "Somebody turn it off! Turn it off!" and Poppy and I watched Mama's face as she looked at those pictures on the screen. Baby after baby after baby. Her face scrunched up while she was holding Rainey's head, and all of a sudden, Mama fell back on the floor, passed out cold. Rainey thought she'd died and so she wailed even longer and harder, and it took five people to carry her outdoors where whisper voices weren't needed.

After a couple minutes, an ambulance came and put Mama in it, though she didn't want to go. "I'm all right, I mean it. I just got lightheaded." She must have been forceful enough because after a while and a glass of water, they let Mama go, and Poppy, Rainey, Mama, and me walked home, slow and quiet, eyes still burning with what we'd seen, souls scarred and changed forever.

It was the longest walk I could ever remember.

Chapter Twenty-four
CONFESSION

"Fritz?" I could hear Mama whispering on the telephone. I was coming into the kitchen to get a sip of water, but I waited at the door. I knew it might not be right to listen but I didn't feel like myself anymore. I was still numbed from the library, my spirit lifeless like Rainey's poor magic cicada.

"I need to talk to you," Mama said. "It's important." She was standing up, arms crossed over her chest, her head leaned against the wall. She was sniffling and got off the phone right quick. I came in after and acted like I hadn't heard, just grabbed my water and headed out to the garden. Mama sat there at the kitchen table and didn't move a muscle. If she knew I was even there, she didn't let on. She was in her own little world.

I wondered what she needed to talk to Uncle Fritz about. Was she going to tell him what had happened today? If so, I didn't want to be anywhere around. I went out back and found Poppy rocking on the porch. He was eyeing the garden like it was his kingdom. He didn't look over at me when I took the other seat, but I could see his face was troubled. Looked like he was trying to smooth out the wrinkles with his hand. "Janie, I can remember when I helped my father plant this garden. We had a lot more vegetables here, squash, green beans . . . We ate off this garden. It's changed a good bit over the years . . . as all things do."

He rocked and rocked and I followed, pushing my toes off the porch boards. A nice breeze flowed through us, and I watched as two yellow butterflies danced in a circle, turning and tussling. Then they flew off to find the bushy lantana. Poppy looked over at me. "You got some hair in your eyes, sweetie. Why don't you put it back so I can see that pretty face?"

I didn't budge, but then after he'd said it, it was starting to bug me. Sly-like, I tucked my hair behind my ears. I pulled my knees up to my chest, held my bare feet, and rocked.

"Your mama's hair's getting longer, don't you think?" he said. "Maybe she's letting it grow out. You know she used to have these long blonde pigtails when she was little. You wanna know how long?"

I didn't feel like talking, but I didn't want to disrespect him so I murmured a faint "Hmm."

"They were so long she had to flop 'em up over her shoulders when she was on the commode, otherwise they'd dunk right in."

I tried not to smile, but I couldn't help it.

"Oh yes, your mother was known for her hair. Everybody always remarked on it—how pretty it was, how lucky she was to have it. Then we moved to Yuma."

"What happened in Yuma?"

"She was about fifteen or so. She chopped her hair off, real close to her head, almost like a boy. To this day I don't know why she did it."

"Maybe she was hot," I said.

"Maybe so. But I mourned that hair."

"You mourned over hair?"

"Not the hair exactly, but what it stood for. For what I lost along with that hair, my sweet little girl who called me Daddy, who would sit on my lap at every meal . . ." He cleared his throat and said, "Anyway, next thing you know my little girl's coming home, announcing she's having a baby. Your grandma and I didn't handle it well. We were just . . . caught off guard, I guess. And then off she went."

I looked at him to see if he was crying or anything. He wasn't, but nearly rubbed the arms of that rocking chair plumb off. " 'Course, all that's over. I'm here with her now and things seem to be going just fine."

"They do?" I had to say it. After the library, the baby photos, screaming, and passing out, I thought for sure things weren't going fine at all. "She doesn't seem to talk to you much."

"Maybe she's still upset with me," he said.

"She doesn't talk to me much, neither. Not since we left town. You think she's upset with me too?"

"She's got a lot on her mind."

"Yeah, I reckon." Just that second I remembered the change purse I'd taken from Mama and felt like I needed to get it back to her. Like maybe I never should have taken it at all. It was only adding to her troubles. I was ashamed all of a sudden and excused myself to the upstairs. I'd hidden it in this secret pocket in the corner of the white hard suitcase, worn in because the seam was coming loose. Mama never would have thought to look there.

I went down to the kitchen to find Mama. I wondered if I should tell her I took her money and apologize or if I should just say, "Look what I found!" That felt a lot like lying, so I figured I just needed to fess up and take whatever came my way.

She wasn't in the kitchen. The stove was cold, with little towels hanging off the handle, nice and neat. They had orange teapots embroidered on the front. On the table there was a glass pitcher of iced tea, dripping sweat on another teapot towel. There were two glasses set out. All of a sudden I remembered Uncle Fritz.

Sure enough, the front door creaked open and I heard Mama say, "So glad you could make it. I know you're busy."

"I was coming over anyway. You look . . . you all right?"

I heard footsteps padding to the kitchen, and my

175

eyes lit up, wanting a way out. I headed for the back door, but there was no time. I slid to the side of the refrigerator and hid behind a little curtain made especially for covering a food pantry. There wasn't much in there except a big old tub of grits and some cans of pickled beets and corn.

"Aagh!" Mama squealed. "My goodness, would you look at this?" My breath was much too loud for somebody trying to hide, and I hoped nobody could hear me. "I lost my change purse back at the hotel! I lost it, I looked everywhere, and here it is?!"

My heart pounded in my chest. *Be still, be still,* I told it. I could hear Mama counting the money I'd accidentally left on the table. Fritz murmured something, but it was so low I couldn't understand. "I must be losing my mind," Mama said, stunned. "I just—"

"Maybe it was old Gertrude, playing a little trick."

"Huh, yeah . . . imagine that. I guess Rainey had it? I can't imagine she would have taken it and not told me when I asked. That's not like her." I hoped to goodness Mama wouldn't suspect me next.

"Maybe she's upset about all this travel and such," Fritz said. "Is she holding up all right? I've got a few children like her in church. They have certain needs when it comes to stability and—oh, now, please don't. I didn't mean anything by it."

"It's not you, Fritz." Mama was crying now. "It's me. I just . . ." I peeked out the slit in the curtain and saw Fritz sitting at the head of the breakfast table. He saw Mama struggling and said in a gentle voice, "It's all right, you can tell me anything you want, anytime you want. Trust me, nothing could shock me." He poured two glasses of tea and pushed one to Mama. I couldn't see her face, but her back hunched over as she sipped.

"Thanks," she said. She set her glass down and seemed to be looking straight at Fritz. His face was kind and attentive. I longed for him to look at me that way.

"Sometimes I forget how much she's affected by my life . . . what happens with me and . . . Oh Fritz, I'm pregnant," Mama said.

"So I gathered from supper," he said.

"I don't know why I'm telling you this, it's just . . ."

"It's okay. Go on."

"I just don't know what I'm going to do. I thought if I got out of town, I could think more clearly. But then today at the library, there was this—oh gosh—big to-do, you just wouldn't believe, and now I'm afraid I've really messed things up . . ."

Fritz didn't speak but drank his tea. The ice in his glass clinked, and the noise was good. A helpful noise. I looked down at my foot, and a spider was walking by. Luckily it was a bitty little thing, so I didn't scream or holler. Or squash him. It walked right past me out onto the floor for a better look at Mama and Fritz.

"I've been trying to find the baby's father," Mama said after a long while. "I don't know why, exactly. Except I used to be in love with him."

"Used to?"

"He lived with us for five years. He was the only daddy we ever had in our house. Then he left."

My daddy! They were talking about my daddy! My ears sharpened to fine points.

"I see," said Fritz. "Well obviously, he came back."

"Yes. About a month ago. I was getting off work, and I saw Marilyn in front of the drugstore."

"Marilyn?"

"His motorcycle. He said it had curves like Marilyn Monroe. I was always so dang jealous of that motorcycle, you never forget a thing like that. Anyway, I waited to see if it was him, and sure enough, out he comes. After all that time."

"How long had it been?"

"Four long years."

I was trying to make sure I'd heard correctly. Daddy came back and I never saw him? My face grew hot, and I thought I might cry. But I didn't. Not yet.

"Goodness," said Fritz.

"I was so angry with him, I just let him have it right there on the sidewalk! And he took it. Every little bit. He listened, and then he teared up some. He said he'd been passing through every couple weeks, just hoping to see me. Said he drove by the house some, but I wasn't sure if I could believe him or not. I mean, I'd know that cycle anywhere. The sound of it, even."

"So, I imagine you two . . . made up."

"Sort of. We cried . . . him, me. We got a motel. I thought he was coming back for good."

"But he left again." Fritz's voice fell flat.

"He left again," Mama repeated. "Funny thing. You know, all that time, I'd imagined what it would be like to have him back. I told myself I'd never fall for it again, I'd never get hurt like that again. But I did. And now . . ."

"Now there's a baby."

Mama put her head down, and Fritz put his hand on her arm. "I know I wasn't there for a lot of years, Priscilla, but for what it's worth, I'm here now. I'm not planning on going anywhere."

"Thank you," she said. "You can't imagine how alone I feel."

I was next to those grits, my mind whirling and twirling like the loop-the-loop at Disney. I was thinking about my daddy being back and not coming to see me. I was thinking about him leaving my mama again. I was so hot I thought my teeth might pop right out! But the thing that hurt me worst of all was hearing Mama say how alone she was feeling. Here I was. I'd been there with her the whole time, from the minute she found out this baby was coming. I'd been right there with her! Helping her! Didn't she even care about that? Well, didn't she?

Chapter Twenty-five
HOT ENOUGH TO BOIL

Sitting there, hiding behind that curtain, listening to the truth about my mama and daddy, I was burning up mad. I felt like as soon as I got out, I didn't quite care if I ever saw them or any other member of the Macy family again. Well, except for Rainey. And Poppy. And well, okay, Mama too. Who was I kidding? They were all I had.

Fritz and Mama walked out on the front porch to talk some more. Frankly, I'd had enough eavesdropping for one day, so I crawled out of the pantry and quickly climbed the stairs, whizzing past the portraits of my ancestors. I rounded the corner and sneaked into Mama's room. I found my list. It appeared she hadn't even looked at it. I folded it carefully and put it in my pocket, then headed out back for a quiet place in the garden.

I had some serious thinking to do. For one, I wished Mama had never met my daddy. Things would have been a whole lot easier that way. But she did meet him, and then he came back again, and she kissed him, and now they were having another baby. Like it or not, there were decisions to be made.

I'd never sat before a list, ready to write, and nothing coming to me. I was finding it hard to keep my list of pros and cons about the baby. Writing what was good and bad about adoption had made me sad. So, so sad. But writing them about abortion nearly did me in. There was a little brother or sister growing inside my mama. Growing little arms, little legs, a little mouth. I kept having flashes of those horrible pictures in my mind. They were worse than anything I'd ever seen in a movie or the newspaper. Anything I could imagine. But they were real. My list was not so fun anymore.

I didn't know why my mother had choices anyway. She was having a baby, like it or not. Babies didn't come from lists or studying or planning. There was magic in making a baby. I may not have known all how it worked, but even I knew that.

There was God in having a baby.

My mother didn't seem to want my help anyway. She hardly looked my way anymore. She was so caught up with having this child, she'd all but forgotten the two she already had. Was this how life would be when she had even less time for us?

I wanted to go home. Now. Even though I loved this house and the garden and the sidewalks and the flowers and the trees, for the first time, I wanted to just leave this place and get back to how things were before.

"You ready to go home, sugar?" asked Poppy, touching my hand and squeezing. He had found me sitting by the strawberries. They climbed out of the ground and over my ankles and made me feel loved. Poppy had this smile on his face like he knew every single thought in my head. Made me wonder if he did.

"Yes, Poppy. Let's go hop on a bus and go on home."

"It's not time to go yet, Grayson." Grandma Mona and her supersonic ears came whirling up behind him. "Priscilla still needs us here. She needs all of us."

"I'll say it again, who are you and what have you done with my wife?" teased Poppy.

Grandma Mona clucked her tongue and said, "Time away from you'll do that for a woman. Fine. You want mean? I'll go back to being mean."

"No, no," said Poppy. "I like it. You used to be that way. Before."

"Before? Before what?" I ask.

"Never you mind, child," said Grandma Mona. "Every family has a few secrets. Every single one."

"But I don't know anything! Every single thing is a secret to me. Why does being eight years old not entitle a person to knowing a thing?" I was being sassy, but I'd been pushed. And they'd pushed me far enough.

Grandma Mona ignored my backtalk and said to Poppy, "She's almost ready anyway."

"Yes, I am," I said. "What am I ready for?"

"Are you sure?" asked Poppy.

"I'm positive. Coming here has been good, no matter what all's gone on. My guess is any day now."

"What's any day now? Is there something gonna happen?" But I realized they weren't even talking about me or to me anymore, so I stomped away, right through the house to the front porch.

Standing there, leaning over the railing and looking at that old lady across the street at the yellow house, I realized I'd become invisible, hopelessly invisible. What to do about Mama's new baby had consumed everybody, even me. But I was done with it. I crumpled my list and threw it hard into the lawn. It was white on green and stuck out like a bat in daytime. I didn't care I'd just littered. So what if it was against the law? I didn't like laws anymore. They had nothing to do with right or wrong. Looking at those dead baby pictures had taught me all I needed to know about the law.

I turned around and firmed my shoulders. I was

going up to that attic. I was not going to be afraid anymore. I was going to see what was up there, like it or not, and if a ghost just happened to be there, then she best not mess with me.

"Come on, Rain, let's go in the attic." She was on the other side of the porch in the gazebo. She'd found a gold beetle and was sticking it in a tissue box. Bugs seemed to calm her, and since we'd come back to the house she'd been outdoors with a small butterfly net, searching, scrambling for peace. Rainey looked up at me proud and showing off her find, then her forehead wrinkled. "The attic? Uh-uh. Ghost up there."

"There's no ghost. Don't you see? There never has been a ghost. They just told us that so we'd be scared and not go up there. But I got a feeling there's more they haven't told us. I think everybody's hiding something in this family, and I'm gonna find out. You coming or not?"

I didn't leave her much choice. She put the lid on her beetle and stuck it under her arm. Her face was different than I'd ever seen it. I could tell she was working hard not to think about those baby pictures too. I wondered how she could even process something so awful. It wasn't in her brainwork to think on things that weren't good and beautiful.

I took her hand and said, "It's just you and me. We're sisters. We'll always be together. No matter what."

"Okay," she said, and we went in the front door. Beside me, Rainey climbed the steps, somber but with purpose. Then she took the lead. I watched her and marveled. I was filled with admiration. For the first time ever, Rainey was setting out to face her fears instead of running to a tree hollow to squelch them away. It was the first time I thought I might have a lot to learn from my big sister, Rainey Dae Macy.

The original staircase leading to the attic in the 1870s Victorian was removed in the 1920s and replaced with a spiral one, or so Poppy had told me. At the top was a narrow door. Rainey and I climbed around and around the stairs with nervous stomachs. We'd never seen a ghost before. What if Gertrude was angry we were coming up? What if she was bent on protecting family secrets? When we got to the top, we swallowed hard because the door was already open.

Chapter Twenty-six
THE ATTIC

The first thing I noticed about the attic was the change in heat. The air was steamy-hot from summer.

"Mama?" said Rainey.

My mother looked at us, and a bead of sweat ran alongside her face.

"What are you doing up here?" she asked.

"Janie want to come."

"Oh, I see. Janie. Well, I thought I told you girls that this attic was no place for you."

Mama was on the floor, legs spread out with books in front of her.

"What are you looking at?" I asked.

"Come here, honey, let me show you some photographs of your family. There are some of me when I was little."

We sat down on the heart pine floor beside her, and I looked around. There were beams overhead running the width of the room, and a pointed ceiling. There were small windows on the front, side, and back of the house. Boxes and dust were stacked in the corners, and under the back window I saw an old loom, a fake Christmas tree, and two mannequin busts.

"Have you seen the ghost?" I whispered. Rainey looked at me and then around the attic room.

"Mama, where the ghost?"

"What ghost? You mean Gertrude?" Rainey nodded, eyes round. "My guess is she left a long time ago. I've been up here a little while and there's no sign of any ghosts. There's nothing to be afraid of, honey. I promise, it's all right."

No ghost. All that fear for nothing? I was almost disappointed. I looked up at the rafters and imagined a pot of boiling oil up there, Gertrude waiting for her husband to walk in so she could murder him. I shivered and looked around for a big pot. I saw none. Then I studied the wood on the floor for grease spots, but there were none of those either. Something was fishy. Either the story had been made up or the boards had been replaced. I thought the floor looked younger than one hundred and forty years, so soon my disappointment in not seeing the ghost of Gertrude was replaced with pure relief. I focused on the books and on Mama's face as she flipped through them. They were filled with Polaroid pictures.

"My father was so handsome, don't you think?" Mama said. "Here we are when I was about four or five at Christmas." She took her time, rolling a finger along each and every picture. "Oh, and look. You see this? This is when I learned to ride a bike. It was right out there on Vinca Lane."

"Where Grandma Mona?" Rainey asked.

Mama turned some more pages. The photos were all of her and Poppy. "I don't know, honey. Maybe, maybe she was the one taking all these pictures. Huh. Come on, it's hot in here."

So we took the photo albums down to Mama's room and spent the next hour looking over them under a cool fan. I learned more about Mama, seeing her as a child. Seeing her with no stress on her face, just happiness. Children were supposed to be that way, happy, I thought. No worries. I watched my mother's face and saw that something was changing. She was settling into this house, sharing her life, her past with us. She was remembering what it felt like to be happy. And in that hour, sitting on the bed next to her, I almost felt close to her again. Almost. She was still only in her own little world.

I wasn't angry anymore about my daddy, though, or about Mama not telling me he'd been back a month ago. She was a grown-up, and grown-ups had reasons for doing things I couldn't understand. I got that. "When did life get so complicated?" Mama said at one point.

I told her I didn't know, but it must be sometime after eight and a half.

When it was time for Rainey to go to work at the grocery store, Mama left me and the albums on her bed, and I spent the whole afternoon soaking up my history and feeling I had roots for once. I remember that feeling because it didn't last but for a few days—when everything I thought I knew was finally put to the test.

Chapter Twenty-seven
THE BURDENS OF APPLE SNAILS

We'd settled in to a little routine in the blue house. Mama would wake first and get breakfast started. It was simple, mostly using up the big container of grits in the pantry with little pats of butter on top, or sometimes a piece of toast with jelly. Occasionally, a sausage patty. Mama was happy all of the sandwiches were gone. Rainey and I would wake up smelling Mama's decaf coffee, and every morning we'd have this tinge of excitement itching just under our rib cages. We spent our days exploring the yard because we weren't allowed to leave it on our own. We learned every square inch of the front and sides of that house, but our favorite place was the garden in the back.

One afternoon, Rainey and I were out back with Poppy when I found an apple snail on the trellis. Rainey pulled it off and held it in her hands. She was squealing and cooing and petting the little thing.

"He sure is cute," I said. "Look at his little eyes, how they poke out. Hey there, buddy, hey there."

"I gon' name it Snaily," said Rainey.

"That's a fine name, Rainey," said Poppy. "And look here. You see this trail of snail slime? He leaves a trail wherever he goes."

"Why?" I asked.

"Maybe so he can find his way home," Poppy said, with crinkles at the edges of his eyes.

"Nah-uh," I said. "Really?"

"I'm just teasing, sweetie."

"Oh no!" said Rainey. She'd been lifting the snail up to check the slime trail on her finger when she'd dropped it on the walkway. She leaned down and picked it up. "Look!"

That poor snail had lost part of its shell on the back.

"Oh goodness, that's too bad," said Poppy, studying it. He was so close I could smell his aftershave. Smelled like pine.

"Is it okay?" I asked.

"I'm afraid not for long."

"Oh no." Rainey was trying not to drop it again. She was getting ready to tear up and kept hopping from one foot to the next as if she was in pain. "Okay, Snaily, you okay."

"Poppy? He's gonna be fine," I said. "See? He's still crawling along."

"Rainey, honey, you see that? See that hole right there?"

"Uh-huh."

"Well that's where the snail breathes. Without that shell, he'll suffocate."

Rainey looked at him like he was speaking a foreign language. She was trying to make sense of this *suffocate* word.

"It means it cain't breathe," I said. "It's gonna die."

Rainey starting rocking her arms like she was rocking a baby and not just a slimy snail. It was sad to watch. She never meant anything any harm.

"An apple snail can't survive without its shell," said Poppy in a slow, smooth voice. "Even though carrying around that big weight on its back looks hard to handle, it's his home. Without it, he'll suffocate and die a slow death."

"Well, what do we do?" I asked. "Can we take him to the vet? Can we put some tape on it?"

" 'Fraid not, honey. Best thing to do would be put him in the freezer . . . or smash it with a rock. Put him out of his misery."

"No, no, no, no!" Rainey started hollering and crying and ran off with that snail in her hand. "I sorry, I sorry, Snaily!" She took off, running around to the front of the house and then down the sidewalk, away from the yellow house and the library. She ran and ran and I ran after her, calling, "Rainey, wait up!" but she wouldn't stop.

Her gait was heavy, so I finally caught up with her. She was already six houses down the street and I said, out of breath, "Rainey, it's me! Hold on. Let me walk with you."

She had tears all down her face and a fixed grimace on her mouth. She stopped, and I looked at that snail in her hand. With all the running, she'd wadded it up in her fist and completely crushed its shell. When she opened her fingers and saw the poor mangled thing, she wailed and flung it into somebody's grass. She wiped her hand off on her shorts and shirt and looked down at her bare feet. They were filthy from all the running. Then she put her hands up on her ears and closed her eyes.

"Come on, Rain. Let's go on home now. Mama's gonna be worried."

She shook her head.

"She's gonna be mad too."

Rainey opened her eyes and searched around. "I go up there," she said, pointing to a big oak tree. It was plopped smack-dab in the middle of the yard of this gray house with bright white trim. The tree was old and big, and the branches at the top did a loop, so even though there was no hollow in it, there was a place for Rainey to want to crawl into. I thought I understood it, and seeing how upset she was, I thought it wouldn't hurt for her to have a rest and find a quiet place to listen to the wind. And maybe God too.

We climbed that tree. It wasn't easy with no shoes, and it being an oak we didn't know real well. It took some time learning where all the places were to put your feet. The only tree we ever climbed was this one with a low branch on it about a foot off the ground. It was at a playground at the Y back home in Cypresswood. We'd climb up and jump off, over and over. After a few minutes, we were high up in that tree in front of the gray house and watching the cars go by. Rainey was perched on a branch about a gazillion feet up, squatting like a bird. Her head was resting on her knees. I was up one branch from her, sitting with my bare feet dangling by her ears. The height was making me dizzy.

"It was just an accident, Rain. The snail, I mean," I said.

"Uh-huh. It dead. Bitsy dead. I no like dead."

"Me neither. I don't ever wanna die. Do you?"

"Huh-uh. I not gonna die."

"Yeah," I said. "Me neither."

We sat in that big tree, for how long, I don't know. But after a while, we heard Mama calling. She was frantic. "Rainey? Rai-ney!" She kept calling and it was getting louder. We knew she'd be up on us any minute.

"Time to get down, I guess," I said.

"Okay," said Rainey.

And before I could say boo, she jumped.

Chapter Twenty-eight
THE PROMISE

To be honest, I don't know how I got down out of that tree, whether I jumped, climbed down, or what. All I knew is I wasn't hurt at all, and I was sitting there on the ground with Rainey's head in my lap when Mama came up on us. She had an apron on and curlers in her hair. There was no makeup on her red-smeared face. "Oh good heavens, Rainey!" She ran up to me and touched Rainey's face. "Rainey! Are you okay? Rainey?"

Rainey's eyes were closed and she wasn't answering Mama.

193

"She jumped," I said. "Just flat-out jumped from way up there. I did too, but I'm okay, Mama."

Mama started wailing, and then I saw what she was looking at. Rainey's left arm was twisted under at an odd angle and turning purple. "Help!" Mama screamed, looking around her. "Heeeeelp uuuuus!" It was a scream I knew I'd never get over. In fact, for the next several days I'd wake in the night, hearing that same scream for help and looking up at Rainey's bunk to see if she was okay.

Her arm was broken in four places and her ankle was sprained. She had to stay off her feet for a while and got a crutch. Once the cast was on her and her head checked out okay, Rainey was enjoying that crutch, except for she couldn't get up the stairs real well. Mama showed her how to scoot up on her rear end and push with one foot, one step at a time. And she absolutely forbade her to slide down the banister, which is what I'd suggested, as it just made good sense, seeing as she wouldn't have to hop.

Mama was doting on Rainey's every need. During the day, she got all her books propped up around her and read *Corduroy* I don't know how many times. She kissed her on the forehead a lot. She smiled at her in a sad sort of way. She sat with her, sang to her, made me feel like I was absolutely nobody. I was starting to wish I'd broken my whole body in that tree. Maybe then Mama'd pay attention to me.

After several days of it, I heard Mama get on the telephone and whisper to an operator for a medical clinic over in Fervor. I heard her say "six to seven weeks." Then she went ahead and made an appointment to go to see a doctor in two weeks. I was happy Mama'd finally made a decision to go see a doctor. Maybe having Rainey break her arm was what she needed to realize she had to take care of herself and that baby she was carrying. Maybe being in the hospital made her not so afraid to meet with a doctor.

Being in that blue gingerbread house with Rainey on a crutch and Poppy and Grandma Mona for conversation, I'd tried to forget about Mama having a baby. If I'm honest, I played a little harder outside when she was around so I wouldn't have to think about the baby much or how much attention Rainey was getting instead of me. When she wasn't babying Rainey, Mama kept to herself, cleaning out cabinets, washing the windows. If I didn't know better, it looked like we might be staying a long while. Who really knew what Mama was thinking? Fritz came by for supper some days and mowed the grass once. I watched him do the whole lawn from start to finish, which took a really long time.

Mama kept those photo albums in her bedroom and looked at them every night before bed.

She'd gone back up in the attic a couple more times, with me following, and we'd brought down more books. I never did see the ghost of Great-Aunt Gertrude and remained a little disappointed about that. Mama brought down some old clothes of Grandma Mona's too. Rainey could sit up and play in the hats and all, but she couldn't wear the dresses and could only put on one shoe. She didn't much care, just held them up to the mirror with one hand and laughed and laughed about how much we looked like Grandma Mona. It was actually fun for a few days after Rainey got more confidence in moving around. We shed our worries together and stuck to ourselves.

Then one morning I woke up early, before Rainey. I climbed down the stairs hoping to catch some time alone with Mama, but she wasn't in the kitchen. Instead, she was sipping her coffee on the front porch. I went over and sat on a rocker beside her. The morning smelled different, cleaner, smelled like grass to me. Cars weren't on the street yet but a few folks were walking their dogs. A breeze floated through the gazebo, casting wild, slow shadows from the trees across my skinny legs.

"It sort of reminds you of the sunporch at home, don't it, Mama?"

She grinned over at me, took a deep breath, and pressed her hand down on mine. It'd been so long since I'd felt her touch. We sat there not talking, just listening to the sounds of Vinca Lane, the birds calling back and forth, the rush of the wind in the maple leaves.

"Looks like it might rain today," she said.

We watched the white clouds rolling in and growing darker. Sitting on that porch, next to Mama, was the closest I'd felt to happy in a long time. Strange thing was, I knew her head wasn't really there, not with me. Maybe she was thinking about Rainey all crippled in her bed. Maybe she was thinking back on when she was a little girl, sitting on those very chairs. Or maybe she was months down the road from now, settled, with all her decision making done.

The only decisions I'd had to make were what clothes to put on. What channels to watch. What books to look at and read. What games to play with Rainey.

But not Mama. Her decisions were harder.

"I love you, Mama," I said, thinking back on the trials of the last couple weeks. "No matter what, I'll always love you."

"You sure are sweet, Miss Janie," said Poppy, sneaking up on us. "What a good, kind heart you have. Such a good daughter. And a wonderful granddaughter."

"And smart," I added, grinning.

He chuckled and agreed. "So smart."

"Might be a doctor or astronaut when I grow

up. Don't you think, Mama? Think I could go all the way to the moon?"

"Wouldn't put it past her," said Grandma Mona, coming out of the house and trying to be grumpy. For some reason, it wasn't working right now. She seemed distracted. "Janie, honey, why don't you go on inside. Play with your sister. She's up now. Your Poppy needs to have a talk with Priscilla."

I looked up at Mama's face. Her eyes were closed like she was concentrating. More slow breathing. Then her hand let up off mine and she said, "Just go. Please."

Poppy was smiling, I could see the silver caps on his molars, but at the same time, his eyes looked sad, moist, and red. "Come here, sugar," he said to me, bending at the knees and squatting with his small, wrinkled hands held out.

I moved to him and he held me by the hips. "Janie Doe Macy. Do you know I'd do anything for you? Do you know you make my whole world go around and around? There's nothing more important to me than you and my family?"

"Yes sir. I guess so."

He held me tighter still. "Don't you ever forget how important you are to this family. Hear me? To this whole wide world. All right? Promise."

"All right, but why—"

"Janie, just promise me."

"I promise. Poppy, what's going on? I—"

He pulled me in to him and hugged me tighter than I'd ever been squeezed. I wrapped my arms around the back of his neck and took in all that warmth. Being held like that didn't happen every day. Or ever. His heat got my head to feeling dizzy, and before I knew it, he pushed me away and cleared his throat. He stood up and turned to Mama. "Mona, take Janie on in now." He gave Grandma Mona a hard kiss on the lips, something I'd never seen him do, then he winked at her, and when he did, a tear rolled down his brown cheek. Grandma Mona and I walked slowly, hand in hand into the house and out back, where Rainey was nibbling on a piece of toast and chasing butterflies. The white lantana seemed to be swallowing her up.

"Go on and help her, Janie," said Grandma Mona. "The net's right there. I'm sure y'all will catch one yet."

"But what's wrong with Poppy?" I said. "Is he going somewhere?"

"Oh goodness. You could say that, sugar. Yes, you could say he's going somewhere."

Chapter Twenty-nine
STUCK IN THE MIDDLE

"I wanna go with him!" I hollered. "Is he going back home!? I wanna go with Poppy!"

"Shhh, shh . . ." Grandma Mona pulled me to her and held me to her bony chest. It was the first time I could remember her doing that in many years. "It's okay," she said.

"But when's he coming back?"

"It'll be a little while. Don't you worry."

I asked and I pleaded, but I heard that sort of nonsense from Grandma Mona until I thought I might keel over. I knew Poppy was gone for good. There was too much secrecy and weirdness going on. Same as when my daddy left. I ran out onto the front porch and looked around for Poppy, but he was gone. No sign of him.

"Mama?" Mama was hunched over, holding her belly. She'd been crying and her face was all swollen. "Mama, you okay? Where'd Poppy go? What'd you say?"

Grandma Mona came and pulled me from behind and said, "Let's give your mama some space, all right? There'll be plenty of time for questions and answers and all that sort of thing after a while."

I decided then and there I didn't like being a kid anymore. No one was honest with kids. No one thought they could handle the truth about grown-up things, but I could! I knew I could. When I became a grown-up someday I'd tell my children everything. I swore to it right then. Mama'd said something to Poppy, and now he'd gone away forever because of it. Here they were, two of the people I loved most in the world, and one was gone and the other remained, and I was stuck in the middle not liking it one bit.

Uncle Fritz called later that morning and said he had some papers for Mama down at the church. Mama said she'd be over after the Bobby Sue party. I'd forgotten all about that. I told her I didn't feel like going to a party, what with Poppy being gone, but she just hummed and showered and acted like nothing at all was wrong. In fact, I wondered about my Mama's state of mind then. How could a person be so unaffected—happy-seeming, even—about their own daddy leaving that very day?

Made no sense to me. I grumped up in my room. I was too mad at everybody to be sad. The real grieving for Poppy hadn't even started yet.

Rainey talked me into coming to the party at that fancy lady's house. She said we could wear makeup and look like Mama. She was excited, and well, when Rainey was excited, it made things that bothered you pale in comparison. I put my thoughts of where Poppy could have gone and when he was coming back on hold, just for Rainey's sake. 'Fact, she didn't seem too upset about Poppy at all, which wasn't like her. Rainey didn't like change. I figured, her being older, they'd told her something they'd withheld from eight-year-old me.

With Rainey's arm broken, the grocery store had only been letting her bag up one or two folks, and then only for the most patient customers because it took her so long. She was tired of being home so much and ready to get out and be useful again. Mama was starting to miss the money, and I could tell from the way she was putting on so she was hoping to fit in with the Bobby Sue gals and maybe even start selling cosmetics. I hadn't seen her excited about the prospects of work in a long, long time, or maybe never.

Mama walked up to Mrs. Arielle's house with a confident swagger. She had on high-heel black shoes, a form-fitting black skirt, and a pink and green blouse with flowers on it. She looked real nice and had worked an extra thirty minutes on her hair alone. It was swooped over smooth across her forehead, then pulled back in a ponytail with curls coming from it. It was strange seeing Mama with real curls on her head. She'd worked nearly as hard on Rainey. Rainey grinned and clip-clopped up the walkway to the house, wearing a long peach-colored dress with no sleeves that Mama was able to stretch over the cast on her arm. She was still limping a little on that twisted foot, but it was better now. She had on hard, white flat shoes that made her walk like a penguin, back and forth. I thought it looked funny, but she liked the way she walked. Rainey felt pretty and special in those shoes, I could tell. And me? Rainey'd asked Mama if we could wear a couple of Grandma Mona's hats. She said yes, so I was wearing a frilly one Grandma Mona gave me with a little net in the front, coming down over my eyebrows. Rainey's had a white ribbon that tied under her chin. "Spiffy" is what Grandma Mona'd called us before we left the gingerbread house.

We'd driven over to the Arielle residence in the Crown Victoria Police Interceptor, and everywhere we turned I looked to see if Poppy was walking or sitting or standing or up in a tree, for all I knew. I looked and looked but didn't find him.

God, wherever Poppy is, let him be okay, I prayed. *Let him come home to us soon.*

The doorbell played music, actual music instead of a ding-dong. I'd never heard of such a thing, but when I heard that music, it didn't surprise me. Instead, it just fit the house. It made sense that the door would announce the house's guests with real-live Dixie. The house was grander than the library even, white with long white columns in front. The grass was greener than it was on Vinca Lane. There were pretty ladies sitting in chairs, holding little pink drinks with umbrellas in them. A couple of them had hats like Rainey and me, but I thought ours were nicer.

"Now don't touch anything, remember?" said Mama. "And use your best manners. Say 'please,' 'thank you,' 'yes, ma'am,' that sort of thing. Okay?" Mama was smiling and talking to us out the side of her mouth as we waited for the door to open. The ladies around us disregarded us until we'd been properly introduced. We were nothing and nobody standing there at the door until spoken to.

"Everyone, this is Priscilla Macy I was telling you about," announced Mrs. Arielle when she opened the door. "We went to elementary school together. Jennifer, you remember Priscilla?"

"Oh my goodness, look at you!" Jennifer squealed. Then another and another, all hugging and carrying on. The ladies oohed and aahed over Mama, how good she looked. I thought she was prettier than all those ladies, to be honest. Most of them were chunky with round bellies and hips and painted-on cheeks, and I thought they needed to lay off the little tea sandwiches and brownie squares. I looked over at Rainey who was cradling her cast with her good arm. She was starting to look sheepish and shy at all the goings-on. I threw my hand out like Vanna White and said, "And this here is Rainey Dae Macy." I smiled at her, and she blushed and loved me back.

"This Janie," she said, whispering and trying to put her good arm out to show me off like I'd done her. "I like the hat," she said, admiring me. I was so glad to have a sister.

Next thing we knew, ladies were coming up left and right, asking how we liked Forest Pines, how Rainey had broken her arm, where we'd gotten our lovely hats.

I sort of liked the attention. I ate it up for a while. Then Mama was real busy cavorting with the ladies, and we were being so good, she let us go off and look around that fancy house all by ourselves.

Turned out that was a big mistake.

Chapter Thirty
PARTY TIME

There was an indoor swimming pool in the back of the house, with screened-in walls around it. Rainey and I stood there marveling that folks could have a swimming pool in their very own house. We looked for bugs but there were none. Rainey thought about getting in and wading around but I reminded her of her cast, how she couldn't get it wet, so she stuck her shoes back on and off we went looking for other such treasures.

We heard the Bobby Sue ladies talking on our

way up the grand white staircase in the foyer. They were humming and chirping in the formal living room that was twice as big as the one we had back on Vinca Lane.

"You know, you have the smoothest skin. What do you use on it, Priscilla?"

"Me? Oh, I . . . just some Ivory soap."

"Ah-ha-ha-ha-ha—" The room erupted in laughter.

"Well, now, see this? I just love this new product here. Gets rid of all those little lines around the eyes. Not that you have any! Because you don't . . ."

"Maryann, why don't you just start selling Bobby Sue? You know all the stuff anyway—"

"Oh, please. I'm not a salesperson."

"The dickens you're not—"

And so on and so forth. Rainey and I couldn't wait to get out of earshot. I was thinking to myself, *I wonder when little girls grow up to the point that their parties aren't any fun anymore?*

Upstairs there was a long hallway to the left and to the right. In many ways, the layout was like the blue gingerbread house, traditional, but this one was much more expansive. I was looking to the right when something caught Rainey's eye and she ran down the hall the other way.

I found her in a blue room. The walls were blue with white clouds and hot-air balloons painted at the top. There was a white crib with blue sheets on it and more of those balloons adorning the sides. Beside the bed was a white bassinet with baby powder on it and a bag of unopened diapers. Rainey stood there, motionless. Her bottom lip was dropped to bug-catching position, so it was a good thing we were indoors.

"The baby room," said Rainey. She turned to me with stars in her eyes. Then she broke out in the biggest grin. With her good arm, she reached into the crib and grabbed a brown teddy bear. She rubbed it against her face and cooed. She handed it to me and picked up the baby powder. She sniffed it and squeezed at the same time so white powder stuck up on her nose and the middle of her forehead. Rainey bent over, sneezing and wiping, then finally stopped, and the smile returned, albeit whiter.

She ran her thick fingers over every inch of that room and then grabbed the baby blanket and sat down in the rocker chair with a stool that moved along with it. "I gonna sit here with baby Jesus. Rock. Rock."

"Rainey, you know this isn't Mama's baby room. This is the lady who lives here's room."

Rainey rocked and tilted her head to the side.

"The baby sleep right there." She pointed to the crib and cradled the teddy bear. *Rock.*

"That lady who lives here, Rainey? Mrs. Arielle with the pink dress on? She must be the one having a baby. Her baby's gonna sleep here. Not Mama's."

Finally, it sank in with Rainey that this was not Mama's baby's room and that another baby would be here instead. She looked around at the blue walls, the white crib, the teddy bear, the diapers, the dresser with little-boy outfits folded on top. It looked like those pictures she'd seen on the Internet, little perfect baby-boy rooms. Suddenly, she looked covetous. She stuck her hand in the air like I'd done a while ago, Vanna White–style, and said, "Baby Jesus need this." Then she stood up and started grabbing things left and right. At that point, there was no talking her down.

". . . told him there was no way I was going back to work, and I—"

". . . now that's just not right. I've never seen anybody get a rash from—"

Rainey and I zipped up and down those stairs like ninjas. Nobody seemed to notice a couple of girls in fancy hats hauling loot out the door. I wasn't stealing the stuff, I was just making sure Rainey didn't hurt herself, what with being one-armed and having a tricky ankle. But you know, that last time we came down, I heard them say, "Priscilla? You've won the free makeover!" Everybody started clapping, and then somebody said, "We should really find—what's her name? Rainbow? She would love to see this."

Next thing you know, Mama's sitting there on a sofa with a lady rubbing a cotton ball over her face, and everybody's turned around staring at me and Rainey, who happens to be skulking down the stairs with a bag of diapers and two blue onesies. The whole baby room was empty, and if Rainey could have brought down the crib and rocker chair, she'd have done that too.

The room grew deadly quiet and Rainey stuck her tongue out, thinking of what to say. Finally, she said, "Mama got baby Jesus in the tummy." And she kept going down the stairs and out the door to our getaway car.

Chapter Thirty-one
THE GETAWAY

"I cannot believe this. I just cannot believe this."

I guess I'd never seen Mama so mad in my lifetime. They'd halfway taken her makeup off, so it looked like she'd melted on one side of her face.

"I have never been so embarrassed in all my life! What were you thinking?"

We'd already cleared the baby items out of the car, and all the Bobby Sue ladies offered to take them back into the house, which I thought was pretty nice. I heard some comments:

"Oh, it's no trouble at all."

"What a shame you can't stay longer."

"I'm sure she didn't mean any harm by it."

"No, I'm sorry," said Mama, shaking. "We've really got to go."

"But your Bobby Sue makeover, Priscilla." They said *makeover* like, who in her right mind would turn down such a door prize?

Mrs. Arielle tapped on the window as we were backing out the driveway, and Mama rolled it down, though I could tell she didn't want to.

"Priscilla, please don't go like this. It's totally understandable."

"I'm sorry, Kelsey, I'm just . . ." Mama held back tears.

"Listen, I'll call you and we'll have coffee, okay? Decaf?" Mrs. Arielle smiled sadly and let Mama know in a single look that she knew she was pregnant and didn't care one bit about her daughters trying to rob her blind at her very own Bobby Sue party. "We're expecting a child too. My husband and I, we're adopting a baby boy. Could be weeks, months . . ."

"I'm happy for you," Mama said, trying to rub the mascara off from under her eye. "But I really just need to go."

"All right. We'll talk soon. Don't you worry about anything. It's no big deal. I promise."

And then off we went in our Crown Victoria that had for some reason developed a squeak that very moment. Funny how I hadn't noticed it before. You couldn't miss us rolling down the drive and squeaking up Mercy Street to Vinca Lane.

"Why did I ever say anything?" Mama said to herself. "Why did I ever say a word about anything?" Rainey and I both knew to stay quiet, that Mama's question was not really one she wanted answered. Just the same, when she settled down I had to set the record straight. "I wasn't stealing, Mama. I tried to tell her that stuff was for some other baby, not yours."

"Baby Jesus need clothes," said Rainey.

Mama let out a long sigh because, well, there was no arguing with that.

It'd been a whole thirty minutes or so since I'd thought about Poppy being gone. And I only remembered him because I was thinking about what Grandma Mona would say about Rainey stealing the baby stuff when she found out. Then I thought of her being back at the blue gingerbread house, probably in the garden or on the back porch with Poppy. That's when I remembered he was gone. My grandfather had left us. He'd left Mama with a baby in her tummy. Again.

I was furious with Poppy. I turned to look at Mama while she was driving and wanted so bad to touch the silky hair in her ponytail, to run it through my fingers, to tell her how sorry I was she was daddyless again, but I didn't. Instead I let her look in her tiny mirror and fix her face. It was pretty much clear of makeup by the time we got to the church.

• • •

We bumped up into a parking lot of a large white building. It said COVENANT CHURCH, PASTOR: FRITZ ROSIER. Mama said, "Now listen, I have got to go in here a few minutes and I do not want any trouble, all right? Please keep your hands to yourself, honey. Don't touch anything." She had turned all the way around and was eyeing Rainey. "Already it's been a long day and it's barely the afternoon. I just want to go in, sign some papers, and let's go back to the house and take a nap. All right?"

Rainey nodded. She fiddled with her fat fingers. She scratched her shoulder underneath the strap that held her cast up. She looked out the window and tried to touch her tongue to her nose. She stopped when she saw the cross on top of the building. She smiled and said, "Jesus' house."

"That's right," said Mama. Then under her breath she said, "God help us."

As we walked up the sidewalk past the round green bushes and marigolds, we heard thunder far off. Mama walked, shoulders hunched over and staring up at the approaching clouds. If I didn't know any better, I'd say she was afraid of getting struck by lightning. And sure enough, when the thunder sounded again, Mama nearly jumped out of her high-heeled shoes.

"Priscilla," said Fritz. He was standing there with the door open. "I'm glad you're here. How would you ladies like a tour of the place? I don't do this with everybody, you know. Only the most important people."

He didn't look like a preacher to me. No long white robes. No little square thingy on his collar. No halo over his head. He just looked like a man, a nice man. He smiled a nice, big, tall smile, and Mama said, "Well . . ." She looked over at me and Rainey. "I guess we don't get to see the insides of a church that often. The behind-the-scenes, I mean."

I'm pretty sure Fritz knew none of us went to church because each of us was staring and pointing at stained-glass windows and red-velvet-covered benches and blue books marked "Hymnal" stuck on the backs of chairs. Rainey and I scooted in and out of every single long pew. We sat in each seat, pretending church was in session while Mama stood up at the front with Fritz and got a feel for what it was like behind the podium.

"Say something, Mama," I said.

"Say something," Rainey copied me.

"Our Father who art in heaven . . ." Uncle Fritz put on a deep preacherly voice, then he stopped and laughed. "Come on, ya'll. There's more to see."

I know it might not have been the nicest thing to think at that moment, what with me already having a daddy and such, even if he was long

213

gone. But sitting there looking up at Uncle Fritz all tall and funny and kind like that, I wished, *I wished* he was my real daddy.

And suddenly, I was sad again. But not as sad as I'd be once we'd found our way to the Macy family graveyard.

What I'd see there would change my life forever.

Chapter Thirty-two
HOLD YOUR BREATH

There was a little graveyard back in Cypresswood within walking distance from our house. Not that we ever walked there. It was overgrown with weeds and such, but from the street we could see white tombstones jutting out of the ground like hands of the dead, reaching for us. Driving by that graveyard, Rainey and I would hold our breaths. Mama did it too. She'd taught us that if we breathed while driving by a graveyard, the spirits of the dead people might rise up out of the ground and take up house in our bodies. Coming in through the mouths, we guessed. For good measure, we always held our noses shut tight too. Just in case.

Mama had to drive past that graveyard every day, both going to and coming from work at the pancake house. I felt sorry for her. Rainey was lucky in that Jerry's Supermarket was the other way down the road. Rainey and I only had to pass it when we were going out of town or to the Y every other Tuesday for skating. 'Course when Rainey did that Special Olympics, we drove by there a lot, seeing as the events were all held at the Y. We got pretty good at knowing exactly when to start holding our breaths and when we could breathe again.

But what were we to do when we came upon a real live graveyard that you walked through? Rainey and I sucked in breaths and pinched our noses shut when Uncle Fritz walked us out back behind the Covenant Church. I'd never seen graves up close. I'd looked at them hard as I could driving by them, but they just looked like stones, wobbled this way and that, sometimes a cross, sometimes an angel. Never up close.

But this. Before us were a hundred or more graves. With dead people under the ground. The very ground we were standing on! Dead people. I stuck my shirt up over my mouth and nose. I was starting to feel dizzy. Rainey looked at me and her eyes bugged out. She was getting ready to lose her breath too. All of a sudden, we ran back inside and hid behind the door. We breathed in air so hard and long I thought my lungs might never fully inflate again. But they did. And Mama came running in after us. She wasn't out of breath at all. In fact, I wondered, had some spirit come and filled her up? She didn't look scared at all, just peaceful. Her golden eyebrows hung there over her blue eyes like halos.

"You all right?" Mama asked us. "What's wrong with you?"

"Cain't breathe," said Rainey.

"You're supposed to hold your breath, Mama!"

"Oh my goodness. Honey, that's just a superstition. I just do it sometimes when we're driving by graveyards because, well, it's what I did as a little girl. Just an old habit. There's no reason to hold your breath here, honey. There's nothing at all scary here. Nothing at all is going to happen to you."

"Ghost," said Rainey.

"No ghosts," said Mama. "I promise. Now come on out here. I have something to show you."

There were two walkways in this graveyard, one led to the left and the other to the right. The graves had little fake flowers in little planters in front of the stones. I thought it wasn't very nice to not have real flowers to honor the dead people, but then again, they were dead and wouldn't know the difference. Then I thought it was real smart to put fake flowers out there so you never had to water them. Very smart indeed. The living people had certainly wised up. Probably why they were still alive.

Mama and Fritz walked along the left path, pointing to stones like they were old friends. "Oh look. Mrs. Abernathy. I remember her. She always invited us in for pie."

"Died in a car accident," said Fritz.

"Oh no. Really? Nicest lady."

And so on and so forth.

Finally, we got to the Macy family ancestors. I wondered if maybe this graveyard was in alphabetical order like the books in the library. If so, it was a real smart way to do it because you'd never lose a loved one, like a Macy stuck between a Jones and a Brigham. Because after all, who really wanted to stay here in this graveyard longer than they needed, trying to find a grave? I suspected we'd been here long enough for whatever spirits who wanted new bodies to come on up in our nostrils and take root. I didn't feel any different, though, so I figured all was well.

"Rainey?" Mama called. Rainey was hunched over a little tiny grave with a name on it, *Baby Jenkins*. I knew it was for a child, and she was starting to understand that too.

"Me and Janie looking at the baby," she said.

"Oh, goodness. How 'bout you girls come on over and look at this. All right?"

Fritz walked over to us and put his arm on Rainey's shoulder. "Remember, this just a resting place. All the folks here in this yard? They believed in the Lord Jesus. They get to be up in heaven with him right now, singing, happy as all get-out." He was smiling like he really believed it too.

"But the baby," Rainey said, sadness filling her eyes.

"Don't you worry about that baby, Rainey. God loves babies and he takes extra-special care of them. Why, do you know, when a baby goes to heaven it gets wings and can fly and smiles all the time?"

"I want wings," said Rainey, cheering a bit.

"I have no doubt that someday, Rainey Dae Macy, you will have wings. No doubt at all. But for now we have living to do. Right? How 'bout we go on over here with your mama?"

I liked what Uncle Fritz said about angels and baby wings and flying and being happy. It sounded like a good place, this heaven. Thinking on it hard made me not so sad or scared around these graves. We were sort of like at a bus stop with all the dead folks already hopped on board and traveled to their destination. I followed him and Rainey over to where Mama was standing. She was looking at us with little tears in her eyes but a smile in the corners of her mouth. Like she was happy and sad at the same time.

"Look right here, honey. Can you read what this says?" Mama pointed to the etched-out words on a tombstone.

"Ad-Ado—"

"Adolph Macy," I said. "That was Poppy's father."

"Adolph Macy was your great-grandfather. He was a war hero."

"His picture's up on the wall in the stairway, Rainey," I said.

"And see this one?" Mama pointed to another stone. "Here's Madeline, his wife. Your great-grandmother. They lived in the very house we're in right now on Vinca Lane."

I listened to her explaining everything and everybody to Rainey, but I was one step ahead. I was already looking for Great-Aunt Gertrude's grave. I was half-expecting her to be sitting right on top of it, saying, "Ooooooh, what went wrong . . . what went wronnnng," like a witch belly-aching over her faulty cauldron. But I didn't see Gertrude's grave. Instead, I saw something that made me stumble.

I fell down on my knees in the soft soil.

I scrunched my eyes up, convinced they were seeing things. I closed them, then opened them again. Then I heard myself wailing as if I was far-off from my body.

I put my hand out and touched the letters in front of me. G-R-A.

Rainey came over and stuck her hand over her right ear. She tried to close the other one by pressing it down to her left shoulder because her hand was in a cast and couldn't be used for closing up ears. She started wailing, too, and I'm not sure if it was because I was crying or because she'd read the name of the man on the headstone in front of us. There were no two ways about it.

Our grandfather, Poppy, was dead.

Chapter Thirty-three
DEAD AND BURIED

To onlookers, the scene in the Covenant Church graveyard that day must have seemed chaos— screaming, crying, carrying on. Rainey and I lay down over that tombstone and bawled. We were ripped up one way and down the other. I'd known in my heart I'd never see Poppy again. *I knew it!* The feeling made me sick inside. I replayed over and over how that very morning he'd said he loved me, how he'd made me promise not to forget how important I was. Well, if I was so important, how come nobody thought to tell me he was dying? How come he didn't tell me himself? I cried and cried until no more tears came, but my body lay shaking, all used up.

Rainey'd worked herself into hysterics, so they had to haul her inside the church and lay her down in a pew. "No wanna dead! No wanna dead!" she kept saying, and Mama and Fritz thought she was saying she didn't want to die, so they made on and on about how she wasn't going to. "You're not gonna die, honey." But that, too, I knew was a lie, because she was going to die someday. We all were. Like Poppy.

"Why didn't you tell me?" I asked Mama. "Why didn't you just tell me he was dying? I could have said good-bye. I could have told him how much I love him!"

Mama stayed quiet, tears streaming down her face. She was stroking Rainey's hair. "I didn't want a big scene," she said finally. "I guess this wasn't such a good idea. I'm so sorry, honey. I didn't want you upset."

She didn't want a big scene? That's why they didn't tell me Poppy was dying? I was a person! A child, yes, but a person anyway! Didn't I have rights? Well, didn't I?

I was too exhausted to fight. I bent down on the church floor and put my head the safest place I could think of, on Mama's lap. I couldn't speak anymore. I'd never felt the loss of something so great. This was worse than when my daddy had left me. Because Poppy had really loved me. He knew me. He loved me *even though* he knew me, how imperfect I was. He showered me with affection. To be honest, he was the only one ever to do that. In thinking of Poppy's being gone, I didn't picture him in heaven, being happy, playing harps and such. I simply felt sorry for myself. I was the sorriest and saddest I'd ever been.

Dead and buried in a single day. I thought Uncle Fritz must be the fastest, tidiest preacher there ever was. We were in his office now. Rainey was lying on a little red sofa, and I was on the floor with my head back on Rainey's legs. Mama was sitting in a hardwood chair across from Fritz's hardwood desk. Mama looked over at us and said quietly, "Honey? I know this might not be the best time, but . . . you know these papers I'm about to sign?" Rainey and I sat up and looked her way. "These papers mean that . . . I mean, my father left me—us—the house on Vinca Lane. It's ours. Can you believe it? We can stay here if you like. Would you like that?"

How Mama could almost look happy, I did not know. If ever I'd had an up-and-down moment where the up part nearly matched the down part, this was it. Hearing that we could live on Vinca Lane forever, but without Poppy, was like getting a brand-new bike but losing your legs to pedal with. There was simply no joy in it. Only cruel mockery.

Two weeks ago if they'd told me I'd have a nice new house in a nice new town, I would have jumped for joy. But now it just didn't matter to me. Not one bit. Life, I was learning fast, did not play by any fair rules.

Before we left his office and Mama had signed whatever she needed to sign, she hugged Uncle

Fritz. Leaned in and squeezed him tight. He was so tall, her face melted into his chest. He held her back stiff-like, as if hugging didn't quite come easy for him, what with being so tall or being a preacher, or being Grandma Mona's son, one.

"I'm so glad you came back," he said. "He knew you would, you know. He prayed you would."

"I just wish it hadn't taken me so long," said Mama. "If I'd just come back a year ago . . . Why didn't he just set out to find me . . . or send you for me if he knew—"

"Sometimes a person has to find her own way back home, Priscilla. It means more that way, having gone on the journey. There's less resentment when we reach out instead of being pulled. Not to mention, if he'd come for you, would it have changed anything?"

"I'm not sure. Maybe. Maybe not. I could have spent more time with him. Told him how I really felt."

"A father always knows," said Fritz. "Even when things are unspoken, a father knows his child's heart. Your daddy knew yours, no matter what you did or didn't say."

On the way out, Uncle Fritz walked us to a place he called his "special place." "It's where I come whenever I'm feeling down," he said. "It makes me happy. Do you have a place like that?"

Rainey nodded and said, "The tree."

We followed him outside and around the church by the parking lot. I wasn't sure how we hadn't seen it before, but there in front of us was a real-life nativity scene, with Joseph, Mary, and a little baby Jesus in the crib. And here it was the middle of June! The manger was sheltered by a large live oak, and there were shepherds and sheep and animals of all sorts.

"Wow," mouthed Rainey. She'd never seen real-life-sized Bible people or animals before. I hadn't either.

"At Christmastime, we light this whole thing up and people come from miles around to see it. You know why?"

"Huh-uh," said Rainey, still gawking.

"Because on Christmas Eve, we replace the Mary, Joseph, the baby Jesus, the shepherds, the animal figures—everything—with real-life ones. Real, live sheep . . ."

"A real, live baby?" I asked.

"Every year we use a different baby . . . whoever in the church has an infant they'll let us borrow. We wrap them up tight so they don't get cold. And you know what?"

"What?" asked Rainey, fascinated now.

Fritz bent down on his knees and touched the little Jesus figure. Rainey followed suit and put her whole hand on his face, caressing it. "Sometimes we have a little boy baby who plays Jesus . . . and sometimes we have a little girl.

Shhhh. Can you believe that? It's funny, and nobody can tell the difference. That's just a little secret between us, all right?" Fritz looked up at Mama, and I did too. There was a sweetness in Mama's eyes. She cared for Fritz. That much was clear.

"And look here. See this manger? Your granddaddy, Grayson Macy, helped me build it."

"Poppy?" I said.

"Yes ma'am, he treated me like his own son. He didn't have to; it's just the kind of man he was. When I went into ministry, it was just natural that I come here to Forest Pines. Your granddaddy sort of took me under his wing." He ran his hand up the woodwork and down again. "Building this manger together, we got to know each other even better . . . I know for a fact he would have been happy to see you girls standing here, admiring his handiwork."

Rainey sniffled, and I did too.

"No need to get sad anymore. Your granddaddy's in a much better place now. And y'all are too. I'm so happy you're going to be living here in Forest Pines, Priscilla. I'm looking forward to spending some time with you girls. You're welcome here at the church whenever you like. Anytime."

We all waved good-bye and turned to go when Fritz called, "You know, it's almost time for picking those peaches. How 'bout we make some homemade ice cream. Would y'all like that? Or peach pie?"

"Ice cream," said Rainey, licking her lips. "No. Pie."

"Either one, I guess," I said.

Fritz was finding how easy it was to soothe Rainey, to tell her the things she wanted to hear. But me? I wasn't quite so easy. I stood there with arms folded across my chest until Mama said, "Oh gracious, I forgot my bag. Wait right here and I'll be out in a second. Just stay here and look at this nice manger."

"I'll have to open the office again," Fritz said, rattling his keys, and off they went, muttering about how often they lose things the older they get.

This was just the opening Rainey'd been looking for, because as soon as they went back inside that church she looked at me, face still stained red from tears, and said, "I take the baby Jesus for Mama. They get new one at Christmas anyways."

Chapter Thirty-four
STEALING BABY JESUS

I did not tell Rainey it was wrong to steal that baby Jesus. It wasn't a real baby, after all. It was a fake, a pretender. A stand-in. But she knew it was stealing, especially after what had happened at Mrs. Arielle's house. That was all too fresh in our minds. So I kept on the lookout while she pulled it from the little cradle and hauled it, one-handed, into the Police Interceptor and hid it down in the backseat. It was the least I could do for her. Rainey'd lost her grandfather, too, that day. If holding that baby could take away just an instant of her sadness, I'd do it. She was my sister, after all, and that's just what sisters do for each other.

As soon as we entered the house, I saw everything in a new light, and I had mixed feelings about that. The house was ours now—we owned the furniture, the walls, the carpets—but Poppy was no longer there. There was no possibility of him ever coming back because he was dead and gone and . . .

Unless.

I looked up at the wall of dead family members along the stairs and thought about Gertrude being a ghost. Not that I'd seen her or anything, but Grandma Mona seemed to think she had at one time. Maybe being a ghost was a real, live thing that could happen to a person. Maybe Poppy, in leaving so quickly, still had some business to tend to. Maybe I was his business. I certainly needed him here. I bent down on the steps right then and there and prayed, *Please, God, let Poppy come back. He can stay in the attic if he needs to, because I know how to get up there. And I won't mind the heat. I just want to see Poppy again. I need him. Please. Amen.*

Mama and Rainey had gone off to the kitchen to have some tea, but I wasn't thirsty. I knew God had heard my prayer. I knew it like you know something deep in your bones. I flew up those stairs, past Mama's room, past Rainey's and my green room and up the spiral staircase. I wound up and up and with each turn got more excited that I was going to see Poppy. Oh, maybe I couldn't hold him or touch him now that he was a ghost, but I could talk to him. Maybe. Maybe I could look in his eyes some more. Maybe I could at least tell him how much I loved him just one last time.

I stood frozen at the top of the stairs. I could hear my heart pounding in my ears. I grabbed onto the knob and turned slowly. Then I pushed in the door. The heat hit me and I inhaled. I didn't mind the heat. I didn't. The door swung open all the way and there, sitting in an old rocking chair by the window on the side of the house, *wasn't* Poppy. It was Grandma Mona. She held a quilt in her hands and she was sewing. She stopped when she saw me, and it was then I realized she might not know anything about Poppy dying. Here I was, having to be the one to break the news to her about her very own husband. I firmed my shoulders and held them tight until they melted back down again, and I said, whimpering, "Oh Grandma Mona. Something terrible has happened."

And I'll never forget how tired and strange she looked when she said, "Do tell, child. Do tell."

Chapter Thirty-five
THE MATRIARCH

{Mona}

"Do tell, child. Do tell," I said.

I'd been waiting for her. I knew where they'd gone, to the church, to the cemetery. I didn't know for sure what she'd see, but I was ready, nonetheless. Janie looked up at me with the saddest brown eyes. Her hair was disheveled and held up on one side with a yellow barrette. She looked even younger than her eight years. "What is it that's so terrible, Janie? You can tell me."

Her eyes darted across the room as if she was wishing for an escape, and then she began crawling up into my lap. It had been years since she'd done this, and I'd missed it so. I set down my sewing and hoisted her up. I held her and hugged her tight. I felt her warmth all through me and I wanted her to feel mine, aside from the immense heat of the attic. I rocked us for a second while she gathered her thoughts.

"Poppy's . . . in heaven," she said and began to cry.

"Wh-what?" I feigned ignorance. "What do you mean?"

She looked me in the eyes then, and it was hard to keep her from seeing inside me. It was hard to watch her so torn up. Nearly broke my heart, but it was as it had to be.

"I saw his grave, Grandma Mona. He's dead! I saw his tombstone with the name *Grayson Macy* on it. I cain't believe they didn't tell you either!"

"Who?" I asked, tearing up.

"Mama and Uncle Fritz! They didn't tell us Poppy was dying! And I never got to say good-bye!"

She started getting worked up and thrashing around. Then she slowed. Finally, perfect still-ness. In that instant, something registered in Janie's face, smart girl. She looked at me and studied the lines in my cheeks and forehead. I'd always been a fairly good liar, but now my face betrayed me. I was trying to look distraught and surprised, but to no avail. She pushed away from me and slid off my lap. "You knew," she said, her voice turned cold. "Didn't you. You knew all along he was sick and you never let on."

"Oh, honey, I—" But before she would even let me explain, she ran out of the attic crying, and down the stairs, probably to Rainey, my other sweet, special grandchild. Rainey was the pot at the end of my rainbow. Just being with her made me feel bright and shiny, and . . .

Well, after Janie was gone, I sat there rocking, pondering my loved ones and all that was before me. As matriarch of the Macy family, much had been asked of me. Much was at stake. But all in its own time. The key to doing anything right was the timing. I'd learned that the hard way. One false move and everything could fall apart.

I didn't so mind Janie being mad at me—she'd certainly been that way before. It was simply the sort of relationship we'd grown into. Over time, meanness had become my necessity. It was easier to grump and fuss and push her away. It made it much harder for her to get close to me.

To peek into my soul.

To see the years of secrets hidden there, waiting like cicadas, ready to rise again.

But only at the proper time.

Part Three

The Macy Family Ghost

Chapter Thirty-six
THE BURDEN SHE BORE

{Mona}

I didn't like lying to my granddaughter. It didn't come natural, lying to the ones I loved.

Back when Grayson and I were living in the Macy house with his mama, Mrs. Madeline Macy, she and I used to take turns making meals, and I remember how she would make this pot roast with so much salt the meat would shrivel and dry up like a little brown—well, you can imagine. One time I tried to lie and tell her it was better than mine—I was trying to smooth her over for something I'd done, something—I can't remember what now. But she could see it on my face, my lips all puckered up. Maybe she knew it, too, how bad it was. Mrs. Madeline never said a word, but she strongly suggested I do the cooking from then on. I cooked every single meal after that. Every night, every day, I stayed in that kitchen, cooking for Grayson and Mrs. Madeline and later Priscilla, up until the very day we left for Yuma.

I love each and every one of my children and grandchildren the same. Each is special in his or her own way. My daughter, Priscilla, is a hard-working woman. Even as a little girl she worked hard at her grades, at her chores. She was the kind of child I never had to discipline. I never had to ask her to clean her room, for it was always kept clean. She was quiet for the most part, usually having a book in her hands, her face just inches from it. I picture her that way sometimes, Priscilla lying on her bedroom floor, head hanging over *Anne of Green Gables*. She was the joy of my life. But when you've done something you regret and it involves a child, you spend the rest of your days trying to make it up to whatever child comes your way—trying to erase the guilt you feel from long ago. Yet there's no making up for it. There's no erasing it.

I wonder what went wrong with Priscilla. Perhaps I doted on her too much when she was younger. Gave her too much freedom. I was afraid to do anything for fear she wouldn't love me anymore. I had a son out there, somewhere. The knowledge was unbearable at times, and I felt undeserving of whatever love I received from Priscilla. I was terrified she might make the same mistakes I'd made someday. And when she was becoming of age and I saw a young woman there, I grew determined to protect her from the world. Perhaps I overcompensated a bit. Overwhelmed her with rules just a little.

Children can sense when a parent suffers. I gladly would have kept silent all my suffering except that when we moved to Yuma, my son

Fritz came to find us, and my deepest secret came spilling out.

How many nights I lay in bed, dreaming of a day when we might be reunited. I prayed every night that Fritz was with a family who loved him. At the same time, I envied those people. They, whoever they were, got to hold him, touch him, look at him in the eyes. They got to know him. I imagined he didn't even remember me anymore. I was torn between hoping he'd forget and hoping there was still a remembrance of me, somewhere inside.

I have no real excuse for giving Fritz away. In my time of grief, after hearing William had died in Vietnam, I was hardly a woman. I was unfit to be his mother. In my eyes, Fritz had lost both parents at the same time. I felt nothing. I looked at my own child and could not summon any emotion. In my grief, I feared I may never feel a thing again and I knew I was no sort of mother for a child to have.

I made sure he was placed with a family before making it final. Fritz was only eighteen months old when I said good-bye to him. I can remember he was wearing the nicest blue sailor smock. I'd made it for him when he was born with the hopes of him growing into it. I'd hoped his father might come home from war and find his new son wearing that outfit, and we'd be a family.

But that didn't happen.

Fritz was asleep in a basket when I handed him to the social worker. We said everything in a hushed voice so as not to wake him up.

The feelings inside me were so dead and gone I never imagined them resurrected, but the very next morning with the light of day coming in the bedroom window, I sat up, waiting for my child to coo from the crib. Suddenly, the most enormous pain I'd ever encountered ripped through my body. I felt the pain of losing my husband fully and completely. And I felt the horrible shattering that no mother should ever feel, that of regret and sadness and fear, to the point I considered jumping from the rooftop just to end my misery. I knew in that instant, sitting in my nightclothes, I'd made the most terrible mistake of my life, giving Fritz away.

But times were different then. There was no undoing it.

Timing. My timing, or God's timing, whoever's timing it was, was hideous. If only I'd been able to feel the pain of losing William twenty-four hours earlier, I might have spared myself a lifetime of regret, and a lifetime away from my precious son Fritz. Of course, then I never would have met Grayson neither.

These are the things some mothers must ponder and bear for years and years. And bear it I do. Still to this day.

Chapter Thirty-seven
THE DEAD WALL

{Janie}

The day we put Poppy's picture up on "the dead wall" was the single worst one of my eight-and-a-half years. Rainey and I had spent the last couple days moping around the house, trying to accept the fact that Poppy was dead and gone. We were mostly quiet, keeping to ourselves, not yet at the reminiscing stage that some grievers make it to. But we did get together long enough to discuss the fact that Poppy's picture was not up on the stairwell.

At suppertime, Rainey asked Mama, "Where Poppy picture? Got put up on the wall." She pointed, and Mama observed her with reverence.

"You know, you are absolutely right. My daddy's picture should be up on that wall and it's not. Is that what you mean, honey?"

Rainey nodded and stuffed her mouth full with dumplings. "Tell you what, after I do the dishes, why don't we go up in the attic and see if there's a big one we can frame and stick up there. Would you like that?"

We both said we would, and Grandma Mona agreed it was a fine idea, so after supper, Rainey and I waited patiently on the stairs for Mama to finish cleaning up. It was a solemn occasion. And quick.

We climbed up to the attic, felt the heat, and didn't hardly look around at all because right there by the door, propped up, was a large, already-framed photo of Poppy. Funny how we hadn't seen that before. He was young and dressed in his bow tie, just like always. Behind him was a corn-field. Grandma Mona said how handsome he was, and Rainey and I teared up at seeing him, and when Mama hung him right next to his daddy, Adolph Macy, we sat there for the rest of the night, staring at the wall, sad as all get-out, missing our grandfather. Knowing that nothing would ever be as good without him around. 'Course, we should have appreciated those moments of calm and quiet. We didn't know things could get even worse than they already were.

Mama had been awful sweet ever since signing those papers at the church. She seemed happy in her new house. She spent much of her time cleaning and making lists of things she needed to fix and things she needed to buy for the house. She bought a newspaper and began circling jobs she could apply for. Some of them were wait-ressing jobs, but some of them weren't—things like *secretary* and *receptionist*. Those were big jobs, and I was proud of her for thinking of trying something different.

She even circled the names of some schools and day care centers. One was at the Covenant Church. I imagined our lives there in Forest Pines, Mama working a new big job, Rainey at the grocery store, me in a new school, and the baby at the church with Fritz. Yes, it all seemed it might work out nicely in the end.

Then one day the doorbell rang.

Rainey and I were up in our room, reading books, and Mama was in the kitchen, cutting up some squash she'd pulled from the garden. We knew it wasn't Fritz, because he never rang the doorbell, just knocked on the door whenever he came over. We thought it might could be Mrs. Arielle coming to call about Bobby Sue cosmetics, or maybe the old lady in the yellow house across the street needing to borrow some sugar, like people do sometimes on TV shows.

But when we came to the top of the stairs and looked down at Mama opening the door, we could see by the way she stood there frozen—the person on the other side was somebody she sure as rain wasn't expecting to see.

"Harlan?" we heard Mama say. "Fritz?"

"Hey, Priscilla. You were right. He sure is a hard man to find."

"Daddy?" I looked over at Grandma Mona. We were all huddled at the top of the steps. I started to dart down to the door.

"Janie!" Grandma Mona said in a hush. "Not now. Come back up here."

I stopped but didn't turn around. My eyes were glued to that front door. I couldn't see my daddy, but I knew he was just on the other side, and the thought of it made me faint, like I might roll right down the stairs and bump into Mama's feet. I turned and looked at Grandma Mona, and she reached for my hand. Numbly, I gave it to her and she walked Rainey and me up the stairs and into Mama's room. She quietly shut the door and stood in front of it.

"Daddy's here, Daddy's here!" I whispered to Rainey, jumping around like I might wet my pants.

"That's enough," said Grandma Mona.

"She said 'Harlan.' That's Daddy's name!"

"I know it, child, I know."

"But she's been looking for him . . . all over everywhere. And she loves him. And now he's back. We're gonna be a family again. With the house and the daddy and everything! Just like the real gingerbread house."

"Gingerbread," said Rainey, trying to smile, but scared at the same time.

Rainey looked at me, and I could tell we were thinking the same thing. We ran to the window with the big tree behind it and opened it up. We stuck our heads out and breathed the cool breeze and tried desperately to see what was going on, but we couldn't see for the porch being there. I loved that porch, but at that moment, I would've given anything if we just didn't have one.

"Girls, that's your mother's private affair down there. It's not good to listen in like this."

But there was no stopping us. In fact, I could tell Grandma Mona was getting closer to that window, too, eavesdropping like we were.

". . . you shouldn't be here . . ."

". . . shouldn't have ran off like that . . ."

". . . can't come in the house, she might see you . . ."

"Priscilla, isn't there something you wanted to say to Harlan?" I heard Uncle Fritz's voice cut clear through like a bell.

"No. Wait." It was my daddy's voice now, low and firm. Hearing it made my body fill up with warm goodness, like blood pumping for the very first time. It spread all over in my cheeks, my arms, my feet. Then it chilled when I heard him say, "There's something I've got to say to you, Priscilla. Something I should have said a long time ago."

Chapter Thirty-eight
RIGHT UNDER THEIR NOSES

{Mona}

It was 1980. We'd just moved to Yuma, Arizona. Grayson was excited about being out in the desert with a whole new ecosystem to learn and fuss over. Me? I missed the trees from back home. I missed the oaks and pines and birds and bugs and everything there was to surround you with greenness and home. I even missed the humidity of South Carolina. But Grayson was happy, and that's what I wanted.

Priscilla was now the prettiest girl in Yuma. She had been the prettiest in Forest Pines, but she'd left all of her friends back there, every single one. They said they'd call and write, and there had been a letter or two, but the letters had already stopped. Priscilla was fifteen years old, in a new place where people didn't know her. It must have been a confusing time for a young girl, but I thought kids were resilient.

Then to top it all off, Fritz, the long-lost brother she never knew about, came and found me. I can only imagine what that must have done to her. I know how it affected me and, temporarily, my marriage to Grayson.

Now, it's not like Priscilla turned bad or was

getting into drugs or anything like that. Not like she came home with tattoos or ears pierced, even. But when Priscilla came home with all that long beautiful blonde hair chopped off, I sucked in my breath and feared the worst. She had changed before my very eyes. She was a different child all of a sudden. She began hanging out with this Johnson boy and his friends. I forbade her from leaving the house at times, but she'd sneak off. It seemed the more I told her she couldn't do something, the more she'd try to do the opposite.

Turned out it wasn't the Johnson boy I should have been worried about at all. It was the strange young man who lived across the street from us. He was right under our noses the whole time, and his name was Harlan Bradfield.

Chapter Thirty-nine
THE BIG QUESTION

{Janie}

Rainey and I were leaning so far out that bedroom window, Grandma Mona had to reel us back in lest we fall. The sky was dark and cloudless above, full of stars. For once in my life, I was glad it was dark because it made it easier to sharpen my senses and listen in on what my daddy was saying on the porch. It's not like it came in all loud and clear because his voice dropped down an octave, and I could only catch a word here or there.

". . . back in Yuma . . . loved you the first time . . . shouldn't have taken me so . . . don't need an answer now . . . marry me?"

A hush lay over the whole town in the instant my father asked my mother to marry him. Rainey and I looked at each other. We stopped breathing just to hear what her answer would be. In those moments of waiting, I was filled with pure hope, hope for a better life, hope for a whole family, hope for the love my mama and Rainey and I so deserved.

And then, without any screaming or crying or calling out, "Yes, Harlan, yes!" I heard the door shut quietly below us. I watched the backs of Uncle Fritz and my daddy as they emerged from the porch, went down the walkway, and got back in Fritz's car to leave.

Every child wants to see her parents together, and I was no different. I lay in bed for three nights, praying Mama would say yes. But she didn't let on what she was thinking. Instead she stared out the windows or lay on the couch holding her belly. She hardly touched her supper at all. She picked weeds here and there in the garden. Grandma Mona'd told us not to ask Mama about Daddy coming over because we weren't supposed to be eavesdropping. She said sometimes grown-ups keep important things to themselves. I said, smart-like, "How come children are the last ones to know anything?" She didn't answer me back.

Daddy never came around at all. Seems like if you'd just asked somebody to marry you, you'd want to spend every second together, or so it seemed to me. I'd wait and watch, listening for Daddy's motorcycle, but never heard a thing. Rainey and I were inseparable those next few days. Her foot was all healed and her arm didn't hurt quite so much anymore, so she could bounce again. We had chalk and played hopscotch out in front of the house for hours at a time, talking about what it would be like to be a family again. Talking about memories we had of Daddy being home. How Mama used to try to look nice all the time. How she'd stay up with him for a while when he came home from the mechanic shop. How she'd kiss him even though he smelled like oil.

"That's true love," I said, "when you can kiss somebody when they smell that way." I threw down my rock and hop-hop-hopped. "Remember how sometimes he'd bring us flowers—daisies and daffodils?"

"Uh-huh," said Rainey. She picked up the rock and threw it. It landed on the number 3. "And the cowbell?"

I told her, how could I forget the cowbell? I hadn't heard it in years, but you never forget a sound like that. It was something Daddy had found in a field, and he kept it in his sock drawer. It would lie quiet most of the time, when Daddy was normal-acting. Other times, he was so sad he'd stay in bed for days on end. Mama'd make excuses to his boss when he couldn't go to work. He would cry sometimes. He would yell some others. Rainey and I would worry. But then, sometimes he would get so happy he'd be nearly bouncing off the walls. His voice would be loud and there'd be no escaping his enthusiasm. He'd shower sometimes two, three times a day. He'd ride that motorcycle fast as he could. He'd love on Mama and make her giggle. He'd eat second helpings at dinnertime. And every morning when he was extra happy like that he'd ring that silly cowbell and wake the whole house. Life was never boring when Daddy was around, only unpredictable.

The more I started thinking about all the faces of Daddy, the more my stomach started jumbling up in a knot. Then it would smooth away with a fresh wash of optimism. *My Mama might finally be getting married*, I thought. *To my very own father.* What could be better than that?

I started wondering about miracles. Coming to the house on Vinca Lane had been a miracle—it was so much nicer than the one in Cypresswood. I pondered how I came out of the tree when Rainey fell and I was just fine. I still didn't have an answer for it. For all I knew, *it* could have been a miracle. In fact, I started adding up all the things that were good about our new lives . . . finding Uncle Fritz, the new baby coming. Not counting Poppy's dying, there seemed to be an abundance of miracles in our family. Yes. I believed. Mama was going to say yes.

The way I learned the news was like this. One day, and I'm not sure which day of the week it was, being summertime, Mrs. Arielle came over to the house. She was dressed in a pink linen suit and she smelled real nice. Mama was expecting her so she'd been working on the house all morning long. She'd gone from no makeup and hair tied back behind her head, to spic-and-span floors along with a painted face and conditioned hair. Mrs. Arielle was pretty. More than her looks I think it was her confidence. She just seemed sure in her shoes. Mama's skin and hair and eyes were even prettier than Mrs. Arielle's, but the fact she seemed so unsure made her shine not quite so bright.

"You know I don't get over this way that often, but this neighborhood is just as nice as it always was. I remember coming over here when we were girls, Priscilla. You still have that swing in the back?"

"No," said Mama. "The branch broke off. Isn't that a shame? Here. Let me show you around. Or

249

would you like something to drink? Iced tea?"

Mama was real good at playing hostess, and I was proud of her. Grandma Mona was rocking out on the back porch and Rainey and I sat in the sewing room, quiet, still, waiting, listening, staying out of Mama's way. After a while, when we heard Mama pulling out a tin of cookies, Rainey said, "Come on." And I followed her.

We strolled into the kitchen and grinned, being real, real good. We wanted to show Mrs. Arielle we weren't always thieves.

"Well hello again," she said, beaming. "I'm so glad you were able to come to my little party."

"Oh no, Kelsey."

"No, I mean it. Y'all were the life of it all. And you know, I brought something for you." Mrs. Arielle stood up and walked into the living room. She fiddled with her purse and then reentered with her hands behind her back. She raised her eyebrows and brought out that teddy bear Rainey had tried to steal.

Rainey grabbed it and rubbed it on her face.

"I thought you might like to have this for your new little brother or sister."

Rainey looked at Mama to see if it was okay, and Mama nodded, a distracted look on her face. "Thank you," said Rainey. She held it out to me and I petted its soft little brown head. Then we turned and ran giggling out back to the garden to show Grandma Mona. While Grandma Mona was admiring that teddy bear and Rainey was chattering about how much she loved it and how the baby was going to love it too, I was standing close to the door, trying to listen some more to Mama's conversation. I couldn't hear much except all of a sudden Mrs. Arielle clapped her hands together and said, "Married? That's wonderful! I'm so happy—"

"Shh . . ." Mama said. ". . . doesn't know anything yet."

I turned to Grandma Mona and Rainey, who was rocking in the chair next to her, cradling that bear. "She's getting married! Mama's getting married!" I whispered. I thought I might burst.

"That'll be the day," said Grandma Mona, and I remember how angry I was at her for spoiling our fun. Here it was the happiest thing to have happened in a long time, if not ever, and this was the way she celebrated? I knew she was mourning over having lost Poppy, but grieving or not, I rekindled my dislike of Grandma Mona right then. Nobody messed with my Mama's being happy.

Chapter Forty
THE VOW MAKER

{Mona}

It's not as if I was being a spoilsport just to be a spoilsport. Sadly, I was considering history and what I knew to be true.

What I knew to be true is that the Bradfield boy would never get married. He didn't have it in him. He was a coward, if you ask me. I could remember watching him play by himself, walking his dog, shooting marbles, always by himself in his driveway across the street from us in Yuma. For a teenaged boy to spend so much time alone, I felt sorry for him. I befriended him. I'd say hello after Priscilla had already left to go somewhere with her friends. I would talk to this boy as if I might be able to help him in some way. You see, Harlan never had a father that I knew of, and his mother suffered a debilitating disorder. Back in the early eighties they weren't talking much yet about bipolar, but that young boy told me all about it. Told me when his mama was having a good spell. Told me just as honest when she was having one of her bad.

I remember one afternoon I had invited Harlan to the front porch and we were sitting on the steps. He was distraught his mother was in bed and having a bad go of it, and he said, "I'll never be like that."

" 'Course you won't," I said.

"And I'll never have children. Never."

"Oh now, don't say that, Harlan. Sure you will. You'll meet a nice girl, you'll settle down—"

"No, I won't, because Mama says if I ever do, I'll be a terrible father. And to add to it, I'll pass along the crazy gene. There's enough crazy in the world, she says."

Can you imagine that? He said it with such conviction. It pretty much summed up Harlan's life sentence. A life of fear and instability. A lifetime of thinking he had nothing to offer a woman or, heaven forbid, a child. No, Harlan always kept the ones who loved him at arm's length. Whether he actually developed a true touch of the disorder I couldn't tell you for sure. All I know is his mother assured him he was a carrier, and that changed his outlook on himself and the whole wide world. And it would affect the Macy family for generations to come.

Chapter Forty-one
LOVE NEVER DIES

{Janie}

Rainey and I heard Mama's footsteps before her knock. We were lying in our beds, talking about everything and nothing, singing silly songs. It was almost like the night before Christmas. We were just as excited.

"Can I come in?" Mama said. She pushed the door open and Rainey and I grinned up at her. I tried not to show that I knew her secret, but I couldn't. I just couldn't. "Listen, there's something I wanted to talk about." Mama stepped up on my mattress to go sit next to Rainey and almost pinched my arm.

"Watch out. You hurt Janie," said Rainey.

"Oh goodness, I'm sorry, Janie. Let me move over here." She stepped over me carefully and sat down. "Now listen up, girls, I've got some big news to tell you."

"Mama get married!" said Rainey.

"Wh-what? How did you—"

"We saw Daddy and everything."

"Oh my goodness. You little stinkbug. I cannot believe . . . well, yes. I know it's been a long time . . . a real long time, but your father came and we talked. He's asked me to marry him, but I told him I'd have to check with you first. He wants us to be a family again. I don't know. I think I'd like that too, but what do you think?"

"Okay, Mama," said Rainey.

"Yes. Tell him yes!" I said.

At this point Mama's face lit up, and she pulled her left hand in front of us and showed off a ring. It was gold with a single diamond on it, not as big as Mrs. Arielle's but a real ring, nonetheless. Mama'd never worn a ring. It made her look like a princess.

We touched that ring and looked up at Mama in awe. She was happy, truly. She was like Cinderella who had found her prince. Out of all my moments of true happiness, that one was the best one yet.

After so many years gone by, it's a strange thing to see your father. It's like this love you felt but set aside comes rushing back along with a whole other feeling—trepidation, shyness, knowing him but not knowing him. Standing there in the living room, looking at my daddy with his brown hair pulled back in a ponytail, clean jeans on, and Uncle Fritz by his side, I forgot all about the questions I'd wanted to ask him over the years like, *where did you go, how could you leave us?* Things like that. Instead, as soon as he smiled and put out his arms, I could see in his eyes he was sorry for being gone so long, and Rainey and I ran to him.

We hugged him as hard as we could. Daddy sat down on the sofa and cried like a little baby. He seemed genuinely shocked we could love him still after all this time. It seemed to me that Rainey and I, mere children, knew something the grown-ups around us didn't. That love never dies. I felt happy they were learning what we already knew.

But Grandma Mona remained the naysayer and sucked all the fun out of everything.

"Don't get too hung up on that boy," she'd tell Mama. "Don't pin your hopes on him. He hasn't changed, Priscilla. People don't change."

But Mama must have thought they could. Mama had changed herself, after all. She was changing every second these days, humming at times, cleaning, crying at others. Pretty soon she started getting ill. She'd try to eat some dry toast but wound up running to the bathroom instead.

Daddy moved onto the couch in the living room and just let Mama do her thing. He watched in horror when she got sick. He'd try to help around the house. He'd read to us. I don't know how many times he read *Corduroy*, and I was tired of the book, but I listened in anyway. It was my daddy's voice. My father. The newness of every-thing was like icing on our gingerbread house. Pinpricks up my spine. Cool chills in the warm air. Stomach jitters. Overwhelming happiness.

Then one day, Mama and Daddy were sitting at the breakfast table, looking at each other in a serious way. Rainey was still in the bathroom, and I sat down beside Daddy and placed my hand on his arm, hoping for love. He was so consumed with what he was thinking, he didn't notice me at all. I pulled my hand away and sat there feeling scolded. Out of place.

"Of course I still want to marry you," he said, "but I just don't think . . ." He breathed out hard and said, "What if something's wrong with the baby? What if I pass along—"

"I don't want to hear another word about that," said Mama. She had put her head in her hands. She looked up and right at me, and I took that as my cue to walk away. Still, I stood quietly in the living room and listened in. "Do you see why I didn't tell you?" she whispered. "Do you see?"

"Yes, yes, I completely understand. You're right . . . as usual. I'm sorry. We're having this baby, and everything will be fine."

"Everything will be fine," said Mama with finality, though there was an edge to her voice.

The wedding was set for July the third. It had been so many years, it seemed no time for wasting. It was to be here at the house with Fritz officiating, and only a few friends in attendance. Rainey and I were going to be flower girls. We'd always wanted to be flower girls, and we practiced by pulling up strays in Mrs. Shoemaker's front yard whenever Mrs. Shoemaker was not around to see us. We'd amassed a small treasure of petals and kept them in a little basket. We'd take turns walking up and down the garden, dropping them one at a time to the left, to the right. Then we'd pick them up, one by one, and do it all over again.

One morning, after we were done practicing and were sure we knew our parts, we sat on the front steps and watched Daddy give Mama a kiss on the cheek. Then he got on his motorcycle and told her he would be back in two days. He was going to take care of his house in the mountains. He was going to get all his stuff and move it to Forest Pines. Then he and Mama were going to do the same with our house in Cypresswood, and we would all be together again under one roof. They were so excited, we all were. It was a very happy time.

But Daddy never came back from the mountains, and Mama cried, and Grandma Mona said she knew it all along. There seemed nothing much to be happy about after that.

Chapter Forty-two
ON THIEVES AND STEALING

When July the third came and went, Mama stayed quiet. Her soft face grew hard along her cheekbones. Her glow from pregnancy had disappeared. To me, she seemed only halfway living, and try as I might to cheer her up or suggest reasons why Daddy had left us, she seemed closed to anything but the fact she'd fallen for it. Again.

There were no fireworks or sparklers for Independence Day, at least not at our house, and two nights went by uneventful and sad. Then one night, I was coming to Mama's bedroom to say good night, but mostly just to check on her. She'd already put us into bed with barely a word. No promptings to say our prayers as if she'd forgotten our routine. I heard her voice, and I stopped just outside her door.

"If it was only about me," I heard her telling somebody, "I would be all right, but it's not. It's not just about me. I brought him here, into my home, into my family again. All I did was create false hopes. I'm embarrassed. I'm angry . . . No, I'm not mad at you, of course not. I don't . . . Fritz, no. I don't want to talk about that right now. I just . . . you wouldn't understand. You cannot possibly. I'll just say this: this is no way to bring a child into the world. It's not supposed to be this way, to feel this way. I'm sure this is not what God intended. This whole thing has been one mistake after another. Now I don't want to hear another word about it."

Without saying good-bye, Mama hung up the phone and closed Fritz out of her life, along with me and Rainey. I tiptoed back to bed and lay there all night thinking, suddenly afraid again of what Mama was going to do about the baby.

● ● ●

Early the next morning, as I was wiping the fog from my eyes, I heard Rainey snoring. I had woken up with something important on my mind, and I needed to talk to somebody about it. If he was still alive, I would have searched the house for Poppy, but he wasn't there for me anymore. I didn't want to talk to Grandma Mona because I was still mad at her, and I couldn't talk to Mama about it. That left Rainey. It was a gamble because I didn't like getting her upset, and I was pretty sure what I had to say wouldn't sit well with her.

I looked up at her sleeping. By her head was an upside-down teddy bear, the one Mrs. Arielle had given her, and against the wall sat the baby doll she'd brought with her from home. Beneath the covers was a lump with a hand sticking out. Every night since she'd taken it, Rainey had slipped the baby Jesus out of his hiding place in the closet and slept with him, remembering to hide him again by morning light.

"Rainey?" I whispered. She didn't answer. I poked her in the back. "Rainey?"

"Mmm," she grumbled.

"I gotta talk about something. Wake up."

Rainey stirred and then struggled to turn over. She stretched with her good arm, yawned, then lay on her side, looking at me with one sleepy eye. Birds were beginning to sing, and by the light coming in atop the curtains, I could tell it was going to be a hot, sunny day.

"Rainey, listen. You know that baby Jesus you stole?"

"I took it," she said, correcting me.

"No, you stole it, Rainey. It belonged to the church and you stole it. You're a thief. You could go to jail."

At this, Rainey's brow furrowed, and she sat up, grabbing the baby Jesus. She hugged him hard, then realized he was the contraband, so she jumped out of bed and stuffed him in the closet, laying a blanket on top of him for safer keeping.

She looked at me and said, "I not go jail."

"You're not, you're not," I said. "Come back over here and sit down." She sat, pajamas twisted, hair mussed, eyes puffy.

"You tell Mama?" she asked.

"No."

"Okay."

"I'm just saying that you stole the baby Jesus, and I was thinking how that's a crime. Stealing, it's a crime, you know, and they send people to jail for stealing things, even a plastic doll. Even something small like that or a piece of chewing gum."

Rainey's chest was starting to heave up and down like she might start crying.

"All I'm saying is . . . you 'member how Poppy and Grandma Mona taught us that new word?

You member those baby pictures we saw in the library? On Google?"

Rainey's bottom lip curled and started shaking. She nodded her head.

"How come *you* could go to jail for stealing that baby Jesus—which you won't, 'cause I'm not gonna tell on you, I promise—but anyway, how come you could go to jail for that, but Mama might could do abortion on her baby and that wouldn't be against the law?"

Rainey shook her head.

"It doesn't seem right to me," I said. "Seems like doing that to a real baby'd be worse than stealing a dumb plastic one."

"Uh-huh." A tear escaped Rainey's left eye and plopped to her chest. "I not go jail."

"And then I started thinking, you know what?"

"What."

"What if Jesus really was in Mama's tummy?"

"Baby Jesus in Mama's tummy," said Rainey.

"I know, but what if he *really* was. I mean, what if Jesus hadn't come two thousand years ago, but he waited to come now. And what if Mary, like Mama, had thought she didn't want to have a baby. She could have un-borned him, and Jesus never would have come into the world. Can you imagine? If Jesus were to come today, he might not have been born at all. There'd be no Christmas, no Easter, no church, nothing like that."

I could see I'd lost Rainey somewhere along the way. She was rubbing her fingers and fretting, looking toward our closed bedroom door. She got up and dug around for her baby Jesus and ran to the dresser, quick like a ninja. She opened the bottom drawer, moved aside some clothes, and stuffed Baby Jesus in a new, better hiding place. She was a criminal now. She knew it. She'd have to be more careful for nobody to find the evidence.

Mama seemed to shut down completely. She'd stay in bed until it was time for her to drive Rainey to work. She wouldn't talk. She'd look out the window for long, long periods of time and tear up at nearly everything . . . the grass growing, a bird chirping, the wind blowing.

Uncle Fritz would call the house and leave her messages saying, "Thought I'd stop by later on, see how you're doing." "Please call me back." "There's nothing we can't handle together. I'm your brother." "Please promise you'll call me before doing anything drastic."

At one point he came to the front door and knocked. "Don't answer that," Mama said in a hushed voice.

"But it Fritz," said Rainey.

"Rainey, please. Just do as your mother says."

After trying the doorknob and finding it

locked, Fritz walked back down to his car and looked at the house real sad-like before getting back in and driving off.

Later that day, Mama picked up the telephone. Rainey and I were at the kitchen table eating some grits that Mama forgot to salt and butter. Rainey's face looked funny as she tried to gum her way through her bowl. "Yuck," she said, and got up to get the butter herself. Mama walked out of the kitchen, the phone cord trailing behind her, and started talking real low. But I could hear her.

"Hi, this is Priscilla Macy. I need to make an appointment. Yes, I realize I canceled the other one, but I've changed my mind now."

Rainey cut two big chunks of butter from the stick and licked her lips as she plopped them in her steaming grits.

"Yes. I'm sure," said Mama. "Between eight and nine weeks. Thank you. Friday? That's . . . two days. Fine, I'll see you then."

Chapter Forty-three
A Purpose in Life

{Mona}

If there's one thing I've learned, it's this: our purpose in life has very little, if anything, to do with ourselves. Sadly, this is a fact most discover much too late. We spend our days making decisions that will better ourselves, our goals, our quality of life, only to find later that those same decisions are the ones we regret the most. This is not an easy lesson. I, in fact, learned it the hard way.

With no one else around to explain things to Janie, it had fallen upon me to teach her what I knew. I wasn't sure how Janie would accept the news about her role in the Macy family and the fact that she did, indeed, have a part to play in it. A very important part.

Now that Harlan had disappeared as I knew he would, and Priscilla had pushed Fritz away and had come up with the cockamamie idea that she had—that she could not bear her baby any longer—well, sure as the stars, I knew it was time again for me to get involved.

I found Priscilla whimpering and babbling one night in the dark. "Oh, dear Lord, there is nothing left for me to do. I'll have to get a job. I'll get a job so I can stick the baby in day care so that I can go to work to pay for the day care! I'll spend the rest of my days slopping pancakes while he's off riding Marilyn." I moved in and sat next to her. She stilled when I put my hand on hers. "Wouldn't it be more humane to . . . why would I want to bring a child into a world with no father, where people don't keep their promises . . . and the world is overcrowded anyway . . . and the terrorists, I mean, it's just a matter of time . . . war and sickness . . . not to mention . . ."

I rubbed her forehead and ran my hand along her crown. "Oh Priscilla, dear child. You are making the biggest mistake of your life if you do this. Or maybe second biggest. Third, counting Harlan—no, fourth, counting cutting your hair when you were younger."

I smiled in the darkness, but she rolled over and shunned me like she was doing everyone who loved her. I took the hint and exited quietly. For a moment, it felt like it did when she was a little girl, except back then she was in the green room. That feeling a mother, a parent, has, of leaving the room with a sleeping child safe behind its doors is like nothing else in the whole world. It's as if in those moments everything makes sense, seems manageable, is worth waking up for the next day. No matter what struggles the daylight will bring, it's that moment of exiting your child's room that refreshes a parent. Fortifies a mother.

But on this evening, middle of July, knowing the trouble my grown-up child had gotten herself into and knowing how hard it would be to dig her out, I walked heavy-footed out the door, the weight of the family on my shoulders. There was no happy feeling to be had.

I walked to the green room where the girls were supposed to be asleep, but when I peeked in, I saw Janie sitting straight up in the dark. Her back was to me and she was facing the faint light from the window. She was holding something in her hands and rocking.

Soon as the door creaked, Janie shuffled and stuck it—whatever it was—under the covers. Rainey was breathing heavy and slow. Janie turned my way.

"Just came to say good night. Wanted to check on you is all."

"I'm fine," she said.

"Janie."

"Huh?"

This was one of the toughest moments I could remember. I just needed to say the first words, to get started and build some momentum.

"Get on up and come with me, child. I've got . . . something to show you."

Chapter Forty-four
MIDNIGHT STROLL

{Janie}

It was nighttime. I barely ever went outside in the nighttime, and certainly never left home when I did it, but on this night, Grandma Mona was with me. I'm not sure why this made me feel better. She wasn't my favorite person, although I knew she loved me if only in her strange way. Family members have to love each other. It's a rule. Maybe having a grown-up say it was okay, no matter who it was, made it all right to be outside in the dark where damp air could make me catch cold and who-knew-what was waiting to grab me. But still. Something inside me knew a young girl never leaves the house in the middle of the night in a strange new town, even if it is to see something "of the utmost importance," like Grandma Mona had said it was.

We had no flashlight, so my eyes searched for any light they could find. The world was surprisingly blue after my eyes adjusted to the darkness. Everything looked different—our gingerbread house was just a dark structure no different from Mrs. Shoemaker's yellow one across the street or the other houses along Vinca Lane. We walked along the sidewalk with the quiet *click-brush, click-brush* of Grandma Mona's old lady shoes. I couldn't see the flowers in the sidewalk cracks. They'd become invisible along with everything I remembered this way. We were headed in the direction of the library and of Uncle Fritz's church.

"Where are we going?" I asked again.

I felt the long, hard fingers of Grandma Mona brush against me, then she took my hand and held it gently. I didn't pull away. The feel of her hand in mine brought back memories of Poppy's small, padded hand, how his heat would calm my soul. Somehow, maybe the simple act of connecting with another human being, even if it was Grandma Mona, was just what I needed now. I held her back, and we walked hand in hand.

"Oh Janie, I know this last month must have been difficult for you—your mother's big news, leaving home, coming here to Forest Pines, and to top it all off, your father. Not to mention Grayson. Oh, I know how close you were to your granddaddy. I'm real sorry for how sad it makes you, missing him the way you do. I miss him too, you know."

"But he's in heaven, and we'll see him again one day. Right?" I said this more to comfort my grandmother, but I found the saying of it to be a comfort for me as well.

"Yes. Absolutely," she said. "We will be with Poppy again one day. He's in heaven, and it's the finest place you ever want to go. Once you get there, you'll never wish to leave again."

"So where are we going now?" I asked one more time.

"Janie, you and I are taking a little walk to go visit with Poppy."

"Visit with Poppy? In heaven?"

"Well, what I mean is . . . some people find comfort in visiting the graves of their loved ones . . . after they're gone."

I stopped in my tracks, and Grandma Mona turned to face me. In the moonlight, I could see a glimmer in her eyes.

"Don't be afraid, child."

"But I don't like cemeteries. There's ghosts and stuff, and it's dark, and anyway, Poppy's not even there. He's in heaven. There's no reason to go, and especially no reason to go at night."

"Janie, I heard every word you said, and I know how you feel." She took my other hand and bent down lower to my face. "I'm going to ask you to trust me right now, and it's not the last time I'm going to ask you this. I know I haven't always seemed like the nicest person, but I love you. I always have. I love your Mama and Rainey, Fritz, and I still love Poppy, even though he's gone. But I need you to trust me right now. I am older than you. There are some things I know that you need to know. So we're going to the church right now. Not another word, please."

And with that we continued walking, and my mind filled with Poppy and headstones and Grandma Mona's eyes glittering in the moonlight. And how I shouldn't speak another word of protest. But my senses grew sharp in the darkness. I could hear the squeaking and flapping of bats, and my eyes searched out lights on front porches and streetlamps. Before I knew it, one foot had led after the other and I could see the well-lit words on the sign for Covenant Church.

A deep chill blew through me. We were here. In the dark. At a cemetery. There was no turning back.

I had never been to a church at night. It was strange how something so glorious-seeming in the day could seem scary and foreboding when the shadows swallowed all the bright-white places. I gripped Grandma Mona's hand tighter and we moved slowly around the church to the left. We walked right past the manger with the Mary, Joseph, and empty hay cradle. I was glad it was dark for just a second so Grandma Mona couldn't see what was missing.

The moon was almost full. Behind the church it illuminated the cemetery and the backs of tombstones, little squares dotting the ground, a tall cross every now and again, a tree, the sidewalks. After a minute or so I started squirming, and

Grandma Mona said, "Let it out, Janie. Take a deep breath."

I gasped and inhaled and coughed, inhaled again.

"You know, I've never been a believer in coming to visit graves," Grandma Mona said. We stood among the tombstones and she paused before taking the path to the left. "Not on a regular basis, anyway. Occasionally I'd come when there was a funeral or shortly thereafter, a couple times maybe, just to assure myself the person wasn't coming back. Like my first husband, William. I remember when I heard he'd passed away, your grandfather brought me and your Uncle Fritz to see his grave all the way in Louisiana just so we could say good-bye and have some closure. That's the kind of man your Poppy was."

"So we're coming here to say good-bye and have closure with Poppy? What's closure?"

"Closure is when you've closed that chapter in your life. When you can move on with your life instead of hanging on to the past and what was left behind there. It's a healthy thing to have closure. Lots of people don't ever get it. But no. We're not here to have closure, Janie."

"We're not?" I was usually smart and good at figuring out what grown-ups had to say, but here, I was stumped.

Grandma Mona put her hands on my shoulders

from behind. She pulled me into her legs and held me tight, wrapping her arms around me. I felt the heat of her all over the back of me, and the cool breeze blowing on my face. We stood there looking over Poppy's grave and all the others, and I felt like running. Then Grandma Mona said, "Oh child, you can say your final good-byes to Poppy. You can try to have some closure there. But what I'm about to tell you might change all that. Honey, we're here so I can tell you a ghost story."

I wondered if there could be anything worse than a ghost story in a graveyard. I craned my neck to look up at her but she didn't look at me, only at Poppy's tombstone. "But I don't want a ghost story," I said. "Not here. Please!"

"Oh honey, I wish it could be different. I do. But I'm afraid there's no other way."

I didn't dare say anything back to her after that. Fear had gripped me and wouldn't let me go.

Chapter Forty-five
FEELING IS BELIEVING

My eyes had adjusted to the darkness. The bright light from the moon cast deep shadows, turning everything white or black, no colors in between. Grandma Mona said, "The reason I brought you here, Janie, is there's something on Poppy's tombstone I want you to see. Like a clue."

"Like a mystery?"

"Exactly. Like a mystery. You're a detective, and you must find your first clue. Now this is what I want you to do. Bend down like I am, honey."

Grandma Mona took my right hand and placed it on the gravestone. I jerked it away. "It's okay," she said. "There's nothing to be afraid of."

"But I don't want to. Cain't we just come back in the morning when we can see?"

The moonlight on the back of the stone made it impossible to read the front.

"No, Janie. I'm sorry. Now, I want you to listen closely. Just because you are not able to see things hidden in the darkness, doesn't mean there aren't things hidden there just the same. I want you to touch this stone and tell me what you learn about it. There are some things you can only learn by feeling. Telling or seeing may not have the same effect."

"But what if there's snakes or something?"

"Janie . . ."

I whispered then, "Or what if a hand reaches out and grabs me?"

"Honey, that'll be my hand if you don't just do what I'm asking you. Now, come on. Be a brave girl and give me your hand."

Against my better judgment, I did just that. Grandma Mona took my hand, and with her fingers out flat and interlaced with mine, we felt the cold hardness of Poppy's tombstone. Along the top it was smooth and then an edge. We drifted down to the front of the stone and my fingers touched an indentation. I followed it around and recognized it as the letter *G*. Then we moved to the next letter and traced it, *R*. I knew what we were doing now. Rainey and I had played the letter-guessing game many times over the years when we were bored. One person would draw a letter with her finger on the other one's back. Then you'd have to guess what the other one was trying to say. We taught ourselves so much about letters and reading that way. I wished I was back at the house, drawing letters on Rainey's back.

Tracing Poppy's name filled me with sadness and wonder at the same time. How could an entire life be brought to this—a cold hard stone in the middle of a quiet field of stones? A name. No color at all, no hint at what a wonderful, kind, loving person my grandfather was.

I let Grandma Mona guide me. We finished *M-A-C-Y*, and I took a deep breath. I started to pull away, but she said, "There's more."

By this point, I had closed my eyes so I could heighten my sense of touch. The next letter I felt was a long skinny line, an *I*, maybe, or a lower-case *L*. The next letter I had to trace a couple times because I couldn't figure it out. I finally realized it was not a letter at all, but a number, 9. Next number, 2, then a 9 again.

"1929," I said.

"That's right. Poppy was born in 1929 at the start of the Great Depression."

We kept going. I felt a little horizontal line. "That's a dash," said Grandma Mona. "It means the expanse of time between then and now." We found some more numbers, this time 2, 0, and 0. I knew we were coming to the last digit of the year of Poppy's death. I had rather enjoyed imagining Poppy's birth and how long ago it was, but the death part had become difficult for me again. I pulled back and Grandma Mona said, "Just one more, honey. I promise. Just one more."

I figured it couldn't hurt, and it might help me to get closure. The stone crevices felt even colder beneath my fingertips. I found the last number and my finger started at the top, then swooped around and looped.

"What number is that?" asked Grandma Mona. "I'm not sure I made it out."

"That's easy," I said. "It's a six."

And as soon as I said it, I realized something was very, very wrong. "They messed up!" I said. "They messed up Poppy's tombstone!"

"Shhh," said Grandma Mona. "There was no mistake. The year is 2006."

"But . . . it's not right!"

"It's right, Janie. Remember I told you I was bringing you here to tell you a ghost story?"

Grandma Mona grew perfectly still, and I could hear the bats crying overhead, darting around desperate for food. "Your grandfather died after a long bout with cancer. He died, Janie, two years ago today."

Chapter Forty-six
THE SEER

{Mona}

What you must understand is, I never wanted any of this, *this* way. I never wanted to have to tell the child that her grandfather she knew and loved was not real in the sense that living, breathing, humans are real, but more along the lines of a happy apparition, a translucent loved one.

We had walked all night after leaving the cemetery. Janie was too wound up to go home and sleep, and rightly so. Every now and again a bird would chirp or a stray car would pass as the night wore on to morning. I knew Priscilla and Rainey were still at home sleeping for a little while yet.

"But how could he be here and we could talk to him and everything?" Janie asked. "I know Poppy was real. I just know he was! I'm not imagining!" She was trying her hardest to piece it all together.

"No, you weren't imagining things. Your grandfather really was here."

"But you said he died two years ago! Why, he came to see us for the first time—"

"Two years ago, correct."

"So, you're saying Poppy died and then came to live with us?"

"That is what I'm saying."

"But why? Why didn't he go straight up to heaven?"

My goodness, children have so many questions. "He came because your mother needed him. Plain and simple. She had unresolved feelings where her father was concerned. He died before she could settle those feelings. Sometimes people have a hard time letting loved ones go. They carry them around, bearing them."

"But he's gone now. Did he die again? Did Poppy die twice?"

"Shhh, shh." I took her hand in mine and squeezed it. "Oh no, Janie. Quite the opposite. He's alive and well up in heaven now."

"But why did he go? Why couldn't he just stay? I miss him."

We were getting ready to pass the Shoemaker house, so I brought my voice down a little. I didn't feel like running into Clarabelle if she happened to arise early.

"Do you remember the last time you saw your grandfather?" I asked her.

"Yes. He said good-bye to me on the porch. He was going to talk with Mama. Did she make him leave?"

"Sweetheart, your Mama never even knew he was there."

"She didn't?"

"Honey, I told you, he was there for her because she couldn't let him go. When she came to this house, your mother finally forgave Grayson for letting her go off into the world alone. And she finally forgave herself for not seeing him before he died. She made peace with your grandfather, honey. That's what set him free."

Janie was breathing heavy now, and I could hear her voice escalating to tears. "How could she not see him? How come I could see him? And you? And Rainey?"

She'd had enough for the night, so I told her truthfully, "There are some people who have the gift of seeing folks who've passed on. They're called seers. I suppose we're some of those people and your mother is not.

"Now come on, let's get you in the bed before you fall asleep walking. I know this is a lot to take in. Let's give it some time. We can talk about it all when you've digested it as much as you can. But remember this, Janie: Tell no one. Not your mother, not Rainey. Can you do that? It's our little secret."

Janie nodded and clasped my hand tighter.

Earlier in the night it had been all I could do to get her to leave the house with me, and here she was, clinging to me. It filled me with such joy, I . . . well . . . who could blame her for not wanting to be with me? I'd been awful to her and everybody else for so long. But finally I could drop my veil. I must say it felt good. We walked back into the house as allies that night, Janie and me, and I led her up the stairs to her bedroom where green light was beginning to spill over everything, the floor, the dresser, the beds. Rainey wasn't awake yet.

My little Janie hugged me before she got into bed, and I kissed her on the forehead, praying her mind could settle after what I'd filled it with. I was hoping with morning light that Janie had the strength I thought she did. Knowing her mama's state of mind, she was going to need every bit.

Chapter Forty-seven
RIPE FOR THE PICKING

{Janie}

I didn't want to sleep at all, but I couldn't help myself. When Rainey woke up, I stirred and heard her moving around, yawning. I tried to open my eyes but I was too tired. I remembered with a jolt the night at the cemetery, walking with Grandma Mona, the fact that my grandfather, the only man who ever really loved me, had been a ghost.

My eyes popped open and my mouth did the same. I started to say something to Rainey, but I stopped myself. Grandma Mona had told me to keep it a secret. Why, I didn't know. I slowly sat up and rubbed my neck. I stared down at my body and saw that I had walked to the graveyard in my pajamas. Then I realized, it was ridiculous to walk to a cemetery in the middle of the night in your pajamas. It must have all been a dream. Of course, it was a dream. My grandfather was a real, live human being. He loved me. He'd held my hand, hugged me, kissed me, just like Grandma Mona.

Grandma Mona was pulling my leg.

That was it. She was playing a cruel joke on me. Maybe she was getting even meaner in her old age. I'd watched it happen, more day by day, year by year.

I plopped back on my pillow. I was so tired I couldn't think straight.

"We pickin' peaches today," said Rainey, sliding her pajama bottoms off and replacing them with a pair of shorts. She struggled to pull her shirt off, and when she did, she just let everything hang out for all to see. I had to look away. Even though Rainey thought like a child most of the time, her body had turned into a woman's, and I didn't think it was right to watch her put on her brassiere and other grown-up-lady things.

"Mama say Fritz can come," she said, excited. "I gonna see Fritz." Then she finished dressing and grabbed some socks and tennis shoes, darting out the door. "Come on!"

I just grunted and rolled over. I was glued to the mattress. I lay there, thinking on all the things that had happened last night. All the things Grandma Mona had said. Then I realized something and sat straight up. She didn't say I couldn't tell Fritz. Or did she? She mentioned Rainey and Mama, but I'm pretty sure she left off Fritz. I sat up again and focused on the light from the window. I'd found the perfect loophole. I could talk to somebody about Poppy's being a ghost without actually breaking my promise.

Mama had made herself look nice for the first time in days. She had her hair brushed and makeup on, and she'd taken her time getting her lips placed just right. She wore a pretty flowered dress that tied in the back. She let the tie go loose as if her belly was growing bigger, but to be honest, I looked and couldn't see anything.

When the doorbell rang, Mama went to open it as nice and proper as she could. "Well, hello, Fritz. I hear there's a tree in the backyard just waiting to be plucked." She smiled a strange smile, like it wasn't really Mama smiling. She didn't say any apologies for not answering his calls or letting him in the house for days, and the whole thing just looked odd to me. I didn't understand grown-ups so well as I thought I did.

Fritz leaned in and she let him kiss her on the cheek. "Thanks for letting me come over," he said, which struck me as funny, seeing as a few weeks ago we were the ones he was inviting into this house. Now *he* was the guest. Fritz had a ball cap on, and he took it off his tall head and set it on a little table beside the front door.

"Uncle Fritz!"

"Hey, Fritz!" Rainey and I ran and hugged him. He was the only man we had left in our lives, and by goodness, we were gonna show him how much we cared so he might choose to stay and not run off.

Before we walked out back, Grandma Mona came down the stairs, and I saw her glaring at me. With her eyes, she was telling me not to say anything. I was telling her right back I needed to talk with her some more about this Poppy-being-a-ghost business. She looked away and said, "Hey there, Fritz. Good to see you, sweetie."

Then we all went to the kitchen to grab some pots and large plastic bowls for picking peaches.

"With your arm still tied up like that, Rainey, I tell you what we'll do. Let's set you a pot on this chair, and when you get a nice peach, you bring it over and put it in here. Okay?" Fritz was rubbing his hands together and seemed like he was having so much fun.

"Okay."

"This is gonna be fun!" I squealed, forgetting my troubles and enjoying being a kid for just a second. Mama was leaning against the trellis, white bowl in hand. She was watching Fritz with amusement.

"Your mama probably knows more about this tree and picking peaches from it than any of us. Right, Priscilla? Why don't you tell us some tips?"

"Oh, Fritz. I don't know any tips. You go ahead."

"Why, sure you do. Tell us about how we should pull the peach off. Should we pull it off the branch if it's hard to pull?"

Mama shook her head no.

"That's right, because if the peach doesn't come easily, it doesn't want to come. It means it's not ready yet. Here. Let me try this one. Yep. See that? Came off real easy. These are the kind you want."

"Like this?" Rainey reached up and grabbed a peach on the tree and pulled it. She got it, but her thumb went right on through.

"Now, hold on, Rainey. Remember what you know about bagging groceries? Are peaches hard or are they soft?"

"Soft," said Rainey, grinning and licking the peach juice off her thumb.

"That's absolutely right. What you wanna do is use this part of your fingers, not the tips, all right?"

Rainey nodded and I did too.

"Okay then. The only thing left to remember is to set the peaches down gently in our bowls and pots, and if you fill one up, let me know. I'll grab you another container."

For being late July, the air was steamy hot as it wore on to lunchtime. My bowl was mostly empty, seeing as I couldn't find any peaches that wanted to come off the tree. Rainey was going to town, though, and I suspected some of hers weren't ripe either, but she pulled them anyway. Fritz was up high on a ladder picking all the peaches on top.

I saw Grandma Mona sitting in the rocking chair next to Mama. The warm breeze kicked up real nice, and the two of them sat there quietly just rocking and rocking. I wanted so bad to talk to Grandma Mona some more about Poppy, but she was beside Mama, and Mama wasn't supposed to know. I thought about climbing the ladder and grabbing Fritz's ear, but Grandma Mona was watching me like a hawk. The novelty of picking peaches had worn off. I was getting sleepy again because I might have had only three minutes of sleep all night. I yawned, and Grandma Mona said, "Don't fall asleep now, Janie. The fun part's about to begin. After picking, there's cutting and freezing and making pie and ice cream."

I said, "Yes, ma'am." And it surprised me that I'd called her *ma'am*. It's the first time in a long time I'd shown her any real respect. I figured if Grandma Mona wasn't lying and actually did know all sorts of secrets about ghosts and life and death, she might be somebody I wanted on my good side.

I was aiming to keep her that way.

Chapter Forty-eight
FRESH PEACH ICE CREAM

Mama, Rainey, and Fritz stood at the kitchen counter like it was an assembly line. Rainey would rinse a peach with her good arm and then hand it to Fritz who dried it off. He would then pass it along to Mama who cut it into pieces and put the pieces in a big yellow bowl. I sat at the table with my head on my arms, trying not to fall asleep.

But actually, I did fall asleep, and when I woke up, the line had disassembled, and Fritz and Rainey were laughing and eating ice cream cones on the back porch.

"Well, sure enough, you missed all the fun," said Grandma Mona.

"But you're the one"—I lowered my voice to a whisper—"you're the one who kept me up all night."

"Here, honey, why don't you try some ice cream? They made it fresh." Grandma Mona had a little bowl right in front of her and stuck a spoon in it. She reached across the table and held it up to my lips. Dutifully, I opened my mouth.

"Now, is that not the best peach ice cream you've ever tasted?"

"Mm-hm." The coldness of the cream woke my senses up.

"Are those the most delicious peaches you've ever had, Janie?"

She fed me another bite, and I licked my lips and said yes they were.

Then Grandma Mona got a strange, wide look in her eye. I swallowed hard because she'd had this same look on her face the night before in the moonlight. At the cemetery. "What's your favorite fruit, Janie? Peaches, strawberries, or blueberries?"

It seemed such an odd question. "Um . . . I don't know. All of them, I guess."

"Not all of them," said Grandma Mona. "Tell me one. Which one do you like the best? Hmm?"

"Peaches, okay? Peaches are my favorite."

Grandma Mona frowned, and her eyes teared up. "Janie, honey. Look right here. You see this bowl of ice cream?"

She pushed it toward me and I told her I did, but really I was getting mighty tired of her strange old-lady games.

"What you just ate was strawberry ice cream, honey. It wasn't peach at all, it was some strawberry left over in the fridge. Now, come on, child, it's time for us to talk. Grab you a pencil and a piece of paper. What I have to say might take a little while."

I followed Grandma Mona up the staircase, my mind and body struggling to keep up with her. I stopped and looked at each and every Macy family portrait. Adolph Macy, Madeline Macy, Great-Aunt Gertrude, who was supposed to be a ghost but I never actually saw, and Poppy, who was supposed to be alive but was actually a ghost. I sighed. At eight-and-a-half-years-old, I thought I knew pretty much everything. The amount of things I didn't know was beginning to add up and make my head feel funny.

We walked toward Mama's room, and Grandma Mona motioned for me to be quiet and tiptoe, so I did. Her bedroom door was closed but I could hear her talking on the other side.

". . . to your place by three. Can you drive me over there? No, she'll be at the grocery store. That should give me enough time to rest and come back and pick her up."

"She's talking to Alisha," whispered Grandma Mona. "She's going to the doctor tomorrow."

"She's going to the doctor for the baby?"

"She's going for the baby, yes." Grandma Mona

took a deep breath and said, "Come on in my room, sweetie."

I wasn't used to her calling me sweetie. It made me feel all upside down. I'd read the book about *Alice in Wonderland* and wondered if I'd fallen down a hole somewhere, unbeknownst to me. I did what Grandma Mona said, and we went to her room and climbed up on the high four-post bed. The tree quilt was lying on top, and I couldn't help but notice it, admire it again.

"Did you sew this?" I asked.

"I did. It shows our lineage. I started it after Priscilla was born. See here? There's your great-great-grandfather Beecham. He was Adolph's father. And over here, this shows my side of the family, the Briggses."

I looked at all the tiny names stitched into the quilt. There were no faces, but for each family member an orange fruit hung on a branch.

"Now go ahead and pull out your paper. I want you to make up a list. You're real good at making lists, just like your mama."

"A list for what?" I asked.

"A list of clues."

"Clues for what?"

"A mystery."

"But Grandma Mona, what's the mystery?" I whined.

"Don't take that tone with me, Janie. This is not easy for me, either. Now, once you have written all the clues, you will know what the mystery is. You will also have your answer to that mystery."

For someone who kept a little girl up at all hours of the night only to throw riddles in her face, I thought Grandma Mona had finally gone off the deep end. But my curiosity was piqued, so I played along.

"Okay." I sat there, hand above blank paper. "What's the first clue?"

I wrote *Mystery* and a question mark at the top of the page and put a number 1 beneath it.

"I told you the first clue last night. At the cemetery."

Hearing her admit that we were actually there sent a chill up my spine. I was beginning to imagine it was all in my head. "Um . . . the first clue was on Poppy's tombstone?"

"Yes, and what was that clue?"

"That he died two years ago? That he was a ghost?" It sounded ridiculous, saying it out loud.

Grandma Mona nodded and motioned for me to write it down. I added next to the number 1, *Poppy was a ghost*. Below it, I added the number 2.

Grandma Mona was looking over at the clock on the wall above the dresser. It was an old-fashioned kind with the pendulum that swung back and forth. I listened to the *tick, tick* and noticed it was almost two o'clock. Grandma Mona sighed and said, "Good. Now what else do you notice in here?"

I looked around the room and said, "I don't know. Can't you just tell me the next clue?"

"What did I tell you about telling you things? You have to feel things, see things for yourself in order to understand." She was starting to get huffy, but she cleared her throat and went on softer. "I'm sorry, honey. I'm usually not under such pressure, but right now I am. I've got a lot to do and a little time to do it. Now, I need you to pay your best attention. Can you do that for me?"

I told her I could, so we went on.

"Now. How 'bout back there at the peach picking. How did it go?"

"Okay, I guess. But I didn't get any peaches. Rainey got a bunch."

"How come you didn't get any peaches, Janie?"

"Mine weren't ripe. They didn't come off easy. I think Rainey was just pulling any old which-a-one."

"I think it was your second clue," she said. "Now, write it down."

"Write what down?"

"That you didn't get any peaches."

Here, I was convinced that Grandma Mona was having a seizure or a stroke of some sort. A great dementia had settled in with the cool night air from the graveyard. I was starting to worry about her, but I wrote down, *Got no peaches* by number 2 anyway, to make her happy.

"Good, good. Now grab your paper and pencil and let's go for a little walk."

"Back to the cemetery? 'Cause I don't want—"

"No, no." She seemed mighty distracted. "We're going on a scavenger hunt."

"Is it a scavenger hunt we're playing or a mystery?" I said it all smarty-like.

She glared at me with clear gray eyes and said, "Mind your manners, child. I know I'm not very good at this. Now, follow me. There are lives at stake."

Chapter Forty-nine
UNDER PRESSURE

{Mona}

They should have given this job to someone else. I didn't think we were making it very far very fast, but I was doing the best I could. Honest. And time was running out. Why, the way things were looking these days, I had no guarantee I'd even be here tomorrow. An old woman must thank her stars for every single morning. I'd learned early on not to take time for granted, that there are forces in the universe unbeknownst to us, working, conspiring . . . I was just happy to still be there in the old house. I'd never felt such urgency.

Janie and I walked out front and turned left onto

the sidewalk. She looked up at me with wary eyes. I could tell she was considering whether I was trustworthy or not. I had to remember to keep my patience with her. I had to remember she was only a child.

"How come we can't let Rainey come on our scavenger hunt?" she asked.

"Because Rainey is spending time with Fritz right now. She needs that."

"But I wanna play with Fritz too. I like him."

"I know you do, honey. I know you do."

I took Janie's hand in mine and we walked. We walked past trees hanging over the sidewalk. We walked past azalea bushes that had bloomed and already withered. We walked past all the houses of the people who lived here once upon a time, the people Priscilla played with as a child, and their parents, moved, scattered all over the earth and heaven by now.

About six houses down, I started to slow. Janie looked over the lawn of a large gray house with bright-white trim. She pointed and said, "There's the tree Rainey fell out of."

"Why, look at that. It sure is," I said. "She's lucky she didn't break her neck and kill herself, isn't she? Look how high it is."

"She's lucky? What about me? I don't even remember coming down! I could've broken my neck too!"

"But you didn't," I said.

"But I could have."

"But you didn't. Hmm. I think we might have us another clue."

"We do?"

"Mm-hmm. Write down that you didn't break your neck coming down out of that tree, and Rainey didn't either." Janie looked at me, eyes wide, and did just that.

"Good girl. Now, because you've been such a good sport, I'm just going to give you your fourth clue flat out."

She kept her pencil poised and stared up at me, eyebrows raised. "Well?"

"You thought you were eating peach ice cream earlier today when it was really what?"

"Strawberry," she said. Janie hesitated, then put her paper and pencil down. She closed her eyes, took half a breath, and said, "Grandma Mona, I don't mean any disrespect, but I don't see where you're going with all this. It's a mistake anybody could have made, strawberries, peaches . . . I'm just so tired today."

"Just write it down," I said. "I've only two more clues to give to you. But for this, we've got to turn around and go back. And sometimes that's the hardest part."

Chapter Fifty
SAVING EARTHWORMS

{Janie}

I had always known Grandma Mona to be mean, meaner than a snake on white-hot asphalt. But I'd never thought of her as being crazy. Until now.

Every list I'd ever made had been helpful in some way. A list of Rainey's toys so she could catalogue them and put them away in an organized fashion. A list of the birds that flew in the hollow tree behind our house in Cypresswood, so we could tell if the new bird feed was working or not. And, of course, the list of options I'd made for Mama and her baby troubles. But this was the strangest list I'd ever made. There were clues to questions I didn't even know. I had played along, but my eyes were closing even as my legs were walking.

"Grandma Mona, can I go take a little nap, please? Maybe we can finish this list a little later."

Grandma Mona just kept on walking. She was wearing a slightly different dress than yesterday, green with ivy crawling all over it. All of her dresses were flowerdy and old-lady-like. Through the slits of my eyelids, she glowed green like the light in our bedroom.

"There'll be plenty of time for rest later, dear."

She hurried her steps and I struggled to keep up.

I yawned and said, "All right, but where are we going now?" As I said it, we walked right past our blue gingerbread house. Napping was out of the question.

"We're going to see Mrs. Shoemaker. Do you know who that is?"

"The old lady who sits on the porch of the yellow house?"

"That's the one."

"But she's mean. And I thought you didn't get along with her."

"She's mean, yes. And once upon a time, we had our differences. But that's pretty much past now."

"What happened?"

Grandma Mona stopped in the sidewalk and assessed me. Then she kept walking and turned her head straight forward. "Her daughter was a year or two older than Priscilla," she said, "and I didn't want my girl around hers. Plain and simple. I thought she was loose and bad news. Said so, too, and my words wound up getting back to Clarabelle's ears. I guess I'm the one who ended up with egg on my face."

"Mama's not loose," I said defensively, not really knowing what it meant. "She's certainly not bad news."

"Oh honey, I know she's not. I didn't mean . . . see? My big mouth always gets me into trouble. Just keep your mouth shut, Mona, keep it shut."

Now she was talking to herself. Wonderful. We

walked in silence for a few seconds more. I could see the yellow house getting larger as we approached it. "What happened to Mrs. Shoemaker's daughter?" I whispered.

"Nothing much. She married an accountant. Had a nice quiet life, I reckon, until they divorced. Far as I know she never had any kids. Lives alone in that big house. With her mother now."

"Oh. Does Mrs. Shoemaker know we're coming over?"

"Well, we'll just have to see, now, won't we?"

When we got up to the yellow house, I couldn't believe my eyes. Earthworms, curled like question marks, littered the driveway. "Look!" I said. I bent down and studied them. I'd never seen so many in my life.

"She must be overwatering her lawn. If there's too much water in the soil, they'll drown. They come up to the surface so they won't die."

"But it's getting hot now and dry. They're dying!"

I heard Grandma Mona go stiff beside me. "Clarabelle," she said, nodding slightly.

"Mona," said Mrs. Shoemaker, nodding back. It was like watching the standoff in a western movie. I wondered which old woman would pull her gun first. Mrs. Shoemaker was sitting in a new porch swing with a long hard bench that had replaced the strange-looking net one from before. She brought the swing to a halt.

"Your daughter's watering the lawn too much," said Grandma Mona.

"What she does with her grass or anything else is her business," said Mrs. Shoemaker. I could feel the heat between these two. "What brings you by on a hot Thursday afternoon, Mona? I see you brought your grandbaby with you."

I was waiting, just waiting for Mrs. Shoemaker to say something about my sister again. I was preparing what I'd say to put her in her place.

"I did, Clarabelle. I believe you've met Janie already?"

"We've been introduced," said Mrs. Shoemaker. "Hello again."

"Hi," I said.

"We were just going for a little walk," said Grandma Mona. "I'm . . . we're learning some new things today, and I had something I needed to tell Janie. I needed a witness and sadly, you fit the bill."

"A witness. Is that right? You've called me some pretty colorful things over the years, Mona, but this is a new one. You've got my attention. Let the witnessing commence."

"Excuse me," I said, "but do you think we could get some of these earthworms off the ground now? They're dying."

"Might have to run go get your sister for a job like that," said Mrs. Shoemaker.

"What's that supposed to mean?" I put my

hands on my hips. Mrs. Shoemaker laughed at me. She plumb laughed at me, and I started fuming. "You mean 'cause my sister's special she's only suited for scooping up worms? Is that what you mean?"

"My goodness, Mona, she is the spittin' image of you, I tell you what."

Grandma Mona took my arm and pulled me to her. "Please, Clarabelle. Just give us a minute." Grandma Mona looked in my eyes, and the sunlight formed a ring around her. I could barely see straight. I used my other hand to rub my eyes.

She smiled. "Janie. Do you have any idea how much I love you?"

I looked down at my feet, at those dying earthworms.

"Well, do you?"

"I guess."

"You guess. I want you to *know*. I want you to know that everything I've ever done was to protect you and your sister and your mama. Look up at me now."

I did as she said. Her eyes were watering. She put her hands on either side of my face. "Oh, honey, never in a million years would I have told you any of this, but I have to now. You're our only hope. Honey, I have another clue for you. I want you to write this down now. Go ahead."

I pulled my pencil and paper out of my pocket and looked at all its craziness.

"Now write exactly what I tell you. Grandma Mona . . ."

Grandma Mona, I wrote dutifully.

". . . is . . ."

is

Part Four

THE CHOICE

Chapter Fifty-one
SPEAKING THE TRUTH

{Mona}

There are certain things little girls should never hear of. Childhood should be childhood through and through. There should never be any thought of troubles, of war, of fornication, of any adult thing that might taint a young mind and take the gentleness out of childhood. But for some children, too many children, there is no such luck. As a very wise man I was once married to used to say, *Wishing something just doesn't make it so.*

Standing there in that worm-filled driveway, I told Janie the truth about me. Ironically, my archnemesis in life was my only ally that day. Much to my regret.

Janie dropped her pencil. She looked up at me, swayed, and I thought she might be about to faint.

"It's true," said Clarabelle Shoemaker. "I know it for a fact."

"But . . . it's impossible," said Janie. She was beginning to tear up. "She's here. We're here. Talking."

"As God is my witness," said Clarabelle, rocking again and pointing to the sky. "Oh how 'bout that? A witness calling a Witness." She chuckled, and I grabbed Janie's hands.

"Come on, Janie," I said. "Let's try to help

these worms now. Come on down here with me."

Janie was glazed over. She was staring from me to Clarabelle, then down at the ground. She was in slow motion, and knowing what the truth was doing to her hurt me down to my core. I wanted to scream and cry at the sky, *Why? Why should a child ever have to go through this?!*

But I didn't. Instead, I said, "Come on, sweetie. Let's pick up these worms now. They're dying."

Janie shook her head and bent down on all fours. She went to pick up a squirming worm. She couldn't quite get her fingers on it. "Janie, I'm having a dickens of a time. Aren't you?"

Janie struggled, convinced the worm was stuck to the ground. She went for another and then another. To no avail. "I cain't pick them up!" she fretted. Then she began crying.

"I can't either," I said. The time had come. There was no more room for stalling.

"Honey, in your heart you already know why I can't pick up these earthworms to save them. But do you know why you can't? Do you know now, honey? Do you understand?"

Clarabelle stood up on her front porch and in all her meanness, blurted it out. I knew there was a special place in hell for her. I watched helplessly as the old woman threw her arms wide, and for all the world to hear, she belted, "Because you're a ghost, too, Janie! You're a ghost, your grandma's a ghost, and even me. Boo!"

Chapter Fifty-two
FLOWERS IN THE SIDEWALK

{Janie}

There were no words. I was in a bad dream. I wanted to wake up, but there was no waking up from this. The sky around me dimmed as if the lights may flick out any second. I saw Mrs. Shoemaker standing on the front porch. She looked much younger—maybe it was her daughter there. On my knees, surrounded by earthworms and question marks, I looked over at Grandma Mona, who was crying. Her eyes were bluer than just a minute ago and her hair was no longer gray, but blonde. Her wrinkles had erased themselves like magic.

"You're . . ." I reached out to touch her face, and she took my hand. She pressed her lips in my palm and kissed it, then took my fingers and ran them along her wet cheeks. "Can you see me, dear? Can you see me?"

"You're young," I said, my knees failing me.

"Yes, I am."

"And so is she." I pointed to Mrs. Shoemaker, who was doing a little jig on the steps. She couldn't have been over fifty years old, when before she'd looked nearly eighty.

Grandma Mona said gently, "You've got new

eyes now, sweetheart. Now that you know. You can see us clearly. You can see us as we really are."

"But I don't understand! Mrs. Shoemaker said you're a ghost. And she's a ghost. And I'm a ghost! Is everybody a ghost? Is nobody real?!"

Grandma Mona pulled me up from the drive and put her arm around me. She held me up as we started walking slowly back down the drive. "Oh, Janie. There's no real ghost here . . . except, maybe her." Grandma Mona turned back and said, "We'll just be going now, Clarabelle. If I don't run up to thank you personally, don't take offense."

"Oh, none taken, Mona. None taken a'tall. Y'all just run along. Enjoy this fine summer day. And give my best to your daughter now."

I was shredded inside. I didn't know what to do, how to act, what to say. I was amazed my feet kept moving along, not making me fall over, for surely I wasn't thinking straight enough to make them move on my own.

"Last night you said Poppy was a ghost," I said, the words coming out slow as if in a dream.

"You're right," said Grandma Mona. "I said that so you might begin to understand. But he wasn't a ghost, not really. Ghosts are generally thought of as, well, people like Great-Aunt Gertrude, who stay here on earth in agony over something they've done or lost or regret. But

306

Poppy, he wasn't that way. He was a ministering spirit—brought here for your mother. We are all spiritual beings, Janie. Every single person, living or not. We are spirits, souls, first and foremost. Some spirits have earthly bodies wrapped around them. Others do not."

"Are you a spirit?" I asked.

"I am."

"Am I . . . a spirit?"

"You are, Janie. You are a beautiful spirit."

"Is Rainey a beautiful spirit?"

"Absolutely. The most beautiful. Just as pretty as you."

"So . . . we're all the same?"

"No. I'm afraid we're not all the same."

I looked up at Grandma Mona again and was startled at how young and pretty she was. I couldn't believe how much she looked like my mama, same blue eyes, same pretty hair.

"How come some spirits have earth bodies and some don't?" I asked.

"Because a person is born into this world with an earthly body. And when the body dies, the spirit goes on, sometimes to heaven, sometimes not."

I stopped under the shade of a crape myrtle and looked at the swaying blossoms. I whispered to Grandma Mona, "Are you . . . dead?" I couldn't believe the sound of my voice—that these words were actually coming out of my mouth. That this was actually a conversation two people might have on the sidewalk in Forest Pines.

"No," said Grandma Mona. "I'm not dead. But my earthly body did die . . . once."

"When?"

"Oh, nearly sixteen years ago, March. About the time I moved in next door to your mama."

"And Mama?"

"Oh no, she's very much alive."

"And Rainey?"

"Rainey's fine. She's full of life and then some."

"And . . . me?"

"Come here, sugar." Grandma Mona reached in and hugged me tight. We rocked back and forth, back and forth, and I was surprised at how strong she felt. "Janie, you are my angel."

Into her dress I breathed, terrified, "But am I dead too?"

Grandma Mona pulled away from me and bent down on her knees right there on the sidewalk filled with cracks and flowers bursting through.

"You . . ." She smiled and brushed a tear away. "You, Janie Doe Macy, my sweet child, my sweetest grandbaby—"

"Grandma Mona? Please?"

"Honey," she said, and she started bawling like I'd never seen her. "You were never even given a chance, child. You were never even born."

Chapter Fifty-three
THE GHOST OF
GREAT-AUNT GERTRUDE

I didn't know what to believe. I surely felt alive, no different than I always had. I broke free from Grandma Mona who was calling after me. I ran faster than I ever had, back up to the house, in the door. "Mama?!" I looked in the sewing and dining rooms. I ran in the kitchen and saw no dishes, only some peaches left sitting on paper towels on the counter. Everything was cleaned up, no sign of ice cream.

"Mama?"

I ran out back and looked in the garden, at the trellis, under the peach tree, on the rockers, but no one was there. I came back inside and called again, louder, "Ma-*ma!*"

I heard a faint "here." I flew up the stairs and looked in Mama's bedroom and ours and the other two, frantically darting here and there, and then I stopped and got quiet. I heard my own breath. I heard something else too. Voices.

Looking up at the attic stairs, I leapt and took them two at a time, and when I got to the door I stood there, staring.

"Hey, Janie," said Rainey. She grinned and waved. She was sitting cross-legged on the floor of the attic with a photo album across her knees.

Mama and Fritz were near her, Mama bent over a box and Fritz flipping pages of another album.

"Mama?" I said. She didn't turn around. "Mama, Grandma Mona said something awful!" I ran to her side and grabbed her arm. I looked up in her face, but she was riffling through a big box. "She said you carried me for two months and then . . . Mama, she said you never let me be born!"

Mama pulled out a large photograph of Grandma Mona and said, "My goodness. Take a look at this one."

She handed it to Fritz, and he said, "Wow. You look so much like her." He looked back and forth from the picture to Mama. "Yep. This is the one. I'll get a frame for it. We can hang it right by your daddy next week."

"But Mama!" I shook her arm, but she never stirred. Never acted like she heard me at all. Fritz didn't seem to notice me neither.

"Janie." I turned around and saw Grandma Mona looking very much like the photograph Fritz was holding, the one that was going up on the dead wall soon. It was true. Grandma Mona was dead.

"Honey, I'm so sorry," said Grandma Mona. "They can't hear you, baby. They don't know . . . you're here."

"But I am here!" I screamed. "I'm right here!"

Rainey stuck her good hand over her ear and

used her knee to cover the other one. She started rocking back and forth. "It's okay, okay," she said.

"Mama!!!" I'd never been so angry and confused. I grabbed a small glass frame of Poppy and threw it across the room. It hit the wall right next to the window and shattered.

Fritz and Mama jolted and turned to look.

"Did you see that?" Mama asked Fritz. She looked over at Rainey, who still had her hand and knee over her ears. "Honey?"

Rainey rocked and rocked and started humming a tune to calm herself down.

"Fritz?" He was standing over by the window with the small frame in his hands. The glass was broken.

"If I didn't see it myself, I wouldn't believe it," said Fritz. "My goodness. Maybe Gertrude really is here. Uh, Gertrude? We don't mean any harm, okay? My goodness, I never thought I'd be saying something like that."

I watched in horror as the person I loved most in the world paid me no attention at all. In fact, she seemed frightened of me. It was true. My mother didn't know I existed. I was no different to her than the ghost of Gertrude, except that Gertrude had actually been alive once.

Chapter Fifty-four
THE FAMILY TREE

"Try not to upset Rainey," said Grandma Mona after she'd coaxed me down from the attic and into her bedroom. "She's the only one who can see us. To her, we're normal family, and nothing else."

My speech had left me. My head was a tornado. Grandma Mona crawled up on the bed and patted a place next to her. I moved close in slow motion, and she hoisted me up, letting me lie in her lap. I felt her legs, her warmth, and tears stung my eyes. Lying there, I realized Mama's lap had never felt warm like this, only there beneath me. I ran my hand over Grandma Mona's knee and held it there, feeling our heat. She said, "There, there now. I know this is difficult for you. I know it is. But you're doing great. I'm so proud of you. And Janie?"

She was waiting for me to look up at her, but I couldn't.

"Janie, honey, I hope you can forgive me . . . for all the things I've said . . . the way I've acted. I know you don't understand, but I'm not a great liar. The only way I could keep the truth from you was to put distance between us. And the only way I knew how to do that was to be mean, just like my mother was to me. It may not have been right, but it's all I could come up with. And heaven knows, for your sake, for everyone's, you couldn't learn who you were until now."

I looked up at her then. Tears were rolling off her face and onto mine.

"You and I were so close once upon a time. We did everything together. Read, walked, laughed. Do you remember? But darn it, you're just too smart of a girl. I knew you'd figure something out, pull the truth out of me if I let you be close to me. Honey, I hope you can forgive me. It's all been a horrible but necessary act. I love you more than there are stars in the sky. I'd do anything for you, for Rainey, and for your mother."

Outside in the hallway, we could hear Fritz, Mama, and Rainey coming down the stairs, and Mama telling Rainey to clean up, it was almost time for supper. Next thing I knew, there was a knock at the door, and Rainey came in. Her bottom lip stuck out when she saw me crying.

"Janie sick," she said, looking from me to Grandma Mona. She came over and petted my head, and I felt pressure from her, but no heat. Again, the tears.

"She's not feeling real well, honey. You go on down and have some supper. You're working at the grocery store in a little while, right?"

"Uh-huh. We havin' noodles."

"Oh, noodles. That sounds very good."

Rainey bent down and put her face in mine. Her

eyes smiled at me. "I go tell Mama you sick." Then she skittered out and down the steps.

Part of me waited for Mama to come up and check on me, and part of me knew that just wasn't going to happen. I sat up a little and stared at the family tree quilt. I noticed something I hadn't before, as if my eyes had only just opened. "Rainey's got a peach," I said. "She's a real girl. Her name is there and everything. I don't have a peach. I'm not a real girl."

"You're real," said Grandma Mona. "You're only—"

"My own mother thinks I'm just Rainey's invisible friend." It was the worst thing I'd ever known. I waited for her to say I was wrong, but instead she stayed silent. "Why am I here?" I said finally. My whole world ground to a halt.

Grandma Mona looked at me with her blue eyes so much like Mama's and said, "You're here because she needs you."

"Rainey?"

"Your mother."

"She doesn't need me. She didn't even want me born. She doesn't even know I'm here."

"You are here, Janie, because your mother feels the void of your loss. Because she regrets what she did eight and a half years ago."

"By kill—"

"By not letting you be born. That's correct."

"She did abortion on me."

314

"She did that. Yes."

I thought I might be ill, thinking of how I was no different than those dead babies I'd seen in the library. I closed my eyes and pressed my face into the quilt, hoping I could just quit breathing. It felt like so much effort.

"Mama doesn't love me." My face scrunched up and Grandma Mona grabbed me in her arms. She held me tight.

"She does love you. She just . . . realized it too late. Honey . . . I was there." She pushed me away and held my shoulders. She bore down into my soul with her eyes. "I was there! I tried to stop her. Oh, Janie, you don't know how hard it was. She was convinced your father would leave her if he found out she was pregnant. It was all she thought she could do at the time . . . for herself, for Rainey, so she could have a father in her life. Honey, I tell you the truth, the moment she did it she knew she'd made the biggest mistake of her life. She realized she loved you, honey, in the instant you were gone. I held you in my arms, and I've loved you as my own from that second on. You have always been loved. I promise you that!"

"You raised me," I said, the truth of it heavy on my heart.

"I did. With Rainey. To her, you've always been her baby sister. You see, Rainey is special in many ways. Her heart is pure. Her faith is simple. She doesn't get bogged down with what should

315

be and what shouldn't . . . what is possible or not. She can see us and love us because she has no barriers between earthly and spiritual matters. It's as if there is a window between us, and Rainey can see right through it. Most people are blinded, but she is not. It's her gift."

I ran out of the room and hurried down the stairs. "Wait, Janie!" Grandma Mona ran after me and caught me in the living room. She held her arms tight around me. I was peeking around the corner at Mama serving Rainey noodles. There were only two bowls on the table. Only two. Sadness swept over me. How could I have been so blind all my life? To have seen only what I wanted to see? How could I not know my own mother ignored me? Were there other children out there just like me? Children who had no idea they didn't even exist?

Rainey slurped some spaghetti. She laughed and got red sauce all over her face. Mama sat there, barely picking at her dinner. She looked over toward us, and I hoped she might see me, but she looked away again. It was true. Rainey was the only living person who knew me. I started thinking about Rainey and me. How we'd always played together. How she'd treated me just like any other kid. She'd loved me unconditionally even though *I* was the special one. I remembered how she would tell Mama to kiss me good night. She'd ask for the night-light only because she knew *I* was afraid of the dark. She'd say things about me, and Mama would humor her. *Good night, Janie. What a pretty dress, Janie.* Mama never even saw me. She was playing along with whatever Rainey had said. My whole life had been a lie.

"I've been in Rainey's life since the very beginning too. I died a week after she was born," Grandma Mona whispered in my ear. "In a car accident. Your mother has mixed feelings about that. She's always been angry at me and missing me at the same time. It's a terrible way to feel."

"It's how I feel about Mama," I said. "Angry. And missing her."

"Yes, I suppose it is."

"But why was Mama angry at you?" I asked.

"Oh, now . . . that is the toughest part of all of this." Grandma Mona took me by the hand and led me back up the stairs to her bedroom. I went willingly. Watching Mama just made me hurt.

Grandma Mona and I stood in front of her window. I looked up at her, but she kept her eyes on the sky. "I'm ashamed to say this, especially to you, but you need to understand." She squeezed my left hand. "Many years ago in Yuma, my mistakes started flooding over me. I thought the most painful thing in the world was to give your baby away, and when Priscilla told us she was pregnant, well, I wanted to spare her that. I told her to have an abortion. I thought I was protecting my

317

child. I told her she was wasting her life. That nobody had to know a thing. Your mother left home to save Rainey's life. To get away from me. And I'm glad she did. As soon as I heard about Rainey being born, I was sorry I'd ever suggested not having her. But by then it was too late. I'd pushed your mother away. I died on the road, Janie—on my way to tell her how sorry I was."

Chapter Fifty-five
THE SPIRIT-FILLED LIFE

Evening had come and the sky was filling with dim stars. I'd never been so tired in my life, but Grandma Mona was keeping me awake. It was torture being stuck in her bedroom, stuffing her square, jagged words into my round-peg head. My head hurt. My heart hurt worse. We were sitting on the floor, propped up against the four-post bed. It was the longest day I'd ever had.

"So where did Poppy go for real?" I asked.

"Up to heaven," said Grandma Mona. "I told you that."

"But if we're—why—"

"Because your mama made peace with her daddy. In the process, she set him free."

"But why are *you* still here?" I asked.

"Because Priscilla hasn't made her peace with me yet. She hasn't made it with you, either. Honey, let me explain something." She took my face in her hand and turned me toward her. I pulled free and laid my head on her shoulder, taking in a deep breath.

"You know how I was saying that everyone is a spirit, a soul?" she asked.

"Uh-huh."

"Well, every soul has a big hole, a void to be filled. Like a puzzle. Do you know what the hole is for?"

"No." I was eight-and-a-half-years-old, for goodness' sake. Up till then, I'd been pleased to know that magic cicadas rise up after seventeen years. Or that mockingbirds sing other birds' songs. This soul-talk was much too much for me.

"Human souls have a hole that needs to be filled up. But a person can fill that hole with one of two things . . . either the Holy Spirit, which is what God promises to believers, or the spirits of ghosts. You mother lives a spirit-filled life, yes, but with the wrong spirits. It's a common mistake. Until she is filled with the one true Holy Spirit from God, she will always hold onto something—you, me, anger, regret, loss."

"So she's only holding on to us because she hasn't made peace with us? Is she gonna make peace with us like she did with Poppy?"

"I don't know, Janie. She might. I certainly hope so."

"But then—"

"Then we'll be set free too. We'll be free to go up

319

to heaven. It's what I've been waiting years for."

"So I have to leave Mama? I don't want to leave Mama! I don't wanna leave!"

"She doesn't know you're here, Janie!" Grandma Mona grabbed my wrists but held me with her eyes. "I know how much you love her, but she doesn't know you at all. All she knows is she grieves over you, every day of her life. I know how she feels. I used to feel the same about giving Fritz away. Honey, don't you want your mama to be happy?"

"Well, yes, but—"

"If and when she makes peace with what she did to you, her grieving will be more bearable. She might be able to move on with her life. Don't you want that for her?"

"I guess, but—"

"I've been praying for it for years, Janie. And I believe it's going to happen. And when it does happen, your mama won't be able to hold on to the things that haunt her anymore."

"Like me."

"Yes. And me."

The only way to describe how I was feeling was that baby in the Bible when the king decreed to cut it in half. I'd never felt so ripped apart in all my so-called life, and I wasn't sure if I could take it or not. Knowing how bad I was hurting, I was surprised the Lord didn't just snatch me up right then and there.

But he didn't.

And I had to go on, knowing I was what stood in the way of Mama ever being happy again. No child should ever feel that way.

"Your Mama won't let me go," said Grandma Mona. "She has unresolved feelings where I'm concerned. For the time being I'm bound here for her. And so are you. If and when she resolves her feelings for us, yes, we will leave this place. I have no guarantees for tomorrow here, and neither do you. Now, I know you're grieving and all sorts of things, but there's a life at stake. There'll be plenty of time to hash through all this feeling business later. Suffice it to say we have even more important things at task. We've got to make a plan now. And this time, it has to work."

I left Grandma Mona's side and moved to the dresser. I saw propped-up photos of her and Poppy when they were younger. When they were alive. I couldn't focus on what Grandma Mona was saying anymore. I didn't care about any plan. I'd just lost my life, my mother. "I have no parents," I said, feeling so empty.

"Rightly so, you are feeling sorry for yourself. But I assure you, you have a father in heaven. You are a child of God, and soon you will come to know what this means in all its glory. As for your earthly father, Harlan, well, he just recently learned of what your mother did to you. She finally told him about the abortion. It's why he left again. He's a very fragile man. Pathetic, if you ask me. Sorry. That was uncalled-for."

"Grandma Mona?" I said, crumbling down onto the bed. "I still love Mama! I love her so much! You don't know how bad this feels. I feel like I'm gonna die."

"Oh honey, if I could change it all, I would, but—"

"But what?"

"Do you remember when we were in the graveyard and I had you feel the words, the texture of the truth about Poppy?" I nodded. "It's important to feel things in order to know them. This pain you're feeling right now . . . would you ever wish this on someone else?"

"No! Never!"

Grandma Mona grew silent. She pursed her lips. She opened her mouth and closed it again. Finally she said, "Janie, time is running out. You have a baby sister in your mother's tummy right now. By this time tomorrow, there will be no more baby. Honey, your mother's not thinking straight. She is so deceived by fear and grief and loneliness, she is planning to end it all. Again."

I grabbed her arm and squeezed, my mouth dropped wide open. I wanted to scream but nothing would come out.

"It's true, Janie. Either your mother will be raising this baby, or you and I will. You are your little sister's only hope in this world."

"But I'm nothing! I'm not even real! I'm just a bad memory for her!"

"Oh, honey, you're not just a bad memory for your mama. You're a light in her life. Why, look out there. See that big moon? You're just as bright as that. Brighter, even. You do what you need to do, Janie Doe. Life is worth saving. You understand that now. Don't let anything stand in your way."

Chapter Fifty-six
SIDEWALK WRITING

The next morning, Friday, Mama woke up at six thirty. I was still up from the night before, waiting for her in the kitchen. At some point in the night, I was no longer tired. Grandma Mona told me the more I learned about myself, the more I'd start to change. Sure enough, I didn't need sleep anymore.

I wasn't hungry either, though I hadn't eaten in a couple days. "The spirit doesn't hunger for food," said Grandma Mona, and anyway, everything had always tasted the same to me, like peaches and strawberries or chicken or cheese. Bland, flavorless. Grandma Mona explained how only certain senses were alive for me in my mother's world—hearing, touch, sight, smell— and once I realized it, I could see colors not even seen in the rainbow, hear music dancing on the wind, smell flowers from miles away. I learned that my grandmother had provided for me all I'd ever needed in the world—spiritual clothes, spiritual paper to write my lists. Everything a child like me would need.

It was hard at first to learn the truth about me. I spent most of the day in tears. But as the night wore on and I finally accepted what Grandma Mona was saying, I felt I'd grown up overnight. Things began to make sense to me—how Mama never reached for me or took me in her arms, why she never saw my lists and notes, or why Uncle Fritz never spoke to me directly. I don't want to say it was a good thing, but at least they weren't ignoring me just to be mean.

Mama was distracted while the sun was rising on Vinca Lane. Her tired eyes danced around the kitchen like they couldn't decide what they wanted to look at. She walked to the counter and scoured the cabinets for a canister of regular Maxwell House.

"See that? She doesn't mind the caffeine anymore, Janie," said Grandma Mona. "She's given up on this baby. Mark my words."

The phone rang, and Mama just looked toward the living room where it sat on a little stand. She didn't move to answer it. Instead, she slowly poured the water into the coffeemaker.

"It's Fritz," said Grandma Mona. "I bet he's worried. He's calling to check in on Priscilla."

I ran into the living room and picked up the receiver. I was able to move nonliving things, no problem. It was the living things I had no control over—peaches, bugs, worms, Mama. This, too, was a mystery explained to me now. I held the phone to my ear and heard Uncle Fritz's voice. "Priscilla? Hello?"

I tried to speak back but I knew he couldn't hear me. "Fritz, it's Janie. Mama's un-bornin' the baby today. You got to come over quick and get her not to do it!"

"Hello? Rainey, is that you?"

"Fritz, come quick!" I hollered. He said one last "Priscilla?" Then he hung up. I sat there like somebody'd kicked me in the stomach.

Rainey came down the stairs with her hair all sticking up. She was holding the teddy bear Mrs. Arielle had given her. She saw me in the living room and said, "Where you sleep?"

"Wasn't really tired," I said.

"Oh."

She stumbled into the kitchen, where Mama was setting out her bowl of grits. She added a blob of butter and salt, just how Rainey liked it.

"Thanks, Mama," said Rainey. "Don't forget Janie."

"Okay, honey." I watched as Mama went to grab a little bowl. She put a dollop of grits in it with no salt, no butter or anything, and set it to the left of Rainey. "Here, Janie. Hope you like it."

I was sitting on the *other* side of the table.

"Janie over there," said Rainey. Mama moved the bowl without giving it another thought. How many times, how many days, had she simply done what Rainey told her, having no idea I was actually by her side?

I got up and left the kitchen. "Where you goin'?" asked Rainey.

"Just outside. I'm not hungry."

"Okay. Be there minute."

I went out on the front porch and sat in a rocking chair under the gazebo. I rocked and rocked. I looked out over the lawn. There was a slight breeze blowing through a weeping willow across the street. I could see Mrs. Shoemaker sitting on her front porch, rocking. She saw me and waved. I did not wave back. To passersby, she and I just looked like wind rocking those rockers and nothing else. I thought how strange it was for living folks, how they never see who's really around them.

I got up and walked into the grass. I stooped down and watched little bugs jumping from one blade of grass to another. I looked in the flower bed behind me. A tiny frog hopped. He hopped again.

"Hi, froggy, don't mind me," I said. "I'm just a ghost. Not the scary kind though. More like Casper the Friendly Ghost. I'm a minister spirit like Poppy was. I've never been a minister or preacher or nothing before, but here I am." The frog stood still, watching me, and his throat went in and out, in and out. I reached for him, but he jumped back in the mulch and hid behind a plant. "I won't hurt you," I said. "I'm just a little girl ghost. I can't do any harm. Grandma Mona says I'm a child of God and it's against my nature to hurt anything, so you don't have to worry about me." I heard the front door open and saw Rainey coming out. " 'Course, my sister, you might want to watch out for her," I whispered. "She's got a good grip."

"Hey, Janie," she said.

"Hey."

"Mama go home Cypresswood when I go work," she said. "She get clothes, stuff, and pick me up."

"That's good," I said. "I guess I'll go with her."

"I wanna come," said Rainey.

"No, Rainey. You got work, remember? I'll help Mama."

She looked at me and thought about this. She bit her fingernail and looked back at the house. "Well, okay. Let play hopscotch."

All morning long, I played hopscotch with my sister. I hugged her often. I laughed with her. I appreciated every bit of her, my big sister. I knew someday I'd have to leave her, but I couldn't think of that right now. Grandma Mona had told me not to think of anything else except how today was the most important day in my life. Today was the day

I would go from being invisible to being a real family hero if all went well in Cypresswood.

"I got an idea, Rainey. Let's write some letters." I motioned for her to pick up the chalk and said, "Bet you don't know how to spell *baby*."

"Do too," she said. Then she proceeded to show me how. She sprawled the word all over the sidewalk in big letters and little letters, upside down and every-which-a-way. Mama'd be forced to see her fortune the minute she tried to leave.

Chapter Fifty-seven
THE BOOK OF LIFE

After the lunch dishes were cleared, Grandma Mona came to find me in the garden by the strawberry patch. I'd been sitting there for a while, letting everything settle in. I was as tight and twisted as a vine around a tree. She bent down and said, "It's almost time to leave, honey."

"I've been thinking," I told her. "You understand all this a lot more than me. I don't know if I can do this right, Grandma Mona. If Mama doesn't even know I'm here, why do I need to go? Why can't you go instead?"

Grandma Mona surprised me by plopping right down on the ground next to me. It was amazing to see her body move like someone younger. The sunlight glowed in her pretty blonde hair.

"Oh, honey," she said. "Because she wouldn't

listen to me. It's just how it is with mothers and daughters. When I whisper in her ear, I'm her voice of condemnation. She's managed to tune me out over the years, but you—you are and have always been her voice of optimism, of hope, of unconditional love. She hears your whispers, feels them, loves them, even. And the love of a child is the only thing that will keep her from doing what she's planning to do today. So you see, it must be you."

I looked up at the peach tree and thought about climbing it. I wanted to hide. This task seemed too big for me.

"You know what else?" she said.

"What?"

"You grandfather left something for you. He asked me to give it to you at just the right time. I think it's now."

"Poppy left something for me?" I looked around at her hands, and she pulled out a folded piece of paper. It did not seem to be regular paper, but an old type, parchment maybe. I opened it slowly and feasted my eyes.

Dear sweet Janie,

If you are reading this, then it's come to the point you must know the truth. How wonderful to learn that you are a child of God, that you have a place here in heaven waiting for you, that you are needed by the ones you love!

Your mother needs you more now than ever.

By now, your Grandma Mona has told you most of what you must know. But there is something else I need to explain about you, your name, in particular. You see, your mother never gave you the name Janie Doe. Your Grandma Mona called you this as a filler, a nickname. Your real name is a powerful thing. Every believer's name is written in the Book of Life, and you, my child, are no different.

There is nothing pleasant about how you came to enter your mother's world, but there's no talking around it either. In order to survive, your mother has pushed the thought of you to the far recesses of her mind. Still, you're constantly with her. She thinks of you whenever she sees a child, when she's shopping for groceries, when she's drifting off to sleep. For an instant she wonders what your life might have been like. But only for an instant. She has never named you because giving you a proper name would mean she'd have to face what she did to you. It would mean having to acknowledge you were a real, live person. But deep in your mother's soul, your name is written there. When she finally hears your true name, she will know it. And she will know you.

Protect your God-given name until the

moment is right. You will know it when the time has come. Your good name is your strongest weapon. Use it to protect the sweet life growing in your mother now.

I will see you soon, sweet Lilly Gray Macy. Be brave and know how much you are loved. Every child has a purpose under heaven. Every child. Fulfill yours, Lilly. Heaven will wait for you.

Poppy

I closed the paper and looked at Grandma Mona through tears. "Poppy," I said. "Poppy's waiting for me. He told me my real name."

She bent down and held my face in her hands. She leaned close, kissed my forehead, and whispered, "You have such a beautiful name. But let's not speak of it just now. You'll know when the time is right."

For feeling so dark and nothing all day, I was surprised to feel so special, the most special I'd ever felt. My name was written in the Book of Life. God himself had given me my name. I wanted to burst with the knowledge. I was no ghost. I was a child of God, an angel sent on a special mission! I ran to find Rainey.

"Be careful of what you tell her, honey," warned Grandma Mona. "No name talk."

"Okay," I said.

I found Rainey brushing her hair in the bathroom upstairs. She smiled at me in the mirror. I wanted to burst. "I have a secret," I whispered.

Her eyes grew large. "What?"

"I cain't tell you. It's a secret, silly."

She furrowed her eyebrows and said, "No fair. Tell me."

I was so happy I thought I might truly explode. I was special, somebody really special! Poppy had said so.

"I'm special," I said after carefully considering my words.

"Uh-huh," said Rainey. She grinned. "Me too."

"Yeah, but I'm a different kind of special." I leaned up in her ear and said, "I'm an angel."

Rainey glowed and said, "I gonna be the angel too!"

"No, Rainey. Maybe someday you will, but I'm already an angel."

Dejected, Rainey put her hairbrush down and plopped down on the toilet seat. "Yeah. You got the wings," she said.

"No, I don't think so, but I'm an angel anyway."

"Yuh-huh, you do. Look." Rainey pointed to my back, and I froze. Slowly, I turned to face the wall. I swiveled my head around until I could see in the mirror.

"I don't see any wings, silly."

"Right there." Rainey stood up and lifted the back of my shirt. "See?"

There, in between my shoulder blades, were

two beautiful golden wings, folded just so. I could not believe my eyes.

"Oh my goodness. You see that? I have wings! I really have wings!"

"Yeah, duh. Everybody know it."

"But how long have I had them? Did they grow overnight?"

Rainey smiled a sly smile and said, "No, silly. You got wings since you the baby."

Then she lifted up her own shirt and struggled to see her back. Rainey mumbled, "I never get wings," and she left the bathroom to go find Mama and tell her it was time for work.

Chapter Fifty-eight
THE LONG ROAD
BACK TO CYPRESSWOOD

The sky was dotted with dark clouds shaped like an army of mice as we left Forest Pines. I watched them, counting thirteen as our Police Interceptor exited the grocery store parking lot and turned right. Rainey was safely inside. Instead of bagging, they'd moved her to stacking products, cans, and occasionally produce until her arm had fully healed. Rainey was happy with this change in duties. It proved to her and everybody else she could do even more.

I sat in the front seat beside Mama. I had watched her walk right over the *baby* words on the sidewalk that Rainey had scribbled. She barely gave them a second glance. Nothing and no one would distract her from what she was setting out to do.

The wind was beginning to pick up and shake the car in gusts. Mama held the wheel a little tighter when that happened. She turned on no music. She barely seemed to breathe. She wore no makeup and had pulled her hair into a clean ponytail behind her neck. She was wearing a blue blouse and a loose skirt disguising her figure. She could have been any woman at all.

"I'm right here, Mama." I put my hand out and touched her arm. It was cold beneath my fingertips. But it was Mama's arm, and I didn't mind. It had always felt the very same way. I was alone in my world, and Mama in hers. It was like those scenes in the movies where the person is being interrogated, and on the other side of the window, people are looking in. I was looking in on Mama's world. She had no idea there were two sides to her mirror.

Just weeks ago, I was so ignorant about my life or lack of it. I remembered driving this same road, but the other way, as a family—Mama, Rainey, Grandma Mona, Poppy, and me. It was the last trip we'd ever take together. I wished I'd known it at the time. I would have appreciated it more, paid attention better. Tears sprang to my eyes when I remembered sitting next to Poppy in the backseat, holding his hand. I thought we were going on an adventure. I was secure in my place in the family, with the people I loved. And now it had all changed. Everything had changed.

Mama breathed in deep and let it out slow. She did this a few more times but never said a word the whole way to Cypresswood.

"Mama, please don't do this," I said as we were pulling into the driveway of Alisha's house. "You can raise this baby. It's not that hard. You did it with Rainey, and you have a nice house now. And did you know you're having another girl?" I touched her shoulder. "I was thinking, Mama. This could be the last Macy there ever is. The baby in your tummy might be the very last one to carry the Macy family name. You can't get rid of her. You just can't! She's a person, like me. Like you. A person!"

Alisha ran to us with a newspaper over her head. She was wearing shorts, and the tops of her legs dimpled and jiggled as she moved. It had begun to rain, and the sound of water on the car roof pummeled my ears. Sounded like my nervous heart.

"Hey, I've missed you," said Alisha.

Mama tried to smile but couldn't. "You too," she said.

"You want me to drive?" Alisha asked.

"No. I'm fine."

After Alisha had buckled in and enlightened us

on all the gossip and trash and complaints about the pancake house, we drove in silence. I had climbed over the seat to the back and was sitting in between, my elbows propped on the console. I didn't like Alisha much. She'd always been no good for Mama, and here she was, helping her make the second biggest mistake of her life. She didn't care about Mama. She didn't care that Mama would regret this decision too, that she'd have to live with it for the rest of her life. She didn't care that Mama suffered deep inside about me and that she was so hardened she couldn't even feel anymore. Alisha didn't care about any of that. A true friend might have suggested these things, but no.

"My cousin James lives in Forest Pines," said Alisha. "Works at the K & W as a manager. You remember meeting him at that party I had a few years back? I'm sure you met him, but you were living with Harlan still. Anyway, he's single. Just got divorced. He remembered you and thought you were pretty hot. Maybe after you get today out of the way, I can set you two up."

"I don't—"

"Mama doesn't want to date your cousin, Alisha. She's in love with my daddy!"

"You don't have to say yes today," said Alisha. "I just thought it might give you something to look forward to. James is a hoot. Not bad looking either."

"Thanks," said Mama. I wished I could kick Alisha right out of the car. I leaned over in her ear, and as loud as I could I yelled, "I don't like you!!! *BOOOOO!*"

Alisha jerked and looked over her shoulder, then back at the road. She stayed quiet after that. We all did, with jangled nerves. All the way to the clinic in Fervor.

To the naked eye of a regular person, I imagined the building looked like any other, white concrete, windows with bars, a sign with a staff and two snakes coiled around it, sad-looking women entering the door, sometimes alone, other times with a man or woman beside them. Some girls were young, real young. They clutched teddy bears and baby dolls as they ducked in from the rain.

But to my eyes, the place looked very different. For every girl or woman who entered there was another person, a spirit who entered right along with them. Some spirits were yelling, others were crying, and still, others begged and pleaded to no avail. We sat there in the car with the windshield wipers flipping back and forth. There was a leaf stuck under the wiper, so every pass made a grating sound. After a while, an angel spirit would leave the building with a bundle in his or her arms, and walk in the rain along the sidewalk until out of sight. The girls with teddy bears would come out in the arms of a mother or father or boyfriend later, crying or glassy-eyed. Doomed and shocked with what they'd done.

Mama watched. She shuddered. Her lip trembled. She felt her stomach and smoothed her hair back. I observed the steady stream of baby bundles floating down the street and saw the hopelessness of it all. Mama couldn't see them. How would I ever be able to accomplish what no one else seemed able to do?

"What time's your appointment?" asked Alisha.

"Right now. Three," said Mama.

"It's three after."

"I know it."

Swish, swish, the wipers went back and forth. The rain turned the road gray, the air gray, the building gray.

"It's raining," said Mama.

"Sure is. We better get out and go on in before it gets any worse."

"Mama. It's raining," I said. "Isn't that what you've been waiting for? To settle down? It's a sign, Mama. You're supposed to keep this baby. Don't go inside. Don't—"

But Mama was opening the car door and stepping out into the rain.

The door slammed closed and I pressed my hands and face to the window. "No, Mama, no!" But she couldn't hear me. I banged on the glass. Some spirits turned and looked at me, but not

Mama, not Alisha. So I did the only thing I could think of. I flipped the switch in our Police Interceptor, and the siren and flashers went off. Mama stopped and cringed. She darted for the car door. Women in the clinic came to the windows to see who was guilty of a crime.

Chapter Fifty-nine
FERVOR

"I don't think I can do this," said Mama. She sat behind the wheel, breathless after turning the siren off. The tears were beginning to flow. Alisha stood outside her window, thunderstruck. The rain was turning her newspaper soggy.

"What in the world happened?" she asked. "Has it ever done that before?"

"No," said Mama. "Not on its own."

"Car's getting old, Priscilla. Real old. Now that you don't have to pay rent, you'll be able to buy a new car. Get rid of this old heap. I got another cousin in Columbia might be willing to take it off your hands."

"Alisha," said Mama, "be quiet. Please."

Mama's eyes were shut. She was gripping the wheel.

"Listen." Alisha stooped down and put her hand on Mama's leg, like she was helping. Like she cared. "You're pregnant, you're hormonal, I know how it is. In an hour, this'll all be over. You'll get back to Forest Pines, pick up Rainey, get on with your life. I know you're scared. The second time's always harder than the first 'cause you know what's coming, right? Like getting a shot or something? But you're having the anesthesia. It won't be that bad. You do have enough money for anesthesia, right? If not, I can spot you."

Mama nodded, eyes still closed.

"Good. Well, let's get on in, then. I gotta be at work at quarter to six."

Mama was stone-faced at the check-in window, and filling out her paperwork, and in the counselor's room. She answered every question with yes or no. I held her hand and whispered in her ear. "I love you, Mama. Don't do this, please."

"Good luck," said a sad old woman to me. She was walking a little bundle out the front door and sniffling all the way.

I closed my eyes and prayed that God would give me the strength to do this. I prayed He would tell me the exact right moment to tell Mama my name. I hadn't heard anything from him yet, and we were getting closer, too close. Alisha sat in the waiting room, reading a magazine as if the world were not about to end. But I knew.

I looked around at all the waiting people. It was a quiet place, no chitchatting, no laughing. Solemn faces waiting their turns. I felt sick to my stomach. My mother was not a bad person. She wasn't! How could she do something like this? How could she think it was all right to do?

A woman holding a clipboard came to the door of the waiting room and said flatly, "Priscilla?"

Mama looked up. She turned to Alisha, who smiled at her. I grabbed Mama's hand and said, "Please, Mama, don't go!" I tugged on her, but she didn't budge my way. Instead, she walked like a robot with the woman holding the clipboard. She led her to a room on the left and told her to take her clothes off and to put on a little gown sitting on the table.

It was then I looked up and saw the window. It was near the ceiling tiles. It had wrought iron bars on it with a heart in the middle. As if love was in this room. There was no love in this room, except the love I had for my mama.

"Mama! I remember that window. I remember it! I was born here, wasn't I? I died here in this very room! Oh, Mama, you can't do this again. You just can't!"

Mama paid me no attention. She undressed and slipped into her gown. She sat up on the table and slowly looked at everything, the tools, the stirrups, the window behind her. She saw the light coming in through the little heart in the wrought iron bars. A tear came down her cheek. "Oh, forgive me, please forgive me."

She shut her eyes hard and held her breath.

"Mama, you have a real, live baby in your

tummy. She's a Macy, Mama. She's my sister. Please don't do this. You can't do this again. I won't let you!" There was an *Us* magazine on the counter, and I pushed it off. It flapped to the floor and Mama opened her eyes. She licked her lips and looked around her, the same way she'd done when I threw the picture of Poppy in the attic.

"Oh my goodness, oh boy," she said over and over and over, arms folded tight in front of her. She was rocking forward and back.

The door began to open. The nurse was coming back in, holding a tray. "Hi, Miss Macy. We doing all right?" She was real happy and chipper this time, like she might be driving an ice cream truck.

Mama just sat there, frozen.

"Good," said the nurse. "Now, we're gonna get you all comfortable and feeling good, okay? Get you nice and relaxed."

I saw the shot on the little tray. Mama eyed it too. That's when I heard-felt something in my soul.

Heaven is forever, Lilly. Your mama needs you now.

I knew it was time.

"Mama," I said, "in this very room, you took my life away eight-and-a-half years ago. But I am real, Mama. I'm a real child. You took my life, and I cain't let you do it again. I just cain't. My name is Lilly Gray Macy, Mama. Lilly Gray Macy! And I forgive you! From the bottom of my heart I forgive you for what you did to me."

Mama pulled her chin up and almost looked in my eyes. I was standing in front of her, touching her knees. "I'm Lilly Gray Macy, Mama. Your real, live child!" I said again, praying she would hear me.

Mama's lips moved. Then she said in a quiet whisper. "Lilly Gray."

"Hmm?" asked the nurse, standing at the counter. She held a shot in her right hand.

"My child's name is Lilly Gray Macy," said Mama, stunned. She looked as if she'd just woken up and realized where she was. She turned and stared at the print of *Meadow with Poppies* by Gustav Klimt hanging on the wall. It was meant, I supposed, to make the place less scary, more flowerdy and happy, as if people didn't die in this room. But I saw it as a sign from God, that Poppy was in heaven and watching over us, watching over Mama.

"That's a pretty name, Miss Macy," said the nurse. "Real pretty. Now this won't hurt at all. But I'll need you to be still for me."

"No," said Mama, crying now. "I can't do this." She slipped off the table, the paper crinkling underneath her.

"Go, Mama, get out of here!" I screamed.

"Oh sugar, I know you're nervous, but this'll do the trick." The nurse moved toward her and touched her on the shoulder. "In just a minute all those jitters will be gone. Now, come have a seat for me."

"No, you don't understand!" said Mama, tears streaming down her face. "I'm not doing this! I'm not going through with it."

The woman stopped and looked at her. She seemed annoyed with this turn of events, as if it was mucking up her schedule. "Let me go get the counselor for you, just wait right here."

"I don't need the counselor! I've made up my mind." Mama grabbed her clothes off the chair and started pulling them on.

"Becky," the nurse called out the door, "we need some help here."

Mama slipped on her shoes and grabbed her big brown leather purse and left the gown on the floor in a heap. I took her hand and we hurried past the nurse, but we were stopped by a woman and a man. One was smiling, the other was not. They took Mama's arms and told her to calm down, it would be all right, and before we entered the hallway, I turned and looked at the room one last time. At the place where my life both ended and began. At the window with the heart in it, where barely any light from heaven comes in. And I said a prayer for the next woman who chose to enter this room and for the child she carried who would never get a chance to choose anything at all.

And I prayed for all the lives that were destroyed here in an instant, women and children and men, for years gone past and years to come.

Chapter Sixty
RISE UP SHINING

I've always wanted to save the world. I once thought I'd go into politics or start my own TV show when I grew up, *The Janie Doe Macy Show*. No, that was too long. Maybe just *Janie*, like *Oprah*. Or, I thought I could be a teacher. I would teach kids to fight in this world—not with each other but for what they believe in. I've learned it's all about what you believe in.

I believe every person—girl, boy, handicapped, healthy, white, black, old, young, everybody—has a little light in them. If it were up to me, I'd save the world by making sure all the little lights shine as bright as they can. That way, heaven could look down and actually see them. Not forget about them, like it seems sometimes. And I'd give everybody wings so they could rise up shining like fireflies and fly all the way to the moon and the stars if they wanted to, or all the way to heaven if they had the itching to go so far.

Maybe someday it will happen. It could.

By the middle of August, Mama was showing real nice. She had a soft little pooch she kept her hand on night and day. Her face began to fill out in a good way. She started with Rainey walking in the mornings for exercise. She began to laugh at

Rainey's antics again. She hugged her a lot more. She invited Fritz over for suppers. Far as I know, she didn't speak a word of what happened in Fervor to him or anybody else. She didn't call Alisha on the phone anymore, which was a good thing, if you ask me. She was trying to get her life in order, and for Mama, it began with the house. Mama scrubbed and cleaned. She was getting her nest ready for the baby to come.

One day she found Baby Jesus hidden in Rainey's drawer. I wondered if she might be mad at Rainey stealing it, and I almost ran to go find Rainey and tell her she'd been found out. But Mama picked up Jesus and studied his face, his halo. She lay him down on Rainey's bed and fell to her knees. She cried then, longer and harder and sadder than I'd ever seen her. She asked for forgiveness. She pleaded. She clenched her fists. She cried until there was nothing left but my name on her lips.

"Lilly Gray," she said, breathless.

"I'm here, Mama."

"Oh sweet child, I am so sorry. I'm just so sorry."

"I know, Mama. I know you are."

"I promise you that I'll do right. I will never do anything bad again."

"I know you won't, Mama. I'm proud of you."

"Oh, dear God. Please forgive me for what I did. Please, how can you ever forgive me?"

"God can forgive you anything, Mama."

She took a deep breath and said through clenched teeth, "I love you, Lilly Gray. You are my angel in heaven. I am just so sorry. Oh, dear God . . ."

And in that instant, even though I was hearing what I'd longed to hear my entire life from Mama, I knew she'd finally made her peace with me. Like she'd done with Poppy.

And I was free to go.

Funny thing about making peace. One person can make it and think *okay, we're done here. We can move on.* But the other person, me, might think *but wait a minute, I don't feel peaceful. I don't want to go.*

That's how I felt. Mama was my mama no matter what. She and Rainey and Grandma Mona were everything I'd ever known. The fact that I was only half-living here in Forest Pines wasn't cause enough for me to want to leave.

"If I'm supposed to go to heaven, wouldn't I want to leave?" I asked Grandma Mona one morning, sitting on the front porch in the gazebo. We were feeling the air turn cooler and watching mockingbirds play in the sky and the younger Mrs. Shoemaker's new cat chasing a squirrel through our yard.

"Yes. I believe you would want to leave. I imagine God'll put the desire in your heart when it's time to go."

"That day . . . in Fervor," I said, "he told me, heaven is forever, but Mama needs me now. He hasn't told me anything different yet."

"Just wait on the Lord," said Grandma Mona, rocking. "That's what I'm doing. You just sit here with me and we'll wait together. However long it takes."

Mama had a nice little belly by the time she found her a good job. Mrs. Arielle had a friend who ran an activity program for children and seniors and adults with special needs. Mama answered the phones in the front office of the Rainbow House, and Rainey got to come for free. She did arts and crafts and made new friends just like her with Down syndrome. She hit it off with one girl in particular, Brenda. Brenda had really bad eyesight and wore thick glasses. She could pronounce her words and read a little better than Rainey, even in glasses, but physically, she was much more impaired. She and Rainey would laugh at nearly everything, at the pictures they drew and funny parts in books. Rainey was making a real friend, and the funny thing was, I wasn't jealous. The old me would have been upset and pouting about losing some of her attention, but no more. Brenda gave me hope that if and when I ever did leave, Rainey would be all right without me.

Mama was doing better too. She liked having a job where she didn't have to stand all day. She was pleasant and pretty and friendly with the people at work. It seems she had finally found herself a good place in the world. We began attending Fritz's church on Sundays. He was a real good preacher, serious sometimes, funny too. I would sit there next to Mama in a pew and close my eyes, listening to his voice. I would play this little game with myself. I knew what Fritz's words would be. Like they came through me a second before they flowed out of him.

"For those who have no eyes for heaven, the taste of Truth is bitter," he said, and I mouthed right along with him. "But for those whose names are written in the Book of Life, the Truth is sweet like honey. It drips from our tongues and covers the world in a froth of joy and glory hallelujah. And all God's people said . . ."

"Amen."

I felt connected to both heaven and earth in the Covenant Church in Forest Pines. Mama did too, and she could finally hold her head up there, knowing the choice she'd made.

Come Christmastime, Fritz offered Rainey "a most important job" in the real, live nativity scene. He said she could be the angel who watched over the baby Jesus. This, to Rainey, was akin to winning the lottery. She'd already returned the plastic baby doll she'd stolen over the summer, but on Christmas Eve, she and I both stood there, angels watching over that real, live baby Jesus. It was a boy named Michael, but nobody really cared about that. People came from far and wide to see what God had brought to Forest Pines, the miracle of the Christmas season. Mary, Joseph, Baby Jesus, two stinky sheep, three wise men, a donkey, and us—me with my golden wings spread out, and Rainey with the big fluffy white ones Mama had sewed by hand and Rainey swore she'd never take off as long as she lived and breathed.

My mother had a baby girl on March the second and named her Lilly Gray. I understood why she did it, and I was happy to have my baby sister named after me. She was small though. For some reason, they had to keep her in the hospital an extra day and give her oxygen. She was yellow, so they put her under lights.

I'll never forget the first time I saw her face. Uncle Fritz, Rainey, Grandma Mona, and I were there in the hospital, waiting for the baby to be born. After three hours, we heard a little wail from the other side of the door, and we cheered in the hallway. A few minutes later a nurse came out, holding the baby in her arms, swaddled up. She didn't let us touch her or look real close while she whisked her to another room, but I saw her, and that was enough. My whole life had been for that moment when my little sister would finally show her face in the world.

Over the next week, Mama was very protective of her. She held her a lot. She let Rainey hold her too, showed her how to hold her head and told her all about the soft spot. She had to ask Rainey to stop kissing the baby, for it was all Rainey could do. She was completely in love with her. She lived and breathed for that baby. If she cried and Mama was holding her, she didn't cover her ears. Instead, she patted her back, her tiny hat-covered head. When Rainey held her, she had to sit down and prop her just so. I would sit beside her on the sofa and touch the baby's tiny fingers. They were cold in my hands, and I'd never been so happy to be holding a cold hand in all my life. It meant she was a real, live baby, not an angel child like me.

Then one night, I was watching over Lilly like I always did. Grandma Mona and I took turns, and this night was mine. I studied how her breathing was slow. How she was dreaming of something wonderful, I was sure. Her crib was lavender, green, and white. Fritz had repainted it for Mama after finding it in the attic, stuffed with boxes. Grandma Mona said my mother had slept in the very same crib when she was little, so it was a special find.

Lilly looked so tiny in that crib. The light coming in from the window grew brighter as if day was coming. But it was the middle of the night.

I moved to the baby's side and put my hand on her little face. It was not quite so cold anymore.

Her tiny chest heaved, then once again. "Baby?" I said. "You okay?" Her little chest was not moving anymore.

"Mama!" I screamed.

The door flew open, and Grandma Mona came rushing in. She looked me in the eye and said without words, *It's time.* Then she opened her mouth and smiled a sad smile. "She's losing her will to live."

"But why? Mama needs her!"

"I don't know, honey. There are some souls who can withstand anything, survivors at all costs. And there are others, like this sweet child, who want nothing more than to go back to heaven, to lie in the warm arms of Father God."

"But this is awful!" I began to cry. I knew how much Mama had been through to have this baby. I knew how hard the whole thing had been, how she'd tried to make peace with what she'd done to me and was ready to move on. But this . . .

"Isn't there anything we can do?" I whimpered.

Grandma Mona stayed quiet until she said, "What does the Lord tell you?"

I listened but heard not a word except the pounding of my own heart. And then we heard a commotion in the hallway, and Mama came in, panting like she'd woken up from a terrible dream. She was clutching her nightgown with one hand and staring big-eyed at the crib. Somehow, she knew.

I leaned over and touched that sweet baby, and all of a sudden I felt her warmth. She felt like Poppy or Grandma Mona had to me. And in an instant, I heard-knew in my soul these words: *You are a survivor, Lilly Gray Macy. Heaven will wait for you, child.*

And I was at peace.

I reached back between the baby's shoulder blades and felt these two little nubs, tiny baby wings. I knew she was too small to fly, so I picked her up and carried her. Across the room we went toward the window, then I heard a cry. I turned back and saw Mama standing at the crib, pleading with her eyes. For just a split second, she saw me, as if peering through a window, and knew who I was.

"Take me instead," she shrieked. "I'll do anything, just leave the baby!"

Grandma Mona wasted no time and grabbed Lilly from me. She handed her to a beautiful glowing angel waiting outside the window.

"No! Please!" Mama wailed. "Please, God!"

And with that, I felt the warm breath of God on the back of my neck. He breathed life into my lungs, my limbs, my heart. Grandma Mona grew cold as she held me in her arms, and she kissed me and lay me back in the crib where all was lavender, green, and happy—where my baby sister lay for nine whole days before me.

In those first moments, the scents of the world

overcame me, and it was the most glorious thing I'd ever felt. I cried my first real, live tears when Mama touched my moving, breathing chest, and I finally felt how warm she was. She wept a river for both of us then, for herself and her real, live girl.

Epilogue
THE WINDOW

{Mona}

In every life there are windows. Between then and now, between dead and gone. There are windows of opportunity, too, chances to see what life could be like—if only. Chances to make things right again, to rebirth, renew, redeem. But timing is everything. And only God knows when the timing is right for you, for me. Knowing when our windows will open—and why and how—is impossible. But being able to recognize a window for what it is, now that is crucial—for when some windows close, they may never be opened again.

It's said there's none greater than he who lays down his life for another. This is the mark of a true hero. The baby I handed out the window that night? That was actually my sweet granddaughter Bonnie Kay. Her name is written in the Book of Life that way, and she's safe in heaven with Poppy now. In my book, she's a hero, because she

gave her life for her sister, Janie. And Janie's a
hero because she saved her sister's life and her
mother's fragile heart. Oh, she'll always be Janie
to me, no matter if they call her Lilly Gray at
school or in heaven. Rainey knows her too. The
next morning after Janie was born, Rainey came
in to find Priscilla holding her in her arms,
rocking and still crying. Rainey got one look at
the baby and scrunched her eyes up. She bent
down close and kissed her on the forehead, then
took her fingers in her own and grinned. "Janie!"
she said. She knew her immediately and has
called her Janie, not Lilly, ever since.

Right now, Rainey and Janie are playing chase
in and out of the pews of the Covenant Church.
Rainey's a young woman now, twenty-two years
old. She's lovely. And Janie's a handful at almost
five. Wild blonde hair and blue eyes like her
Mama. She might look different, but she's still
the same child to me. I've never seen so much
energy in all my life. She sees me and knows me.
She knows Rainey too. She's stubborn and smart
and loving—and she remembers her life before
she came here. She articulates it too. How, I do
not know. I do not understand all the mysteries of
God.

As for Harlan, I imagine he's out hiding somewhere in the North Carolina mountains, unable to
face Priscilla and everything that comes along
with her—Rainey, Janie, leaving again. How the

man can live without his flesh and blood by his side, I'll never know. They're angels, those girls, I tell you the truth. And as such, they'll probably welcome him with open arms if and when he ever does return.

Priscilla and Fritz are sitting in his office with the door slightly ajar so they can hear if there's trouble in the sanctuary. Priscilla's hair is long again, and she's pulling it, twisting it in her fingers. She's asking him about past lives, and I'm sitting here in the shadows grinning because I know what he'll say. He's my son, after all, and a preacher, to boot.

"But she talks about my father, Fritz. You and I both know she never saw my father alive."

Fritz looks at her and says nothing. He's amused.

"Rainey refuses to call her by her real name," says Priscilla. "She insists she's Janie. Remember her invisible friend? As if she's come to life or something . . ."

"I guess I've heard stranger things, Priscilla. Invisible friends can be very real."

"Oh really? Well, do you know she talks to *our mother* as if she's here in the room with us? *Grandma Mona this* and *Grandma Mona that*. As if she's still alive. And Rainey does the very same thing! I feel like I'm outnumbered. Haunted. What if the house really is haunted?"

"Oh, Priscilla. After all this time, what does it

really matter? If something wanted to get you, it've gotten you by now." He smirks and crinkles his eyes.

"No, really, I . . . I hear doors creaking and . . . and water running. I go to check it out but it's not running anymore. I'm—maybe I'm going crazy."

Fritz stops and clears his throat. "You're not going crazy." I wait to see if my children will look for me or at me, but they don't. They're blind as ever. Priscilla stands and moves to the window. She bites a nail and watches three mockingbirds chase off doves on the church lawn.

"The house is old," says Fritz. "Very old. It's settling. And your girls? They're special. God made each of your girls exactly the way he wanted. Who knows? Maybe they have some ability to know things or see things that you and I cannot. Children have a faith that you and I find hard to come by. Rainey has a heart of gold, and that Lilly, well, she's practically a prodigy with her speech and memory. Brilliant, if you ask me."

"But the window, Fritz!" Priscilla turns and glares at him, clutching her chest. "Lilly can't know about that, no one does. She draws pictures of a window with a heart in it—the very same one that shows up in my dreams. Here. See?" She pulls a folded piece of paper from her purse. "Lilly wasn't even born yet when . . . There's no possible way she can know about the window. Right?"

"Priscilla," says Fritz gently. He stands and moves to her side, never touching her. His voice gets very low. "I'm your brother. Yes, I'm a preacher, but I'm your brother first and foremost. Please tell me what happened with this window. Just confess it and get it out in the open. It will lose its power over you if you simply speak of it. I promise you, this window will lose its power."

"I . . ." Priscilla shakes her head and crosses her arms, holding herself.

"Oh, come on, honey," I say from my chair. "Do us all a favor and just tell him what you did. You can talk about it now. You can tell him how I was the one who put that awful idea in your head the first time. You can tell him how angry you are at me, at yourself still. Just say it, child, and I'll be on my way. Please say the word . . ."

Priscilla looks at Fritz with blurry eyes and opens her mouth. Then the door swings open and Rainey chases a giggling four-and-a-half-year-old child to her mama's side. She's clutching a handful of colored construction papers.

"Look, Mama! See? I drew you and me and—"

"Oh, how nice. I'll look in just a minute, sweetie. Okay?" Priscilla wraps her arms around Janie and hoists her to her hip, smiling and kissing her on the neck. Then she says, "Maybe someday we can talk about it, Fritz. But not yet. Maybe someday."

And just like that, I watch as her window closes

again—and mine too. For how long, I don't know. I suppose I will be here in Forest Pines alongside my loved ones until tomorrow or forever . . . whichever one comes first. The way it looks now, I'll be watching over my grandbabies for years and years to come. But I imagine there could be worse things than that. Oh yes, I imagine there are worse things.

"Come over here by the light," I say to my sweet Janie, "and show your Grandma Mona what pretty pictures you drew. Oh, this one here's my favorite. Is it a car?"

Acknowledgments

This book was not an easy one to write, though honestly, none of them are. As always, I have people in my life who helped me in the making of *Saving Cicadas*. I'd like to thank a dear teacher I had in grade school, Sunny Littlejohn, for reminding me to read *To Kill a Mockingbird*. To Phyllis Sippel at Sun City, thank you for being so open and supportive, and for inadvertently providing me with the most powerful part of this book. To Julie Weinheimer, my blessing of a neighbor, I appreciate your prayers for my writing. They helped me through. And to God, thank you for sending the cicadas in full force near Black Mountain, NC. Your timing is always perfect.

Thank you, Amanda Bostic, for allowing me to write such a story, and Rachelle Gardner, for helping me shape it into a finer book. At Thomas Nelson, there is an amazing fiction team that packages and produces on a superbly professional level. I am grateful to you and so pleased to be partnering with you on both the inside and outside of my books.

To all the booksellers who support me, to my

agent, Mark Gilroy, who believes in me, and to my lovely publicists, Marjory and Peter Wentworth, and Katie Bond—God bless you for all that you do to spread the news about this Southern girl and my fancy words.

To my husband, Brian Seitz, and children, Olivia and Cole, I love you. Please know I write because I want the world to be a better place for you. And again, to my amazing mother, Miriam Lucas, thank you for reading my work and giving me unending encouragement and helpful critique. In the end, I am still your child and only want to see you happy.

A Note from the Author

Includes spoilers. Please don't read this until after you finish the novel.

When I was a child, I hardly ever questioned what the grown-ups around me were doing. I just went along with them. I took no part in the decision-making, but I felt deeply my parents' suffering or joy brought on by the decisions they made. All a child really wants is for her parent to be happy. That's pretty much it. I remember that helpless feeling that many children experience when I didn't understand my parents' world. But on the flip side, being a child, things were simpler then. Summers were longer. There were no gray answers, only black or white.

Growing up in the seventies I remember fretting over that song on the radio that declared "Short People" had no reason to live. Why, I was short, only about four feet. Later at the ripe old age of eight and-a-half, I remember watching the news one night and hearing about the AIDS epidemic. I was confounded. I could not understand what could possibly be so wrong with those delicious-looking chocolate candy appetite suppressants (remember AYDs?). Before then, I'd wanted so badly to be old enough to go on a diet, just so I could taste them.

In all seriousness, I remember the first time someone I knew got pregnant—a teenager—and I recall a grown-up declaring her a "bad girl." Make no mistake. Teenage pregnancy, and in fact, all pregnancy, is a serious matter to those involved. There are no good girls and bad girls. No good boys or bad boys either in these circumstances. Only lives that are changed forever . . . for better or worse.

This book explores some of society's toughest challenges. I'll admit—abortion, adoption, and unplanned pregnancy are not things I woke up one morning thinking, gee, I'd really like to write a novel about that! No. But I do remember the feeling I had when I read Harper Lee's *To Kill a Mockingbird* and saw the truth of racial prejudice through a child's eyes. How powerful it became. Sometimes, viewing the world through a child's eyes clears away the gray and brings us closer to the truth. Abortion, no matter which side you are on, is arguably the most divisive debate of our time, much like racial equality was to Harper Lee's era. I don't shy away from tough subjects, and when I felt led to write about pregnancy, I asked myself—in a story that's been told a thousand times over, whose voice is it that still hasn't been heard?

As a result, my beloved Janie Doe Macy was born. My goal was to weave a modern fable that would allow Janie's voice—that voice that hasn't been heard—to touch your soul in a way that was strong, relevant, and memorable. To do that, I utilized some plot twists in this story that I know would not occur in real life. The story is fantastical in that sense because the Bible is clear that angels are created beings and that we humans do not become angels either in this life or after we die. But the beauty of fiction, of this modern fable, is that it can affect us in new and powerful ways because it allows us to look at the heart of an issue in a way that is not part of our normal, everyday experience. If you've finished the story you know that the way I chose to tell it was meant to give insight into the voice of the unborn. If you are curious about more in-depth insights into angels, I encourage you to dive into Scripture.

I have learned from Janie. I have loved her. And I know I will never, ever forget her. My sincere hope is that you, my reader, might never forget her either.

Reading Group Guide

1. The first line of the book is "Do you believe in past lives?" Discuss this theme of "past lives" in *Saving Cicadas*. Who has them? What power do "past lives" play in the characters' lives? What power do they have in our own lives?

2. *Saving Cicadas* is narrated by a child. Do you remember something you thought as a child that was incorrect? Do you remember the first time you learned a difficult truth? Janie and Rainey see the world in black and white, right or wrong. When do shades of gray begin to cloud our vision? Is it possible to view the world in black and white again? Should we?

3. What are the challenges Priscilla faces when she learns that she's pregnant? How does she deal with the news?

4. Rainey has Down's Syndrome. In what ways does this affect her character? Her future? How does it affect her family dynamics?

What challenges do special needs children present? What blessings do they offer? Have you been touched in your own life by someone with Down's Syndrome? In what way?

5. What are Priscilla's choices regarding her pregnancy? Do you believe every woman has the right to choose? Does every woman face the same choices or are they weighted based on circumstance? How does making a poor choice affect future choices?

6. Do you know of someone who has faced an unplanned pregnancy? If so, what choice did she make? How did her choice affect her in the long run?

7. What is the most powerful scene in the book for you?

8. With which character do you most relate? Priscilla, Mona, Rainey, or Janie?

9. The Internet allows us access to all sorts of information. Do you think it can affect the choices we make? If you did not grow up with the Internet, do you feel you were as informed as are the youth of today? How might your life have been different?

10. What is Poppy's role in this book? What about Grandma Mona's? Why did she seem to change so much?

11. Discuss the character of Harlan. Though he's gone, does he play an important part in the Macy family?

12. There is a theme of angels and being "spirit-filled" in *Saving Cicadas*. How does this theme affect the way you view the characters, especially Janie? How do these fictional angels differ from the ones you encounter in the Bible?

13. Why is it so hard for Priscilla to go back home to Forest Pines? Is it important for people to go back home? Why or why not?

14. Discuss the role of fear in this book. Who is fearful? Of what? Does fear affect the decisions the characters make? Is anyone courageous?

15. Who is the true heroine of this book? Does she get what she wants in the end?

16. Discuss faith or lack thereof as it relates to Fritz, Priscilla, Janie, and Rainey.

17. In the end, does Priscilla share her secret of the window? Why or why not?

18. Why do you think the title is *Saving Cicadas*? Is it possible to save cicadas? Who is attempting to save them?

Center Point Publishing
600 Brooks Road ● PO Box 1
Thorndike ME 04986-0001 USA

(207) 568-3717

US & Canada:
1 800 929-9108
www.centerpointlargeprint.com